Praise for *Welcome to Last Chance*

"An outstanding debut novel! *Welcome to Last Chance* gives us a warm but never sentimental view of small-town life, sprinkled with characters full of quirks and faults—all seen through the eyes of a tough but fragile heroine. Cathleen Armstrong has crafted a story to cherish."

—**Sarah Sundin**, award-winning author of *With Every Letter*

"Armstrong's style is as comfortable as a pair of well-worn jeans. *Welcome to Last Chance* welcomes readers into its pages for a relaxing, rewarding story about a girl looking for a better life and the life she finds in Last Chance."

—**Crosswalk.com**

"Readers will enjoy the simplicity of Last Chance and the complexity of Lainie's character."

—*New York Journal of Books*

"Armstrong's enjoyable debut will pull readers into the joys—and trials—of a small town."

—*RT Book Reviews*

"With equal parts hope, charm, and tender faith, Cathleen Armstrong spins a tale as warm and welcoming as a roadside cafe on a dusty highway. Exit from the fast lane and visit Last Chance. It's a place you won't soon forget."

—**Lisa Wingate**, bestselling and award-winning author of *Firefly Island* and *Blue Moon Bay*

"Cathleen Armstrong packs a lot into her debut novel: the suspense of danger lurking on the edges of Lainie Davis's life, a touch of can-this-really-go-anywhere romance, small-town friendships becoming like family, and the disappointment of family being less than ideal. With an eclectic cast of characters and well-developed plot, *Welcome to Last Chance* pulls the reader in from the first blink of the warning light on the dashboard of Lainie's car to the happily-ever-after waiting at the end of her last chance to get her life right."

—**Beth K. Vogt,** author of *Catch a Falling Star* and *Wish You Were Here*

ONE MORE
LAST CHANCE

Books by
Cathleen Armstrong

Welcome to Last Chance
One More Last Chance

ONE MORE LAST CHANCE

A Novel

CATHLEEN ARMSTRONG

Revell

a division of Baker Publishing Group
Grand Rapids, Michigan

© 2014 by Cathleen Armstrong

Published by Revell
a division of Baker Publishing Group
P.O. Box 6287, Grand Rapids, MI 49516-6287
www.revellbooks.com

Printed in the United States of America

Library of Congress Cataloging-in-Publication Data
Armstrong, Cathleen.
    One more last chance : a novel / Cathleen Armstrong.
        pages cm. — (A place to call home ; #2)
    ISBN 978-0-8007-2247-0 (pbk.)
    1. Self-realization in women—Fiction. I. Title.
PS3601.R5747O64 2014
813'.6—dc23   2013044756

This is a work of fiction. Names, characters, incidents, and dialogues are products of the author's imagination and are not to be construed as real. Any resemblance to actual events or persons, living or dead, is entirely coincidental.

14 15 16 17 18 19 20   7 6 5 4 3 2 1

For Rebecca, Amy, Sarah, Jacob, Dylan,
Eli, Luke, and Lydia Cathleen.

Thank you for the joy.

1

The day the new owner of the Dip 'n' Dine tried to put line-caught trout dusted with blue cornmeal and lightly napped in a tricolor chile cream on the menu was the day his cook nearly hung up his apron for good.

"I don't know who you think is going to cook that stuff, but it's not going to be me." Carlos Montoya folded his arms and leaned against his prep table.

Chris Reed looked out the window and sighed. Fayette had warned him when he bought the diner from her that he'd have to go slow if he wanted to change anything. And yes, he understood that people could get set in their ways. But for crying out loud, it had been weeks already. Six long weeks, in fact, of tiptoeing around the prima donna in the kitchen as if Chris were a none-too-bright busboy instead of the new owner. It was time to take charge. He raised himself up to his full six foot four and tried to make his smile warm yet authoritative.

"Let's just give it a try. I have a feeling it'll be a hit. If you're right and it's not, well, at least we tried to shake things up a little."

"Some folks think things don't need any shaking up. Some folks think things are just fine the way they are. But if you're set on turning this place into some kind of fancy Santa Fe bistro, you just might have to find yourself another cook. Excuse me, better make that *chef*." Carlos's glare grew darker, and Chris noticed that Pete, the nephew who helped Carlos in the kitchen, edged closer to his uncle in a show of solidarity.

Chris opened his mouth, but before he could say another word, Juanita Sheppard, his part-time waitress and full-time interpreter of all things Last Chance, stuck her head in the kitchen. "Chris, we've got a little problem out here. Could I see you a minute?"

Chris took a last look at Carlos, now standing shoulder to shoulder with Pete. His own shoulders sagged and he shook his head as he pushed through the swinging door into the dining room of the Dip 'n' Dine where Juanita was waiting for him.

Juanita glanced at the kitchen door and gestured for Chris to follow her to a far corner of the room. She waited till he was close enough to hear a whisper that was so loud Carlos could probably hear it too. "I hope you don't mind my butting in, but I couldn't help hearing you and Carlos talking in there."

Chris didn't say anything. Whether he minded Juanita butting in or not probably didn't make much difference. He waited for her to say what was on her mind.

"Personally, I think that fish dish you were talking about sounds scrumptious. I'd order it in a minute." Juanita put her hand on Chris's arm. "And I think if you make just a couple changes, people will gobble it up, and Carlos might feel better about making it too."

"Changes? Like what?" Chris tried to keep his voice even.

"Well, first of all, use yellow cornmeal. That blue stuff just looks nasty when it's fried. Food was never meant to be that color. Then, instead of going to the work of making all those sauces, just stir pickle relish into some mayonnaise. Fast and easy and gourmet as you please."

Chris just looked at Juanita.

She beamed. "So what do you think?"

"I think you're talking about fried fish and tartar sauce."

"Use your imagination, Chris. Fancy it up like you did with that blue corn stuff. I'm telling you, it'll be a winner. And you'll get to keep your cook." She leaned in and lowered her whisper to a level only Chris could hear. "Fayette spoiled Carlos rotten, of course, but just between you and me, every restaurant within fifty miles of Last Chance has tried to take him away from here. He's turned down every one because he liked working at the Dip 'n' Dine. And he's liked working here because no one ever got in his way. Just a word to the wise."

The front door opened and Juanita patted his arm. "I've got customers that need tending. If I think of something, I'll let you know. But I don't think changing the menu is your answer. You'd probably wind up having to raise your prices, and that'll just make folks mad."

Chris sighed and straightened his shoulders before stopping by a table to say hello on his way to the kitchen. He could at least try to look like the owner, even if no one really believed it.

Carlos looked up from the pot of green chile stew he was stirring and glowered at Chris when he came through the door. Chris lifted his hand in a resigned wave. "Okay, Carlos, no blue corn trout. But keep an open mind, okay? Have you ever heard the saying, 'Unless things change, they die'?"

Carlos went back to his stirring. "Can't say I have, boss. But have you ever heard the saying, 'If it ain't broke, don't fix it'?" His grin softened his words, but Chris got the message. Things weren't going to change much at the Dip 'n' Dine, not with Carlos in the kitchen. He gritted his teeth and went to cross blue cornmeal off his food order. The row of cookbooks he had set up for inspiration on the shelf over his desk mocked him, and his dream of gradually turning the Dip 'n' Dine into a destination restaurant seemed in danger of wafting away in the fragrant steam of green chile stew.

The bell on the front door jingled and Chris winced. That bell was one of the first things he had intended to deep-six when he took possession of his restaurant, but now he found himself second-guessing even that. Who might be offended and raise a ruckus if the door opened without that irritating jangle?

"Well, good morning, Elizabeth." Juanita's voice carried through the window into the kitchen. "And here's our new college graduate. Congratulations, Miss Sarah."

Chris half-raised from his chair to see Juanita hugging what appeared from the back to be a young teenager. She couldn't have been much more than five feet tall, and if it weren't for the cascade of dark curls around her shoulders, she could have been taken for a twelve-year-old boy. When Juanita let her go and she turned around and found Chris staring at her, he fell back in his chair like he had been caught spying. *Smooth move, Reed.* He rubbed his forehead. *Handled just like the owner of a successful establishment. One thing's for sure, though—that is no twelve-year-old boy.*

"So what can I get you ladies?" Juanita's voice carried into the kitchen.

"Gran and I both want the green chile stew. Carlos hasn't changed his Monday special, has he?" The voice was surprisingly low and husky for such a tiny person.

"Not yet, but the way things are going, you never can tell." Juanita's conspiratorial whisper could be heard in every corner of the Dip 'n' Dine. "Chris and Carlos had a dust-up just a while ago that left me wondering what might happen around here. You wouldn't believe the stuff Chris wants to put on the menu."

"Well, it can take a while to settle in when new management takes over." Elizabeth Cooley's wise old voice entered the conversation. "I'm sure they'll get things all worked out before too long."

"Well, I sure hope so. Fayette poured her life and soul into this place, and I'd sure hate to see it go to pot the minute she leaves town."

Chris shoved his chair back and stood up. *That's it.* Time to forget his embarrassment and get out there and stop Juanita before she had the whole town in an uproar over the future of the Dip 'n' Dine.

"Miss Elizabeth, good to see you." His smile was broad and, he hoped, assured as he crossed the room. "Did I hear you ladies say you wanted a bowl of green chile stew? Juanita, you want to take care of that?" He tried to look strong and confident as he turned to Elizabeth's dining companion and extended his hand. "I don't believe we've met. I'm Chris Reed."

Her hand felt cool and smooth. "I'm Sarah Cooley. Glad to see you're all right. You disappeared so fast a minute ago, I thought you'd slipped."

Shoot, she had noticed his duck. "I, uh, dropped my pen."

One corner of her mouth turned up. "Ah."

And she knew a lie when she heard one. Why couldn't he leave bad enough alone?

"Sarah is my granddaughter, Chris." If Elizabeth was aware of the torment Sarah was putting him through, she chose to ignore it. "She just graduated from State, and she's going to teach second grade at the elementary school. You probably met her at Fayette's wedding, but you were so busy catering that you might not remember."

"Well, if I did, it's nice to see you again." He looked up as

Juanita appeared with two bowls of green chile stew and a basket of tortillas. "Enjoy your lunch."

Chris headed back to the kitchen. No, he had never met Sarah. If he had ever looked into those eyes, which were somewhere between hazel and khaki, he'd have remembered.

—⚍—

"What a doofus." Sarah grabbed a thick, hot tortilla from the basket and buttered it. "Who does he think he is, anyway?"

"Shhh." Elizabeth lowered her voice to just above a whisper. "He can hear you."

"So?" But she did lower her voice. "Did you see him march in here with that slop-eating grin on his face, just like he owned the place?"

"He does own the place." The expression on Elizabeth's face left little doubt in her granddaughter's mind that she may have just crossed the lines of propriety. "And I must say, you've picked up some rather colorful language at college."

"Sorry, Gran. I'll watch it." She jabbed her spoon into the stew. "But it just burns me that some big-city stranger thinks he can come in here and run roughshod over what the people of Last Chance want. That's just bullying. People can figure out for themselves what they want. They don't need anyone else telling them what's good for them."

"Sweetheart, settle down. Whatever else you might say about Chris, he's not a bully. I've just known him a little while, but he seems to be one of the nicest young men I've met in a long time." Elizabeth reached across the table to place a warm hand on Sarah's arm. "And besides, not one thing has changed at the Dip 'n' Dine so far. You are getting way too worked up about this. What's the matter?"

14

Sarah shook her head, surprised at the tears that welled up. "I don't know. I guess I was counting on Last Chance to be the one place where things didn't change. I didn't realize how much I missed it."

Elizabeth looked doubtful. "I don't know. You seem to be awfully upset about a menu change or two that hasn't even happened yet. Are you sure there's not something else bothering you?"

"No, I'm fine, really." Sarah took a deep breath and smiled at her grandmother. "You're right. I'm way overreacting. I guess I'm still tired from finals and graduation and everything." She lowered her voice to a whisper that barely reached across the table. "But really, why would he even come here if all he wants to do is change everything? Why not just stay where he was and leave us alone?"

Her grandmother smiled and picked up her spoon. "I like Chris. He's confident, all right, but it takes a lot of courage to just pack up and follow your dream like he did. I know. I was a big-city girl too, remember. And from a city a lot bigger than Albuquerque. Everyone thought I was crazy when I answered that ad to teach school 'way out west,' but Randolph Scott and John Wayne had made me fall in love with cowboys, so I came. And here I still am."

Sarah grinned. "So was it everything you thought it would be?"

"Yes, and then some. Real ranchers do a whole lot more work than those movie cowboys ever did, but I wouldn't trade my life, hard as it was, for any other you could name."

"You didn't teach very long."

"No, I married your granddad as soon as school was out that first year, and that was that."

"That will not be me." Sarah helped herself to another tortilla. "I don't know if I'll ever get married, but I won't let it interfere with my career if I do."

"Well, times have changed." Elizabeth looked up and smiled as Juanita appeared with the iced tea pitcher. "Thank you, I will have a little more."

"You all doing all right over here? Need some more tortillas? How's that stew tasting?" She filled each glass with a practiced pour.

Sarah sat back. "The stew is phenomenal. I'd have more if I had anyplace to put another bite. But I'll be back tomorrow. I plan to be back for lunch every day this week until I've worked my way through the daily specials. Then I might do it again next week. I've really missed Carlos's cooking."

"That should make our new owner real happy." Juanita may have thought she was whispering. "I've seen him walk past the kitchen window half a dozen times looking in here at you. I must say it didn't take him long to figure out who the biggest rancher's youngest daughter was."

"Juanita!" Elizabeth sounded shocked. "You are making a lot of assumptions."

"I just call it as I see it. You should know that about me by now." She winked at Sarah as the sound of a bell indicated an order was ready, then turned toward the kitchen. "Not that you aren't as cute as a bug's ear, of course. That just makes it icing on the cake."

———

Chris stood in the kitchen and watched Juanita approach the window where no order awaited as if every word she had just said hadn't reverberated from the rafters. The puzzled look on her face as she looked over the empty shelf changed to one of mild concern when she saw his face.

"Something wrong, Chris?"

Something wrong? Chris didn't trust himself to open his mouth. He took a deep breath to try to calm himself, gritted his teeth, and jerked his head toward the back door.

By the time Chris closed the door behind them and he and Juanita were alone on the back steps, Juanita really did look worried.

"Chris, what in the world is the matter? You look like you're about to go off like a Fourth of July skyrocket."

He gave himself another few seconds without saying anything.

Juanita reached for the doorknob. "Should I get Carlos?"

Chris shook his head and placed his hand on the door. He was calmer now, but he still needed one more deep breath. "Juanita, you know how much I've relied on you here as I've been getting on my feet. I counted on you to help me find my place here in Last Chance, and you've done a great job."

Juanita's expression relaxed a bit. "Well, thank you, Chris. I knew how hard it would be for an absolute stranger to know how we do things around here. Glad I could help."

Chris nodded. "But as much as I rely on you, we need to get a few things straight if you're going to continue working here."

Juanita's mouth pinched up and she seemed to swell to twice her size as she took in air through her nose. "Are you fixing to fire me? Because I'll quit in a heartbeat if you want me to."

"No, that's not what I'm saying. I want you to keep on working here. Like I said, I rely on you." Chris shook his head to clear it. How did he get on the defensive?

"Then would you please tell me why you dragged me out here? I have customers waiting on their lunch, you know."

Chris took a deep breath and tried again. "I didn't say anything when you overheard my conversation with Carlos this morning."

"Oh, is that what this is all about?" Juanita waved a dismissive hand. "Well, I'm sorry if I stepped on your toes. But you yourself said you don't have the faintest clue of how we like things at the Dip 'n' Dine. I was just trying to help."

"And as I said, I appreciate your efforts." When had he ever said he hadn't the faintest clue? "But what I don't appreciate, and what cannot continue, is your going out there and discussing things you overhear with the patrons."

"Patrons? You mean Elizabeth? She's one of my oldest friends. I don't keep secrets from my friends, and if keeping secrets is part of this job, well then——"

Chris held up his hand to stop her. If he heard one more threatened resignation today, he'd probably take them all up on it, and then what would he do with the lunch crowd?

"Look, Juanita, I'm not telling you to keep secrets from anybody, just to——" He was about to say "use good judgment," but Juanita cut him off in mid-phrase.

"Well, I should hope not. Because as much as I love this job, deceit and deception have never been anything I could tolerate, and frankly, I'm surprised that you even ask it. I am as honest and as open as the day is long."

"Deceit and what? What are you talking about?" Chris knew they were speaking English, but nothing was making sense. "I'm just saying don't talk about private restaurant business in front of the customers. Does being honest and open mean telling everything you hear to everyone you see?"

"Of course not, Chris. I am discretion itself. I thought we were talking about a conversation I had with my oldest friend that you listened in on."

"As did everyone else who was in the restaurant at the time."

"I was whispering."

"I could hear you in the kitchen!" Chris could feel beads of sweat break out on his forehead. He dug in his pocket for his handkerchief.

Juanita was silent a long moment as she considered what he said. "Okay. I see what you mean. If the whole town knows all the problems we're having right now, the Dip 'n' Dine might go belly-up before you have a chance to get adjusted to the way we do things around here." She smiled and patted his arm again. "But don't you worry. You are doing fine. You'll be up to speed in no time."

"There's one more thing."

Juanita had turned to go into the kitchen, but she paused with her hand on the doorknob.

"The comment about the biggest rancher's youngest daughter was completely out of line."

Juanita finally had the grace to look embarrassed. "Oh, that, well, I was only—"

"*Completely* out of line."

She puffed up again like she was going back on the attack, but she seemed to think better of it this time and only nodded before opening the door and disappearing into the kitchen.

Chris sank onto the back step and gazed out across the brush of the high desert behind the Dip 'n' Dine. The craggy mountains across the valley were already beginning to stretch blue shadows across the desert floor. It was beautiful in its own austere way and one of the things that had made him fall in love with Last Chance the first time he saw it. But it had never occurred to him that people tempered by the harsh and unforgiving landscape might be just a bit inflexible themselves. What had he gotten himself into? It had taken every dime of the modest inheritance his grandparents had left him, plus every dime he had been able to save, to buy this place. He was just allowing himself to wonder for the first time if he may have made a mistake, ranchers' beautiful daughters notwithstanding, when the back door opened again and Juanita stuck her head out for one last observation.

"Although I have to say, Chris, eavesdroppers never hear any good of themselves. Just a word to the wise."

2

You know, I like this cute little car." Elizabeth slid into the passenger side of the compact Ford and snapped her seat belt. "It suits you."

"I think so too." Sarah waved at the driver of a passing extended cab pickup and pulled out onto the road. "I'm done hauling horses, and as long as they keep the road to the ranch house graded, this will get me anywhere I need to go."

"You're not planning on living at the ranch after school starts, are you?"

"Nope. I'm a town girl now. There's not a lot to choose from here, but there are a couple places I'm looking at this afternoon. Want to come?"

"I thought you might come live with me. You practically lived with me anyway your senior year of high school, and we got along fine. And think of the money you'll be able to save."

"I loved staying with you in high school." Sarah glanced at her grandmother and smiled. "I got to have a real senior year that way. But I'm all grown up now. I need my own space."

"I don't know what you think you'll be doing at your place that you couldn't do at mine." Elizabeth arched an eyebrow. "I'm not sure I understand all this need for your 'own space.'"

"Says the lady who hotfooted it to town the minute Mom took

over the kitchen at the ranch." Sarah grinned. "Face it, Gran. I got a lot more than my middle name from you, and there you have it."

"Well, I'm not sure you'll find that an unmixed blessing, but if you think you're at all like me, I couldn't be more pleased."

"I have an appointment to see a place in about five minutes." Sarah slowed as she reached Elizabeth's house. "Do you want me to drop you off, or would you like to come?"

"Oh, I'd love to come. I hope it's nearby."

"This close enough?" Sarah came to a stop two doors down.

"Really? The Carter house? I knew his kids were fixing it up, but I thought it was to sell. Are you buying something?"

"I wish. No, they decided to hold on to it awhile to see if the market improves. Meanwhile, they're offering it for rent. Let's go see."

"Oh my. There's no carpeting." Elizabeth stepped through the door that Mike Carter held open for her.

"Nope." He looked around in satisfaction. "Can you believe it? We took up that dark yellow shag and found hardwood underneath. We sanded and refinished the floors all through the house."

"You'll need a lot of rugs just to keep the noise down." Elizabeth looked uncertain as their footsteps reverberated through the house.

"Well, I love it. And rugs won't be a problem." Sarah headed toward the kitchen.

"I would've liked to have done a lot more in here, but we didn't want to price it completely out of the market here in Last Chance." Mike followed her. "We did put in new sinks and a dishwasher, though. And the stove and refrigerator are new."

A quick tour of the two bedrooms and the single bath with new fixtures brought them back to the living room.

"And the fireplace works, of course?"

"Yep, draws like a champ." Mike looked around. It was clear he saw the refurbished little house as a work of art.

Sarah had to agree. "I love it. When can I move in?"

"I have the lease there on the kitchen counter. Let's get it signed and I'll hand the keys over now."

———∞———

"Look at this!" Sarah held her key chain up and jangled it. "My very own key to my very own house." She placed another key on Elizabeth's kitchen table. "And you, madam, may keep the spare key."

Elizabeth turned from the refrigerator holding a pitcher of iced tea. "That's a good idea. Hang it on the hook by the door, would you, honey? And while you're up, get a couple glasses."

Sarah did as she was bid. "And since we're talking keys, I think it would be a good idea if I had one of yours."

"Why?"

"Just in case. You never know. If you needed help in the middle of the night, I could come. Which reminds me, I brought you something." She reached for the bag she had brought in with her and handed it to her grandmother.

"What is this?" Elizabeth pulled a box from the plastic bag.

"It's a new phone to put by your bed."

"I have a phone by my bed and it works just fine."

"And it's worked just fine since the Nixon administration. There have been a few improvements to the system made since then."

"What else do I need? It rings; I answer it. I dial; someone else answers. That's what phones are supposed to do."

"But look at this." Sarah took the box and opened it. "This has speed dial. One button and you get 9-1-1. One button and you get me. You can program other numbers in too. And look, it even has voice mail."

"Oh, for pity's sake. What is the big hurry? I can dial seven numbers almost as fast as you can push a button or two."

"Because, dear Gran, I'm trying to make it easier for you to stay right here where you want to be." Sarah put both hands on her grandmother's shoulders and looked into her eyes. "I shouldn't say this, but I heard Mom and Dad talking about whether you should be living by yourself. They think it might be time for you to move back to the ranch."

"Oh, they do, do they?" Elizabeth's blue eyes shot sparks. "And do I have any say in this, or were they just going to come down and toss me in the back of the truck?"

"Don't get all upset." Sarah kissed her grandmother on the forehead. "It was just a conversation. No one is going to force you to do anything you don't want to do. But you have to admit, knowing I could get here in two minutes flat will certainly help put their minds at ease."

"Is that why you took the Carter house? So you could babysit me?"

"No, Gran, I took it because it is hands-down the cutest house in Last Chance. The fact that you live two doors down is the cherry on top. After all, you're my BFF."

"I don't even know what that means." Elizabeth still didn't look happy.

Sarah laughed and gave her a hug. "It means we're best friends forever."

Elizabeth shook her head and looked in the box. "Black? At least the pink one in my bedroom goes with the bedspread."

Sarah took the package from her and extracted the phone so her grandmother could see it better. "It's the function that's important, Gran, not the color. All the new phones are black. See how sleek and modern it looks?"

"Mmm-hmm, nothing says *modern* like a black phone."

"And look. It's cordless." Sarah tried to keep her voice cheerful. When Gran got her heels dug in, moving sunrise could be easier. "You can put the receiver right there on the table next to your recliner and never have to budge when the phone rings."

Elizabeth didn't look convinced, but she did take the receiver and hold it to her ear. "I guess it's comfortable enough. And light."

Sarah saw her advantage and pressed it. "And my number's not the only one you can program in. You'll be able to reach the ranch, the church, and any of your friends by pressing a button or two. Just think, you can call Ray and Lainie in Santa Fe without having to hunt up your address book. Just punch two buttons."

Elizabeth sighed and got to her feet. "Well, let's go plug it in and see how it works. But you're sure it doesn't come in pink?"

—⁂—

Chris turned off the neon Dip 'n' Dine sign and returned Juanita's wave as she got into her car and drove away. It had been one long day. He wandered into the kitchen where Carlos was getting ready to give the floor a final scrub.

"You can leave that, Carlos. I'll do it before I go."

"It's no problem, boss." Carlos went right on filling his bucket. "I just scrub my way out the back door. Be done in no time."

Chris tied on an apron. "I'll get it for you tonight. I feel like doing some cooking. It relaxes me."

Carlos looked at him as if he had just said he was going to burn the place down. "Here? In my kitchen?"

"Yep. That little electric stove at my house doesn't do it for me."

"But I've already cleaned the stove."

"I know how to clean a stove."

Carlos did not look happy. At all. "No one cleans my kitchen but me. Not even the crew that does the dining room sets foot in here. You know that."

Chris opened the refrigerator and removed some chicken breasts and mushrooms. He put them on the counter and turned to face his fuming cook. "Look, I know how to clean a kitchen. I've cleaned more kitchens than you can count for some of the fussiest chefs on the planet. And believe it or not, since I do own this restaurant, I'm pretty particular about how clean it is myself. You'll never know I was here. Now, go on home. See you tomorrow."

Carlos glared at his bucket, at his stove, and finally at Chris. Grabbing his hat off a hook by the door, he yanked the back door open. "Maybe."

Chris ignored the resounding slam of the back door. Counting Carlos's earlier warning, Pete's show of solidarity, Juanita's two offers to quit when he talked to her this morning, and now this, he'd had five threatened resignations since breakfast. And that was just today. He slipped his smartphone into the dock on his desk and adjusted the sound. As the soft wailing of a saxophone insinuated itself throughout the kitchen, he felt his shoulders ease. He had a feeling that if his love of cool jazz were known, he'd be considered even more of an outsider than he already was, but an evening in the kitchen with Davis or Brubeck relaxed him in a way nothing else did. He unrolled his own set of knives and got to work.

It was nearly 10:30 before he turned off his music and put his phone back in his pocket. Foil freezer containers were stacked on the counter, ready for him to take home. That was the trouble

26

with getting creative in the kitchen. It was impossible to cook only enough for one. But the individual containers would provide him with fallback meals on those days when he didn't feel like cooking. And truthfully, it was hard to get excited about cooking on the little four-burner electric stove in the mobile home Fayette had sold him when he bought the Dip 'n' Dine from her.

He stood in the doorway and gave the kitchen one last look. If Carlos found any fault with this kitchen in the morning, it would be because he felt he had to make a point, not because anything was wrong. Chris sighed, picked up his food, and let himself out the back door.

Last Chance was absolutely silent. He could have walked down the center of Main Street all the way home for all the traffic there was. He had been told that the High Lonesome Saloon across the road had once been open late at night, but it had been closed since before he arrived in Last Chance. Now it sat abandoned and boarded up in its weed-infested parking lot. Chris got into his Jeep and pulled out onto the deserted street to head home. It was at times like this, when he was through with work and away from the Dip 'n' Dine, that he missed having someone to talk to. Unbidden, the image of Sarah Cooley surfaced in his mind. She sure was a little bitty thing. If she wasn't going to be teaching second graders, there was a good chance some of her students might be nearly as tall as she was. He winced as he remembered how she took him down. Size would never stop Sarah Cooley from taking charge.

He parked his car in the carport attached to the yellow-and-white singlewide, gathered his food, and went inside. It was way too frilly for his taste. Fayette had lived there for nearly twenty years, and it looked every bit a woman's home. One of these days, when he had time, he'd have to change some things.

The fifteen hours or so he had just spent at the Dip 'n' Dine settled on his back and shoulders like a lead jacket. He didn't even feel like heating up one of the meals he had brought home with him. He'd just scramble a few eggs and hit the sack. That alarm clock was going to go off awfully early.

Settling himself at the kitchen table with his plate of eggs, Chris bowed his head. Even after a day like this one, he still had a lot to be thankful for. He had almost finished his quick meal when his phone rang. He took it from his pocket and frowned at the screen. This was awfully late for a phone call, even from his sister. He hoped nothing was wrong.

"Hi, Uncle Chris!" The voice chirping in his ear made him smile.

"Olivia! What are you doing up?" He glanced at his watch. "It's 11:00."

"Oh, Mom lets me stay up as long as I want in the summer. I hardly ever go to bed before midnight."

"So is everything okay?" Chris couldn't shake the feeling that all was not as it should be. "Where's your mom?"

If a seven-year-old's voice could drip with contempt, Olivia's did. "Oh, she's out with Jase. Where else?"

"You're with a babysitter, right?" Even as Chris asked the question, he knew the answer was a no-brainer for most parents yet anything but that for his sister.

"A babysitter? What for? I'm no baby." Her words were more confident than her tone.

"You're not by yourself." His statement was more to reassure himself than to ask for clarification.

"Yes, but don't worry, I know the rules. Keep the door locked. Don't open it for anyone. Don't use the stove. And if anyone tries to break in, call 9-1-1."

Chris took a deep breath. Kaitlyn had been only seventeen when Olivia was born, and he had tried to cut her some slack as she learned parenting on the fly, but this went beyond careless parenting well into child endangerment. Their parents had never been much help. Consumed with their own careers, they had always depended on Chris to look after Kaitlyn. He was only four years older than her, but he had tried. And he had to admit he had come up short.

He plugged his phone into the charger and put it on speaker. "Listen, Olivia. I'm right here, and I'll stay on the phone till your mom gets home. You put your phone on speaker too, and we'll just pretend we're together, okay? Are we watching television?"

"Yeah, but it's kind of scary. Someone just got killed."

"Well then, let's turn that off right now. What's your favorite movie?"

"*Pocahontas*. I have the DVD."

"Put it on, and we can watch it together. You can tell me all about it."

"Okay." Her voice had gone back to chirping, and he listened to the bustle as she moved around finding her movie. Finally, as music that could only come from Disney filled the room, she was back. "Okay, there's all these people getting ready to get on a boat, see . . ."

Chris wasn't sure how long he sat listening to Olivia narrate her movie. The pauses between her comments became longer and her voice grew sleepy. She finally drifted off to sleep, and Chris smiled as her snores came to him over the phone. For a little girl, she made an awful lot of noise.

He turned his own television on with the sound almost off so he could hear everything that went on in Kaitlyn's apartment and tried to stay awake. Despite his efforts, he must have dozed, because he was suddenly aware of Kaitlyn's voice in the room.

"Kaitlyn!"

The voice on the other end stopped for a moment. "Chris? Is that you?"

"Yes, it's me. Pick up the phone and turn off the speaker." He jabbed at the speaker button on his own phone and waited until she came back on the line. It was just past midnight.

"Chris. What's going on?"

"Why don't you tell me? What do you mean leaving Olivia alone? She's seven years old, for crying out loud."

Kaitlyn laughed. "Oh, don't worry about Livvy. Sometimes I think she's the grown-up."

"Well, she's not a grown-up. She's seven. What if something happened?"

"I've gone over all that with her. She knows how to get help if she needs it."

"Even if nothing happens, Kaitlyn, leaving her alone is illegal. The authorities would have every reason to find you an unfit mother and take Olivia away from you. Do you realize that?" Chris found himself wishing he could reach through the phone and shake some sense into his sister.

"Look, I don't need a lecture from you." Kaitlyn's voice took on the same petulance she used when he'd tried to rein her in when they were kids. "You have no idea what it's like being tied down with a kid all the time. I'm only twenty-four. I have a right to live my life too, you know."

Chris sighed and rubbed a pain that had begun between his eyes. He didn't know where Olivia was, but she didn't need to be hearing the things Kaitlyn was saying, although he didn't imagine it would be the first time she heard them.

"Okay, it's late. You need to see to Olivia and I need to get to bed. But don't leave her alone anymore. Got that? She's just a little kid, and she was scared. That's why she called me."

The voice on the other end of the line softened. "Well, there's no one better to go to when you're scared. I've known that all my life. But I'll find a sitter next time, promise."

"You'd better." Chris felt his rage, if not his frustration, slip away in spite of himself. He never could stay mad at Kaitlyn long. That was probably why she always did exactly as she pleased. Well, not where Olivia was concerned. Not if he could help it. "Olivia is a precious gift. I hope you realize that. And if you ever need any help with her, all you have to do is let me know. Understand?"

"I understand. And don't think I won't take you up on that."

"You do that."

"Love you, Chris."

"Love you too. And give Olivia a kiss for me." Chris hung up the phone and leaned back in his chair. If he could gather just an ounce or two of strength, maybe he could get to bed.

3

D id you find enough to at least get started?" Nancy Jo Cooley looked up from the bread she was kneading when Sarah came through the back door.

"I found a ton. There were some great midcentury modern pieces in that shed. I had no idea all that was out there."

"Midcentury modern?" Nancy Jo swiped the back of her hand across her nose, leaving a flour smear. "You're not talking about that awful blond bedroom set, are you?"

"And the coffee tables, and the turquoise sofa is still in good shape. And there's even a Formica and chrome kitchen table." Sarah practically danced with excitement. "I marked everything I wanted with that blue painter's tape that was out there. The guys said they could load it on the truck and bring it to town tomorrow."

"I can't believe you want that awful old stuff from the fifties. Gran was still hanging on to her big-city ways when she went clear to Albuquerque to buy it and then had it shipped down. It made the ranch quite the showplace, but by the time I married your dad, it was ready for the shed. Did you see the oak dining table with the claw feet? The bentwood rocker? I think those pieces are so much nicer than that so-called modern stuff."

"Oh, shoot. They've already taken up the gold shag carpet. Otherwise the oak would be perfect, especially with a macramé plant hanger or two." Sarah poured herself a cup of coffee and set another where her mother could reach it. "Nope. I'm thrilled with the midcentury modern. Wait till you see how it looks in my house."

"Did you go through the linen closet too? There are plenty of sheets and towels you can have." Nancy Jo gave the bread dough a final thump and set it to rise under a damp cloth before rinsing her hands. "Thanks for the coffee, honey. I'm ready for a break." She smiled at the familiar ringtone coming from Sarah's purse. "Is that Brandon? Tell him hi from me."

Sarah didn't answer either the phone or her mother, and if Nancy Jo noticed, she didn't say anything. "I think I'm going to get all new linens. I'm going up to San Ramon this afternoon for that, as well as shelf paper and whatever else I decide I need. Want to come?"

"I wish I could. It sounds like fun. But I've got way too much to do around here."

Sarah got up and squeezed her mother's shoulders before she put her cup in the sink. "Well, I'm sure it won't be the last time I head up there for something for the house. I'll give you some warning next time, and maybe we can make a day of it."

"Do. I'd like that." Nancy Jo took a sip of coffee. "Oh, since you seem to like that old stuff, did you find the dishes?"

"Dishes?"

"Gran has a box of Fiesta ware out there somewhere. It's not a complete set anymore, but there should be enough to set a table."

"Real Fiesta? Just sitting in a box in the shed? You've got to be kidding. If it's out there, I'm taking it with me now." Sarah was already off the porch and on her way to the shed by the time the door slammed behind her.

The kitchen, Chris guessed, had passed muster. Not only did Carlos have nothing to say about it, but he actually seemed cheerful as he worked. Chris even caught him whistling softly. Nevertheless, discretion being the better part of valor, Chris decided to stay out of his way. That was the course of action Fayette had recommended anyway, and though he had no intention of abdicating the kitchen of his own restaurant, taking a day off from battle now and then would not hurt. It could even help in the long run.

When the front door opened and in breezed Rita Sandoval, the mayor of Last Chance, Chris held his breath. Earlier, before anyone else arrived at the diner, he had taken down the bell over the door. So far no one had said anything, but he had learned already that nothing ever got past Rita. She stopped in the doorway, looked up, swung the door back and forth a few times, shrugged, and bustled on in. Chris slowly exhaled, feeling absurdly pleased that at least one change he wanted to make at the Dip 'n' Dine had slipped by.

"Sarah Cooley's not here, is she?" Rita looked around and gave a sharp nod. "Good. I stopped by Elizabeth's and she said Sarah was going to come in for lunch on her way to San Ramon this afternoon."

"No, we haven't seen Sarah today, have we, Chris?" Juanita's voice oozed innocence, but Chris felt his ears growing hot anyway.

"Good. Then I'll make this fast. Sarah's moving into the Carter place this week, and we're going to give her a pounding on Saturday night."

Chris had no idea what a pounding was, but he was pretty sure it couldn't be as violent as it sounded. Last Chance just didn't seem like that kind of place.

Rita plopped her ever-present clipboard on the counter. "I'd rather everyone sign up for what they're going to bring so we don't get twenty-five pounds of tea and not an ounce of sugar to go with it, but people in this town can be so hardheaded when it comes to taking the tiniest suggestion, so I'll just let it be what it is and hope for the best."

"Rita, I do believe you're getting soft. You start letting people make up their own minds about things, and the whole town's likely to go to pot." Juanita picked up the clipboard and looked at it. "You can put me down for two jars of my homemade green chile salsa, and of course I'll bring my specialty for the potluck table."

"Terrific. We can never have too much lime Jell-O with cottage cheese and marshmallows." Clearly Rita recognized a dig when she heard one and had no trouble giving as good as she got.

"What about you, Chris?" Juanita either didn't get the jab or chose to ignore it. "You're invited too, you know. The whole town comes to these things. You bring a pound of something for the pantry and a dish for the potluck. It's like a surprise housewarming."

"I don't know. I've only met Sarah once. I'm sure she'll want to see all her old friends." When Chris talked to Sarah again—and he fully intended to—he didn't want it to be in front of a room full of attentive strangers.

"Oh, but you have to come, Chris. She'll think you're hiding from her." Juanita appeared to be working hard to hide a smile. "You wouldn't want that, would you?"

Chris took a deep breath and opened his mouth to speak, but Rita held up a hand and interrupted. "Shhh, here she comes. Remember, 6:00 Saturday evening. Everyone's meeting at Elizabeth's, and we'll walk over together."

She stopped on her way out to give Sarah a hug and then caught Chris's eye over Sarah's head and mouthed something that looked strangely like "Be there or be square."

"What's Rita up to this time?" Sarah smiled as she came in. "I noticed the clipboard."

"Oh, you know Rita." Juanita waved a dismissive hand. "She's always got some project or another going."

When Sarah glanced at him and looked away, Chris realized he was staring. Was his mouth even hanging open? He wasn't sure if he was completely captivated or just falling asleep on his feet, but he had to admit she did look good.

"I hear you're heading up to San Ramon this afternoon to do some shopping. How's the house shaping up?" Juanita handed Sarah a menu that she didn't bother to open.

"How did you know I was going to San Ramon?" Even with her brow furrowed, Sarah looked cute.

If Juanita knew she had blundered, she gave no clue. "How does anyone know anything around here? I think it just blows on the wind. Now, have you had time to look at that menu?"

Sarah held her puzzled frown for a second longer before she accepted the truth of Juanita's observation and let her face relax into a smile. "Don't need the menu. I'm still working my way through the specials."

"Huevos rancheros it is, then. And since Carlos gets his chile from Russ and me, you know it will be the best you've ever put in your mouth."

—◦◦◦—

"My mouth is watering already." Sarah handed the menu back to Juanita. If that big goof of an owner didn't stop staring at her, she was going to have to do something. She wasn't sure what yet, but it wouldn't be taking her business elsewhere, since (a) there was no "elsewhere" and (b) she was here first, darn it. If anyone needed to go elsewhere, it was Chris. Her earliest memories included ice cream at the Dip 'n' Dine on Saturday afternoons. Fayette had been a waitress then before she bought the place, and Sarah was just beginning to realize how much she was going to miss her.

She glanced at Chris, who had stopped by another table to chat for a moment with the customers. Fayette used to do that all the time, of course, but it was different when she did it. Fayette was friendly and down-home. You felt she was plain glad to see you. This guy acted friendly, but Sarah didn't believe it. She had seen guys just like him all her life—big guys with way more looks than brains who thought of no one but themselves and who expected the world to part like the Red Sea just because they swaggered through it. She caught him looking at her again and stared back, opening her eyes as wide as she could get them. He actually blushed and looked away. *Take that, you big doofus, and start packing.*

"Here you go. Eggs over easy. I forgot to ask, but they're best that way." Juanita appeared with a steaming plate of huevos rancheros and a basket of thick flour tortillas.

"Thanks, Juanita." Sarah spread her napkin over her lap. "I meant to tell you how nice it is to see a friendly face in here. When did you start working here?"

"Well, I volunteered, of course, with the rest of the church when Fayette was spending all that time with Matthew at the hospital. Then after she sold the place, I found I missed it. Well, not so much the work as the people. With the kids all grown and gone and the business end of the farm all computerized, I wasn't as busy as I once was. I just work a few days a week anyway."

Sarah kept her voice at a low murmur. "How is it working for . . . ?" She tilted her head toward the kitchen.

"Chris?" Sarah saw him look over at the mention of his name

37

and wished Juanita would lower her voice. "Oh, he's doing all right. He's a little green right now, but he's coming along." A ding came from the kitchen and Juanita rolled her eyes. "Well, either I have an order ready, or Chris wants to bless me out again for talking about him to the customers. His one weakness, other than wanting to change every last thing, is that he's a bit touchy. You enjoy those eggs, now."

Juanita went to the kitchen where there was indeed an order waiting for her, and Sarah turned her attention to her huevos rancheros. Juanita was right. They were outstanding, and Sarah sopped up every bit of egg and green chile with the thick tortillas.

She didn't have time to think of ways to get Chris out of the Dip 'n' Dine and out of Last Chance, because every time someone came in, they stopped by the table to welcome her back. It was surprising how many knew she had taken the Carter place and how many even remarked on her pending trip that afternoon to San Ramon. Juanita was right. There were no secrets in Last Chance.

4

Sarah did a double take when she walked through her living room Saturday evening and glanced out her front window. Something was up. Cars were parked up and down her quiet street, though none directly in front of her house. She saw the Watsons hurry past without looking up, Les holding a plastic grocery bag and Evelyn carrying what looked like a Bundt cake. Someone was obviously having a party tonight, and since she hadn't heard a word about it, she was pretty sure who it was.

Looking around her small living room, Sarah smiled in satisfaction. She had worked hard over the last few days and was pleased with her work. She had been able to get most of the spots out of the turquoise sofa and covered those that remained with cushions of coral and lime green. Some of the Fiesta ware was on display in the kitchen, and the rest sat on freshly papered shelves. She quickly shoved the few boxes she still had to unpack into the spare room and shut the door. There. It looked like she'd been settled forever.

It wasn't till she was adjusting her new towels in the bathroom that she glanced in the mirror. The house might have been ready, but with her stained T-shirt and cutoff jeans, her hair drawn back in a careless ponytail, and not a smidgen of makeup, Sarah clearly was not. She raced to her bedroom to change and had just fluffed her curls around her face and begun applying a light coat of lip gloss when the low rumble of a crowd trying to be silent and the doorbell told her that her party was about to begin.

The surprised look Sarah had practiced in the mirror as she got dressed was totally unnecessary, because as her guests poured through the front door, their attention and exclamations turned to the little house she had worked so hard to fix up. Everyone's attention but that new owner of the Dip 'n' Dine, Chris. At six-something, he stood out in the crowd like a sore thumb, and he was looking at her, not her house. Who invited him, anyway?

"Oh my goodness, I haven't seen this furniture in years. What in the world made you bring all this down?" Elizabeth had a slight smile on her face as she looked around.

"It's the latest thing, Gran." Sarah gave her grandmother a hug. "All the stores are filled with midcentury replicas, and look! I've got a houseful of the real thing. Isn't that great?"

"Well, I was sure proud of it." Elizabeth ran her fingers across the kidney-shaped coffee table. "I can't say your granddad was all that tickled with it, though. He let me get it, but he always said it made him feel like he was company in his own house. It does look cute in here, though."

"Okay, everybody." Rita emerged from a reconnaissance visit to the kitchen. "We're going to need every inch of the counters as well as the table to set up the potluck dishes, so just put your poundings over there by the fireplace."

"Um, this should get in the freezer right away." Chris held up the small cooler he was holding.

Rita sighed. Clearly, she did not like to be interrupted when she was in full organizational mode. "What do you have there, Chris? Ice cream?"

With every eye in the room on him, Chris stood taller than ever.

And to Sarah's ears, he sounded as cocky as ever. "No, these are a couple dinners I made up and froze." He smiled a half smile. "Don't worry. I taped the heating instructions to the covers."

He may have thought he was fooling everyone with that aw-shucks grin of his, but Sarah knew a patronizing attitude when she was confronted with one. Boy, did she. And she was done with it. "Oh, thanks." Her voice and smile were so bright they were almost brittle. "I can't even boil water without instructions."

Everyone laughed, and Chris's smile faded a bit. "Okay, then, I'll stick these in the freezer real quick."

Conversation bubbled around her again, and Rita continued her efforts to take charge, but Sarah felt a twinge of guilt as Chris disappeared into the kitchen. She tried to avoid meeting her grandmother's eye but knew that wouldn't do her any good in the long run. Elizabeth had definite ideas about the obligations of hospitality and would have plenty to say about the way Sarah had spoken to Chris in front of the other guests. She shifted uncomfortably. She hadn't been very nice, and truth be told, boiling water was just about the only thing in the kitchen she didn't need instructions for.

Sarah tried to make her way toward Chris when he came back from the kitchen, but he stayed to the edge of the room, and as soon as she could extricate herself from one group of guests, another claimed her attention to ask about her plans for the fall or to talk about what she had done to the house they continued to call the Carter place.

"I don't care what anyone says, this is real cute." Juanita took Sarah's arm as she tried to slip past. "And you are surely not the first young person to set up housekeeping with a bunch of old stuff nobody else wanted. You wouldn't believe some of the furniture

Russ and I started out with. But don't you worry. You'll have your own before you know it."

"Thanks, Juanita." Sarah saw no point in trying to explain mid-century modern to Juanita. She was getting tired of explaining, anyway. Let people think what they wanted. She was happy, and it was her house.

She had almost made it across the room to at least speak to Chris when Rita clapped her hands to get everyone's attention. "Okay, everything's all set and we're ready to eat. Pastor, would you ask the blessing?"

The room fell silent, and Brother Parker's slow drawl asked God's blessing on Sarah, on the little house that would shelter her, and on the food prepared and offered by so many loving hands. Sarah's eyes filled as that love settled around her like a warm embrace. She blinked back her tears and looked up as everyone joined in the amen. Chris was smiling at her, and for some reason, his smile didn't look quite so cocky. In fact, he had rather a nice smile, and she found herself returning it.

—⚏—

"That breeze feels nice. It got warm in here with all those people." Elizabeth sat at the Formica and chrome kitchen table sipping iced tea and watching Sarah put away all her pantry goods. The cool night wind coming through the back door ruffled the new curtains and brought the sound of crickets.

"It was amazing. I don't think I'll have to grocery shop till Christmas." Sarah tried to squeeze another box of cornmeal into the already crowded cupboard. "It almost makes me want to learn to cook."

"Oh, here. You'll need this." Elizabeth took a pad of paper

from her purse. "It's the guest list. I couldn't write down what they brought since it was all in bags and whatnot, but I think this is one time when a generic thank-you might be acceptable."

"Thank-you notes?" Sarah knew the answer before her grandmother spoke.

"If you sit right down tomorrow afternoon and get them taken care of, they'll be behind you before you know it."

Sarah picked up the pad and flipped a page. "There are an awful lot of names here."

"And each and every person on that list brought you a gift for your pantry and prepared a dish for the potluck. They spent a lot more time on you than you'll spend writing them their note."

"Yes, but there's only one of me and there's . . ." Sarah sighed and gave up. She hated writing thank-you notes, but she knew from a lifetime of experience that it would be easier to do as her grandmother suggested: sit right down tomorrow after church and get them done. If she didn't, she'd have to explain to Gran why she hadn't written them yet every single time she saw her. And Gran lived just two doors down.

"And since we're talking about common courtesy . . ." Gran raised an eyebrow and Sarah braced herself. *Here it comes.* "What in this world were you thinking poking fun at Chris that way this evening? Everyone else knew you were just teasing him a little, but he's new and doesn't know you like we do. He probably thought he'd done something wrong."

Sarah bit her lip. Even with her scolding, Gran was giving her way too much credit. If Chris thought he had messed up, it was because that was exactly what she'd intended for him to think. And thinking about it now made her feel rotten. She cleared her throat.

"Yeah, that was uncalled-for. I guess I should apologize."

"Well, it wouldn't hurt to clear things up."

Sarah plopped into a chair across the table from Elizabeth. "But Gran, he's just out of place here. Tonight there was a room full of faces I've known all my life—and Chris Reed. Everyone else is all normal sized, and there he is sticking out of the crowd like a Wack-A-Mole. We've all been going to the Dip 'n' Dine for the daily specials forever, and he wants to come in and change every last thing."

"He does? Who'd you hear that from?"

"Juanita. You heard her."

"Well, you might want to take that with a grain of salt—at least till those changes start happening. But here's a tip: the quickest way to help someone stop being a stranger is to make him feel at home."

Sarah just looked at her grandmother. The day she won an argument with Gran was going be a red-letter day indeed. She shook her head and sighed. "Want some more iced tea?"

Elizabeth got to her feet. "No, it's late and I need to get on home. Church tomorrow."

"I'll walk you." Sarah stood up and carried her glass to the sink.

"There's no need. I know the way."

"But I want to. It's a beautiful night, and I love thinking you're only two doors down."

Sarah waited on the sidewalk as Elizabeth made her careful way down the porch steps, then tucked her hand in her grandmother's elbow as they walked down the street. She opened the gate to Elizabeth's yard, and Gran gave her hand a pat as she pulled her elbow away.

"I can take it from here, honey. The porch light's on and the sidewalk's lit up. You go on home."

Sam, Elizabeth's giant gray tabby, came bounding off the steps with a large moth in his mouth, and Sarah stood at the gate listening to her grandmother fuss at him all the way up her walk.

"If you think you're going to bring that thing in my house, you've got another think coming, buster. So just drop it now, or plan on staying outside with it."

As if Sam understood, he dropped his prey and trotted past Elizabeth through the front door. She turned and waved at Sarah, still waiting by the gate. "Good night, sweet girl. I'm going to love having you for my neighbor."

"Me too. Shall I pick you up for church in the morning?"

In the glare of the porch light, Elizabeth looked tired, and for the first time Sarah noticed that her indomitable grandmother was starting to look frail. Her smile, though, beamed strong and warm, even from the porch. "I'd love that. See you tomorrow."

Sarah watched the screen door close behind Elizabeth and started back down the street. The night wind, the lullaby of her childhood, rustled the leaves of the cottonwood tree, and overhead the sky was nearly white with stars. Her cousin Ray was the one who knew the stars, and she could never look at a night sky without remembering him patiently pointing out the constellations when she was a little girl and telling her the stories that accompanied them—stories of mighty hunters, of women too vain to put down their mirrors, of golden-fleeced rams. That was the Last Chance that lived in her heart, that called her home when her strength failed her, a Last Chance as unchanging as the rocky hills that sheltered it and the sky that arched overhead. But Last Chance *had* changed. Ray was married now and living with his new wife in Santa Fe. Gran was actually beginning to look old, even if no one dared admit it. And then, of course, there was the Dip 'n' Dine. If anyone was the poster child for change in Last Chance, it was Chris Reed, and that alone was enough to make her want him gone. The insufferable arrogance and that smug know-it-all attitude just made it that much easier.

———✺———

Chris leaned back in the one chair Fayette had left him that he liked, an overstuffed rocker, and closed his eyes. Tomorrow was Sunday, and he thanked the Lord for a day of rest. He had come to Last Chance prepared for the physical work required to run a restaurant. He was certainly no stranger to hard work. It was the other stuff that caught him off guard and really exhausted him. Temperamental chefs, he knew, but everybody in this town seemed to want a say in the way he ran his restaurant. And they were all agreed: he was doing it wrong.

That party tonight felt almost as tiring as the day at the Dip 'n' Dine that preceded it. And now that he thought about it, the chicken breast with artichoke hearts and mushrooms probably wasn't the best choice for the pounding if he wanted to stop being the outsider. Cooks like Carlos worked a man's job and were to be respected. Chefs, on the other hand, were a different breed entirely. He should have just picked up a jar of mayonnaise.

He may have made some progress in spite of himself, though, thanks to Brother Parker. The pastor had taken him under his wing and seemed to know just which groups of guests they should join. That Chris was a three-letter man in high school and had played on a couple championship teams just seemed to fall naturally into the conversation, and Chris noticed a change in people's attitudes. He may not have been one of the guys just yet, but they didn't act as if he had just landed from Mars either.

Chris's phone buzzed, and he smiled as he pulled it out of his pocket. He had told Olivia to call him at 9:00, and she was right on time.

"Hey, Liverhead. How's it going?"

"Fine. And I told you not to call me Liverhead. Liver is disgusting."

"Okay, I'll try to remember. But you're wrong about liver. Liver is delectable."

"Yuck. And you are weird."

Chris laughed out loud. Olivia never failed to delight him. "So where's your mom? Is she home?"

"Yeah, right. What do you think?"

"And?"

"And she made me have a babysitter. Like I'm three years old or something."

"Good. Let me talk to her."

"She's on her own phone right now. She's been talking since Mom left."

"Well, tell her to put down her phone and talk to me. Right now." Chris heard Olivia's sigh of exasperation and a mumbled conversation he couldn't quite understand before a voice came back on the line.

"Hello?"

"Hi. This is Olivia's Uncle Chris. You're the babysitter?"

"Yeah."

Man, she didn't sound any older than Olivia. "How old are you?"

"Twelve."

"Twelve?"

"Nearly."

Chris took a deep breath to calm down. It wasn't the babysitter's fault that she was only eleven, or that someone had hired her to babysit when she needed a babysitter herself. But if there were two babies looking after each other, they could at least do a good job of it. "Okay, look. I want you to hang up your phone. Do you hear me?"

"Okay. I'm almost out of battery anyway."

"Then you and Olivia put in one of *her* movies to watch until her mom gets home. Got that?"

"Uh-huh."

"And if there is any problem whatsoever, you call me. Understand?"

"Okay."

"Now put Olivia back on, and *hang up your phone*!"

Chris repeated his instructions to Olivia and listened to the good-night kiss she sent over the wire before she hung up. She was so little.

He gritted his teeth to the grinding point as he jabbed at his sister's number on his contact list. It went straight to voice mail, of course. If Olivia weren't three hundred miles away in Scottsdale, he'd be sitting on the sofa waiting for Kaitlyn when she got home. He loved his sister, but Olivia deserved better.

5

There was something in the air Sunday mornings that made them different from the rest of the week. Sarah had no idea what it was or why this was so, but she had no doubt that if she were taken out of some sensory deprivation chamber, taken to the middle of Last Chance, and asked "What day is it?" she would know.

"I saw Lurlene up at San Ramon this week at the beauty parlor." Elizabeth, sitting next to Sarah in the front seat, broke the silence of the empty streets. "She said to say hi and to tell you how sorry she was to have to miss your party. She had a church music conference in El Paso from Wednesday through last night."

Sarah glanced across at her grandmother and grinned. "Still trying to recruit me for the choir, is she?"

"Well, no." Elizabeth kept her eyes forward. "I don't believe that came up."

Sarah laughed. The Cooley family was known to be musically gifted, and it had taken her years to realize that the gift may have passed her by. But even if she was the last to know she couldn't carry a tune, she never let it stop her. She sang loudly and with gusto, just never at anyone's particular request.

"See?" Sarah parked her car under the elms. "We got here in plenty of time."

"Well, I wouldn't say 'plenty,' but we did get here before the service started."

"Ah, Gran, come on. What would you have done if we'd gotten here fifteen minutes earlier? You just sat on your front porch instead of in your pew, that's all."

"I just don't like feeling rushed." Elizabeth opened her door to get out. "And if a person says she's coming by at a certain time, then that's when I look for her to come by."

Sarah made sure she was looking the other way before she rolled her eyes. No need to make things worse. "Okay, Gran. I'm sorry I was late. I'll be more careful from now on."

That appeared to be all Elizabeth was waiting for, and her smile returned. "Well, as you said, no harm done. We made it in time."

As Sarah followed her grandmother down the aisle, she began to wonder if she might have made a mistake in moving so close. She loved Gran more than anyone she could name, and the idea of being able to care for Gran the way she had cared for Sarah had given her deep satisfaction. But Gran didn't seem clear on who was taking care of whom.

The choir was already filing in as they took their seats in the third row on the left. Maybe they *had* cut it a little bit close. Lurlene, the worship leader, turned to the congregation and in moments the sounds of praise and worship filled the old wooden building.

Even over the enthusiastic voices filling the church, one strong baritone stood out and Sarah had to turn to see who it belonged to. Chris, of course. Who else? What a show-off. Well, knowing Lurlene, it wouldn't be long before he was up in the choir, and truth be told, Sarah wasn't really looking forward to seeing him stand out up there every time she came to church.

Sarah deliberately turned her attention to the rest of the service. Chris got on her last nerve just by breathing the same air she did, but that would not completely dominate her return to

Last Chance. She would not let it. She owed him an apology, and he would get one. After this very service if she could manage it. Then she would go on about her business and let him go about his. She had friends in town, even if most of them were married now. She had Gran to look after. And in just a few weeks she'd have a classroom of second graders to teach. She had a full life. A deep sense of peace settled over her and remained until Lurlene signaled the final hymn. Chris's voice filled the church again. How irritating could one man be?

Brother Parker raised his hands and pronounced the benediction, but not even that restored the fleeting sense of peace Sarah had experienced earlier. She was still out of sorts when Rita caught up with her.

"Hey, Miss Sarah. I hope we didn't leave you with too much of a mess to clean up last night."

Sarah smiled. The house had been left immaculate. Rita saw to that. But that wasn't what she was looking for, and Sarah knew it. "Everything was perfect, of course. I can't believe you did that for me. Thank you so much!" She gave the wiry redhead a hug.

"And were you really surprised? Did anyone give it away?"

"No one said a single word." Sarah was thankful for a question she could answer easily. "I was just blown away by everything. I still am."

"Well, we love you and we're glad you're home to stay, and we want you to know it. Did you get everything you need?"

"Everything I need and then some."

"Then we did what we set out to do." Rita beamed at her and then waved as she looked past Sarah at someone behind her. "Oops. There's someone I need to catch before they leave." She patted Sarah's arm as she left. "Glad you had a good time last night, honey."

Sarah took a deep breath. Rita was a whirlwind. She blew in, then she blew out again, and Sarah always needed a moment to regroup when she did. Elizabeth had gone on, and Sarah could see her talking to Brother Parker at the door.

As she passed the pew where he had been sitting, Chris Reed stepped out into the aisle and joined her. She lacked about three inches in reaching his shoulder. Good night, he was tall. Almost instinctively, she moved over to put space between them. She didn't like the feeling of being overpowered.

"Good morning." He smiled down at her.

"Hi." Did he do that on purpose? Loom over people like that?

"I wanted to thank you for the party last night. It was a lot of fun."

"Hey, I was as much a guest as anyone. It just happened to be at my house, that's all. The one you want to thank is Rita. She was the one who put it all together."

"I'll do that."

They had reached the vestibule, and Sarah was able to put a couple more feet between them. She could deal with Chris more easily if she didn't have to look up to do it. "I do owe you an apology, though."

Chris raised an inquisitive eyebrow.

"Yeah, the crack about the instructions was uncalled-for. It was a poor joke and I'm sorry." There. She had said it, and now she could be done with Chris Reed.

"Oh, that." There was that aw-shucks grin again. "Well, I sure didn't mean to imply you couldn't cook. I was just trying to make it easy for you."

She couldn't help it. She smiled back. "Well, I appreciate it. Because you know what? I do need written instructions to boil water."

"It's not nearly as hard as it looks, but I could write out the instructions for that too, if you want me to."

Chris's furrowed brow and the concern in his eyes confused Sarah. Surely he knew she was joking. Then she noticed the tiny grin tugging at the corner of his mouth, and she burst out laughing.

"You do that. And don't forget the part about filling the kettle first. That's the bit that I really struggle with." Through the church doors Sarah could see that Elizabeth had finished her conversation with the pastor and was making her careful way across the parking lot. She tossed Chris a hurried wave. "Gotta go. Again, sorry for the cheap shot, and thanks for the . . . ?"

"Boneless chicken breast with mushrooms and artichokes."

"Uh, right, that." Sarah turned and, stopping at the door for only the briefest handshake with Brother Parker, raced to catch up with Elizabeth.

—⁂—

Chris watched her go, wanting to kick himself. Why did he have to sound like a menu? Why couldn't he have just said "chicken"? Everyone likes chicken. And why did he, one of the fastest and most agile running backs his high school had ever fielded, and a smart guy too, always feel like a knuckle-dragging Neanderthal whenever Sarah Cooley was around?

"Well, that was a heavy sigh." Chris turned to find Lurlene entering the vestibule and smiling at him.

"Hi, Lurlene." He decided to ignore the comment about his sigh. What could he say to explain it, anyway? "It was a good service today. And I especially liked the offertory. I don't think I've ever heard the choir sound better."

"Funny you should mention that, Chris, because that's just what I wanted to talk to you about."

Uh-oh.

"You have a very nice voice, do you know that? And I'll just say it straight out. We sure could use you in the choir."

"Thanks, Lurlene, but I just don't see how I can take on anything else right now. I just don't have the bandwidth. I'm still trying to get my feet on the ground at the Dip 'n' Dine."

"Well, yes, I have heard a little bit about that."

Oh you have, have you? And where would that come from, as if I didn't know?

Lurlene smiled and patted his arm. "You're doing just fine. We're proud to have you in Last Chance. And the choir's not going anywhere. We'll be here when you're ready for us."

Chris wanted to hug Lurlene. Her encouraging words made him realize how few he had heard since he arrived in Last Chance. It almost made him want to join the choir, just to please her. Almost. He smiled instead.

"I'll remember that."

"And here's one more thing for you to remember." Lurlene had walked with him to the door and paused before she went to her own car. "If God has something for you to do, he's going to give you the wherewithal to do it, whether it's the time, the energy, or the bandwidth, whatever that is. That's your filter, not how you feel about things."

Chris watched her go before heading to his Jeep. For a few seconds he had thought that she understood how overwhelmed he was, that she might be concerned about him as a person, not just a baritone. He couldn't blame her, though. She was devoted to the choir.

He had just climbed into the front seat when Lurlene drove by and leaned out her window. "And I'm not talking about the choir, either!"

With a wave, Lurlene drove out of the parking lot, and Chris watched her go. Okay, then, if she wasn't talking about the choir, then what? The image of Sarah Cooley floated through his mind again. Could Lurlene possibly have seen something there? Could she have been encouraging Chris to follow up on that?

Chris turned the ignition key and shoved the gearshift into Reverse. *Get real, Reed. The only thing anyone could have noticed about you and Sarah Cooley is that she pretty much can't stand you. Lurlene just meant what she said—let God decide what you have the bandwidth for.*

———

"Was that Chris Reed I saw you talking to after church?" Elizabeth settled herself in the front seat as Sarah started her car.

"Well, there aren't too many other behemoths floating around, so I guess it must have been him that you saw." For a moment Sarah thought she may have gone too far. Gran let a lot go by, but when you crossed the line from sassy to what she considered disrespectful, she yanked you up short. But Gran seemed ready to let this one pass.

"Did you get things straightened out with him?"

"I guess. At any rate, I said I was sorry, and he said okay, so we're done."

"Did you invite him over for coffee or something?"

"Good heavens, why would I do that?"

"Oh, I don't know. Just to be friendly, I guess. There aren't that many single young people in town, and he doesn't have much of a social life here."

"Well, I sure don't see it as my job to provide him with one. Are you matchmaking, Gran?"

"Of course not. I just think he's a nice young man and he seems lonely to me. I know between Carlos and Juanita, they're giving him fits at the Dip 'n' Dine, and he doesn't seem to have much of a life beyond that. A friendly cup of coffee might go a long way toward making him feel at home in Last Chance, that's all."

"Well, I have to say this." Sarah stopped in her grandmother's driveway. "I don't think he's quite as stuck on himself as I once did. He does have a sense of humor. But do you know what was in those packages he brought?" She lowered her voice to an affected baritone. "Boneless chicken breast with artichokes and mushrooms."

"Sounds good. Different anyway." Elizabeth gathered her belongings and prepared to climb out.

"Want to come have lunch with me? We could have chicken with artichokes and mushrooms."

"Not today, sweet girl. I'm just too tired for anything. It seems I can pretty much do anything I ever could, but it just takes me longer and longer to recover."

"Are you okay?" Sarah covered Elizabeth's hand with her own. She wanted to take care of Gran, but that didn't mean Gran was supposed to get old.

"I'm fine." Elizabeth opened the door. "I just need my nap. You can come back this evening for some waffles, if you want. But you should know I'm going to call Chris Reed as soon as I get up and invite him too. I think that boy could use some company."

"Wish I could." Actually, those waffles were sounding good until Gran mentioned inviting Chris. "But I really need to get finished with my unpacking. School's going to be starting soon, and I won't have time then."

Elizabeth just nodded. "Suit yourself, honey, but you have to eat something, so if you decide you have time, just come on over."

Sarah watched her grandmother go into the house before head-

56

ing down the street to her own place. She never could shake the feeling that Gran could see right into her soul, and she felt the tiniest twinge of guilt. Truthfully, she did have some more boxes to unpack, but she knew that wasn't really what was keeping her from Gran's. Gran would never admit it, but if she wasn't actually into matchmaking, she was certainly providing the opportunities.

She slipped off her shoes at the door and padded into the kitchen. It smelled like coffee, and sunlight spilled through the window and left a wide patch of light on the linoleum floor. She found herself humming as she opened the refrigerator and took out some of last night's leftovers. She loved her little house. She loved being back in Last Chance. She loved knowing that she'd be teaching her first class in a few weeks, and she even loved the fact that she had squared things up with Chris and could let him go his way while she went hers. A sense of well-being filled her to the bursting point and poured out in song. Who cared whether or not it was on key? This was her house.

The muffled ring of her phone summoned her to the living room. Still singing, she danced her way back to the sofa where she had tossed her purse and dug through till she found her phone. The song died, and so did the dance. For a long moment she stared at the name and face that appeared on the screen. The ring stopped, probably heading to voice mail. Sarah turned off the ringer, knowing it would just chime again, and buried it under the lime green throw pillow. One of these days, she would take the call, but she wasn't up to it just yet. She just needed more time.

6

The sun was just slipping behind the mountains on the horizon to the west when Sarah collapsed her last cardboard box, poured herself a glass of iced tea, and plopped down in front of the little window air conditioner in her living room. She propped her feet on her coffee table and leaned back against the cushions. It was done. She was all moved in. She closed her eyes and let the cool air and the gentle drone lull her almost to sleep.

The lime green pillow under her elbow vibrated, and she peeked under it to find the still silenced phone. She smiled at the slightly annoyed face filling the screen. Gran hated getting her picture taken.

"Hey, there. What's up?"

"Hello, sweet girl. I didn't wake you, did I?" Gran firmly believed that Sunday afternoons were made for naps as surely as Sunday mornings were made for worship services.

"Nope, I'm just sitting here drinking some tea."

"Well, I was just wondering . . . did you happen to get any syrup last night?"

"Two or three bottles. Why? Need some?"

"I've got about enough for one waffle. I'm so put out with myself. I didn't even think about it when I invited Chris over. If you could lend me a bottle, I'll replace it next time I go shopping."

"No need. I've got more syrup than I'll ever use. Just give me a little time to clean up, and I'll bring it over."

"Thank you, honey. There's no rush. I won't need it for another hour or so."

Sarah hung up the phone and headed down the hall to the bathroom. She stopped just before she got there. Why was she cleaning up to run a bottle of syrup down to Gran's, unless she was falling into Gran's matchmaking plans? And despite her grandmother's protests to the contrary, she was pretty sure Gran was matchmaking.

Sarah turned on her heel, grabbed a bottle of syrup from her stuffed cupboard, and ran down the street to Elizabeth's house.

Elizabeth was sitting in her recliner crocheting and watching television when Sarah came through the front door. She looked up in surprise.

"Well, Sarah! I thought you were coming over later."

"You know, I just want to take a shower, climb into something comfortable, and kick back. I thought I'd run this down first."

"But I was hoping to talk you into staying for supper." Elizabeth rested her crocheting on her lap and looked up, clearly disappointed.

"Gran, what am I going to do with you?" Sarah gave her grandmother an exasperated smile. "I've already told you that trying to play matchmaker between me and Chris Reed is a waste of time. I am not interested."

"And I've already told you that I am not matchmaking. I just thought it might be more of a party with you here, that's all."

A twinge of guilt poked Sarah somewhere in her middle, but she refused to give in to it. Even if Elizabeth had absolutely no intention of matching her up with Chris—and she had to admit she'd never known her grandmother to tell even a half-truth—she didn't want Chris getting any ideas. She was not so naïve or so clueless that she didn't know what Chris's puppy dog stares meant, and if he came for dinner and found her here, he just might think she was being served up with a side of sausage. The thought made her shudder and completely erased the twinge of guilt.

"I'm sorry, Gran." Sarah tried to make her smile conciliatory. "But I really am beat. I would be terrible company, I promise you. But we'll have waffles next Sunday for sure. In fact, if you let me borrow your waffle iron, I'll fix them for you and we'll eat at my house."

"Well, all right then." Elizabeth seemed to know her battle was lost. "Go on home and get some rest. But I have to say, if you end the Lord's Day more tired than you began it, you might need to rethink the way you spend it."

Sarah tried not to heave the sigh that filled her chest. Gran could be so . . . Granish. "It's been a really busy week with moving and all, but I'm settled in now. This coming week should be easier. I'm going to run up to San Ramon one day to get some things to decorate my classroom. Want to come?"

Elizabeth's smile lost all trace of disappointment. "I'd love to. Fixing up the classroom was one of my favorite parts of teaching, although back then we didn't have near what you all have today."

"Great." Sarah set the syrup on the table and headed out the door. "I'll give you a call and we can decide when to go."

"You do that." Elizabeth picked up her crocheting again. "Shall I tell Chris you said hi?"

Sarah stuck her head back in the door. "No."

—⁂—

Chris parked in front of Elizabeth Cooley's just before six. This was his first invitation to a meal with anyone since he arrived in

Last Chance. That in itself wasn't too unusual. Chefs, he had discovered, didn't get many dinner invitations, and neither, it seemed, did chefs-turned-diner-owners.

Elizabeth and the aroma of freshly brewed coffee met him at the door. Her eyes lit up at the flowers he held. "Well, aren't you sweet? These are just lovely. Come with me to the kitchen while I put them in some water."

Chris followed. His mom had told him never to accept a dinner invitation and go empty-handed—to always take wine or flowers. And since he had a feeling Elizabeth wouldn't appreciate wine, that left flowers. The only problem was, there was no place in Last Chance to buy flowers, and the only place in San Ramon he could find that was open was the grocery store. They seemed to please her, though.

When Elizabeth set the flowers in the middle of the table, Chris noticed it was set for two. He tried not to let his disappointment show. Elizabeth had not mentioned that anyone else would be here, but, face it, ever since she had called him this afternoon, he'd been hoping to see Sarah here. He had made one bad impression after another, and a nice, relaxed evening away from the diner might have given him just the chance he needed to finally get her to stop looking at him as if he really needed a keeper.

Elizabeth stopped talking, and he realized she had asked him about his family. He tried to regroup his thoughts and hoped he was answering the right question.

"They're in Scottsdale. My parents have their own real estate company, which keeps them really busy, and I have one sister, Kaitlyn. She has a little girl, Olivia." Thinking about Olivia always made him smile, and Elizabeth seemed to pick up on his delight right away.

"I bet she's darling. How old is she?"

"She's seven. I don't know that I'd call her 'darling,' though. I think of darling as someone in a fluffy dress sitting on a cushion, and that's definitely not Olivia. She's so smart she scares me, but she hasn't had an easy time of it, and she's a tough little cookie. She's been sent home for fighting more than once. I worry about her."

Elizabeth smiled. "Sounds like you need to worry more about the other kids. Olivia's doing okay."

She plugged in her waffle iron, set a mug of coffee on the table next to Chris, and started stirring up the waffle batter before she returned the conversation to Olivia.

"You didn't mention a brother-in-law. Is Olivia's dad in the picture?"

Chris shook his head. "Nope. Both he and Kaitlyn were just kids, and he ran. Kaitlyn's done this pretty much on her own."

"But your folks were there." It was more a question than a statement.

Chris shrugged. Ordinarily he was fiercely protective of his family. He had built a high wall around them in his heart and stood guard, sword drawn, daring any outsider to judge or even criticize. But Elizabeth wasn't coming across as doing either. She just seemed interested and warm, and he felt himself relaxing a bit. "Well, they gave her and Olivia a home, of course, until Kaitlyn could get out on her own. And they put her through beauty school so she could take care of herself and Olivia, but they're too busy to babysit and stuff, if that's what you mean."

"Do you get to see them often?"

"Not as often as I'd like. I tried to get them to move out here with me, but they wouldn't even move to Albuquerque. There's no way I could get them to a place like Last Chance." Chris felt his ears grow red as soon as the words were out of his mouth. *Nice. Eat a lady's waffles and insult her town in one fell swoop.*

But if he had offended Elizabeth, she gave no sign; she just nodded.

"Well, Last Chance isn't for everyone, that's for sure. And I, for one, am glad. If it were, it wouldn't be Last Chance. It would be just another big city in the desert. Not that we wouldn't love to have your sister and Olivia here in Last Chance, of course." She put a cast iron skillet on the stove and took a paper package from the refrigerator. "Now, how about putting those chef skills to work and frying us up some sausage? It should be done about the time the first waffles are ready."

Chris was grateful for the task. He had talked more openly about his family to Elizabeth than he had ever talked to anyone, and even though she was easy to talk to, he was glad to leave the subject.

The conversation never did return to his family. It just slipped from one easy subject to another as they ate their waffles and sausage and then as Chris, over Elizabeth's protests, helped with the dishes. Finally they stood on her front porch in the deepening dusk of the long summer twilight as he said his good-byes.

As he turned to head down the walk to his Jeep, Elizabeth raised her arm in a wave, and he looked to see Sarah in her front yard watering her flowers. He also gave what he hoped looked like a casual yet friendly wave and got in his Jeep. He had turned his Jeep around to park in front of Elizabeth's house, so he was pointed away from Sarah's house.

Almost too embarrassed to admit to himself he was doing so, he swung the Jeep into another U-turn so he could nonchalantly drive by Sarah's house as if he had someplace to go in that direction. He lifted his hand in another easy wave as he drove by, and she returned it. *Perfect, Reed. Cool, casual. Oh, yeah, you live here. I'd forgotten.* He drove to the corner, signaled, and turned into a cul-de-sac. There was nothing he could do but turn the Jeep around and head back the way he came. Sarah was still in her front yard watching him approach. This time he didn't wave. Or even look at her as he passed.

—m—

Sarah shook her head as she watched Chris drive past the second time. What in the world was he doing? But as the taillights disappeared around the corner, she dissolved into laughter. Not a ladylike chuckle either, but the kind of loud belly laugh that made her mother look at her and sigh. If Chris Reed were even half as cool as he tried to be, he'd be an obnoxious jerk, but he was such a doofus, she almost felt sorry for him.

"Was that Chris going by again? What was he doing?" When Elizabeth had seen Sarah in her yard, she had walked on down.

"Beats me." Sarah grinned. "Maybe he just wanted a tour of the neighborhood."

"Well, that's just the strangest thing. There's nothing down there but the Watsons' house. Why would he want to see the Watsons' house?"

Sarah gave her grandmother a one-armed hug. "I don't know. Why don't you come sit on the porch with me for a while and have a glass of tea. You can tell me all about your dinner party."

"I'd hardly call a few waffles and sausage a dinner party." Elizabeth started up the walk with Sarah. "But Chris is a nice young man. He brought me flowers."

"Did he, now? Maybe I'm not the one you should be thinking about matching Chris up with."

Sarah had only to glance at her grandmother's face to realize she had crossed the line. Gran was not amused. "I think that's enough about Chris and matchmaking, don't you? He's clearly been taught some manners, and I find that refreshing."

Not quite sure how she was to take the "refreshing use of good manners" comment, Sarah left her grandmother rocking on the front porch and went into the house to get them both some iced tea. When she got back, Gran, in typical Gran fashion, had moved beyond her admonishment as if it had never happened. Her sigh was as contented as her smile as she accepted the icy glass.

"Thank you, darlin'. This is so nice. I have to admit that when you left for college, I was afraid Last Chance had seen the last of you, to live anyway. So many of our young people leave."

Sarah, rocking beside her, nodded. "Well, there's not a lot to keep people here once they get out of school. A few of my friends from high school stayed to work the family ranch or chile farm, but most are long gone."

"I guess that's one reason why I've taken to Chris Reed like I have." Elizabeth set her glass on the small table between the chairs. "When young people come into the town, instead of leaving it all the time, it makes me think that maybe we're going to be okay."

Sarah put her hand on her grandmother's arm and gave it a tiny shake. "Of course we're going to be okay. Nothing's going to happen to Last Chance. Ask Rita! She's got a dozen schemes going at a time to keep Last Chance revitalized."

Elizabeth smiled into the dusk, "Well, you're right about Rita. If she has anything to say about it, we'll be putting up skyscrapers on Main Street by Christmas."

"See? And have you ever known anyone who can say no to Rita for long? Last Chance isn't going anywhere."

"Maybe not. After all, the Dip 'n' Dine got some new blood. Who knows what else might happen?"

Sarah felt a little air go out of her bubble. "Well, just because Last Chance isn't going anywhere doesn't mean everything has to change, does it?"

Elizabeth patted her granddaughter's arm. "Darlin', things are always changing. That's the nature of life. Sometimes they change toward more life, sometimes they go the other way, but nothing ever stays the same."

"Last Chance has."

"Oh, no, it hasn't. When I first got here, Last Chance was a thriving ranching and farming community. We had a bank, a couple restaurants, neither of them the Dip 'n' Dine, a dry goods store, and I don't remember what all. Then came the drought and the interstate going through up by San Ramon, and we shrunk. Then the chile cannery opened, and we grew again. Then it closed down, and we got to be about where we are now."

"I don't remember all that."

"Well, you weren't even here for most of it. And you were pretty little when the cannery closed. But as you say, Last Chance is still here, and with young people like you and, yes, Chris coming in, I imagine we'll do fine."

Sarah took a sip of her iced tea and didn't say anything. Gran may have been right about change being the nature of life, but she didn't have to like it much.

Elizabeth looked at the trim gold watch on her wrist and set her empty glass back down. "I guess I better get on home. It's been quite a day for both of us, and one of my shows is fixing to come on."

"Let me walk you home."

"No, darlin'. We need to get this settled. I hope we do a whole lot of back-and-forthing between our houses, but you're not going to walk me every time. I'm not an invalid, and I know my own way home."

"I was afraid you were going to be that way. Hang on." Sarah ducked into the house and was back in a minute. "Here. I bought you a flashlight. Promise you'll use it, and I won't bug you about walking you home."

Elizabeth turned it on and off a couple times, then focused the beam on the walk in front of her. "Hmm! This might be nice. Thank you, darlin'."

Sarah watched her grandmother follow the pool of light down the walk. Sam must have joined her when she reached her gate because the gentle fussing Elizabeth always directed toward her cat floated back down the street, followed a moment later by the sound of Elizabeth's front screen opening and closing.

Sarah moved her little table to a spot in front of her chair and propped her feet up on it. It felt good to be on her own porch. She could go in or stay out. It was totally up to her. She leaned back and closed her eyes as the night wind sprang up and ruffled her hair and the events of the day played like a movie through her mind. When she got to the part where Chris Reed had driven himself into a cul-de-sac and then had to drive back by her house as if he had meant to do it, she started giggling.

Still giggling, she got to her feet and went back inside. Gran was right about one thing: as much as Sarah loved her grandmother, she did miss hanging out with people her own age, and face it, pickings were slim in Last Chance when it came to young people. Maybe she would invite Chris over sometime. She'd be right up front that all she was looking for was a friend, and he did make her laugh.

7

You know, you really should think about joining the choir." The first of the Monday morning breakfast crowd had turned their attention to the plates of eggs, biscuits, and green chile in front of them, and Juanita took a minute to join Chris in the kitchen.

Chris, hunched in front of his computer, just grunted his response.

"Seriously." Once Juanita had a good idea, she didn't waste it by just letting it drop. "In the first place, you have a really good voice, and since Ed Preston went to live with his daughter, we are short in the men department. And in the second place, it would do you a world of good, PR-wise. Folks would start seeing you as someone who wanted to be a part of Last Chance, not just some big-city outsider come in to make a fast buck."

Chris closed his account page and sighed. The only word of Juanita's description that seemed to fit him at all was "outsider." He didn't feel like a big-city boy at all, and no way was anyone ever going to make a fast buck off the Dip 'n' Dine.

"So what do you think? Choir practice Wednesday? 8:00?"

Chris leaned back in his chair so he could look up at Juanita. "I already had this conversation with Lurlene. Maybe someday, but not right now. But if and when I do, it sure won't be to promote the restaurant."

"Well, that's not what I meant at all, and I should hope you'd know that." Juanita's mouth had pinched up and she blinked a few times for emphasis. "Russ and I both have devoted ourselves to that choir for more than thirty years, and I'd be the last to suggest using it for anything but praise and worship. I only meant to suggest it wouldn't hurt for people to see that you care about some of the same things they do. And that's all I meant."

Juanita tapped her finger with a sharp rap on his desk as she said "only" and "all I meant," and Chris realized he had really blundered this time. But, come on, she was the one who'd used the word PR. He really wanted to let the whole thing drop and get back to his books, but Juanita stood in front of his desk, arms crossed over her chest and sucking in air through her nose. This was not going away. He stood up and perched on the edge of his desk so she'd stop looking down on him and making him feel like she was going to send him to his room.

"Look, Juanita, I apologize. I really do. If I'd been listening a little closer, I wouldn't have misunderstood." He flapped a half-hearted hand toward his computer. "I'm just, I don't know, frustrated, I guess."

Juanita deflated to normal size, and concern replaced her war mask. As she often confessed, concern for others always took precedence over any personal affront she might feel.

"What's wrong, Chris? Everything's okay with the Dip 'n' Dine, isn't it?"

Chris shrugged. "Yeah, everything's okay—barely. Pretty much what Fayette had led me to believe, anyway. I just want to take things beyond 'okay.'"

"By changing up the menu and all?"

"Well, yeah, for starters. And I still don't think that's a bad idea."

"Not happening." Carlos chimed in from the prep table where

he was already at work on lunch. "It's all I can do to keep up with the things that are already on the menu. Adding a bunch of new stuff would just shut the kitchen down."

"I'm not talking about a bunch of new stuff. Just a dish or two."

"Nope."

"What if we brought in more help?"

"Nope. I got all the help I can work with now. Things are going fine. Just don't mess it up and we'll be okay."

"But we won't be okay." Chris took a deep breath and tried again. "The number of customers hasn't changed much, up or down, in twenty years."

"Well, Last Chance is only so big, Chris." Juanita, still in the kitchen, had to put in her two cents' worth. "There may not be a ton of customers, but they're faithful to this place. You should be grateful."

"And I am." Chris always felt way out of his depth when he got into a discussion with Juanita. "But if you have the same customers wanting to pay the same price for the same food year after year while the cost of running this place is going through the roof, sooner or later we're going under, and we're getting closer to that every month. Something's got to give." He sighed. He would not let it go down the drain without a fight.

"Been thinking, boss." Carlos, still at his prep table, broke the stillness a few minutes later. "I've been here at the Dip 'n' Dine for a good many years now, and I'd like to keep on. I'm getting too old to break in another owner. I'd forgotten till you got here how much work that was."

Chris looked over. "Yeah?"

"Yeah. So what if we worked with what we had?"

Chris waited.

"I mean, some things just aren't going to change. The menu, for one thing." Carlos glanced up to make sure Chris got his point. "And Juanita's right about the prices not changing. You can take the prices up a few cents every now and then. The customers will think that's only fair. But you can't raise 'em enough to do you any good. Folks won't have it."

"Yeah, we covered that." If Carlos had a point to make, he was sure taking his time about it.

"So what I was thinking is the only thing to do is get more customers in here."

"Okay. Any ideas?"

"What if we kept the diner open late, maybe once a month or so, and did something special? Had us a big fiesta."

Chris straightened up. He could almost feel the gears whirring. "I like that idea, Carlos. We could do something completely different each time. Maybe bring in live music."

Carlos grinned. "Yeah, I have a big old smoker I could bring if we wanted to do a barbecue."

"We could sell tickets in advance to build up the buzz, and then sell them at the door too."

"And, of course, the beauty of it is that you could charge a little more for the tickets too. Folks'd be buying a ticket for a party, not ordering off a menu."

Chris stared. Carlos had just said more in five minutes than he usually said in the course of a full day.

Chris could feel his excitement building. This could be what he was looking for. "It would take a ton of planning, though. How soon do you think we could pull this off?"

"Ask her." Carlos jutted his chin at the front door where Rita had just breezed in, clipboard in hand. "Now, I gotta get back to work."

Chris grinned and pushed through the door to the dining room. Rita's eyes lit up when she saw him, but she had just opened her mouth to say her signature phrase when Chris beat her to it.

"Rita! Just the one I've been wanting to see."

—⚏—

Chris drove into the carport of his mobile home and sat in the front seat of his Jeep gathering strength to get out and go inside. It had been another long day, but he felt more encouraged at the end of this one than he had in a long time. Rita, as he had known she would, took the fiesta idea and ran with it. And after he had been assured that the event would take place at the Dip 'n' Dine, inside or out, and that he would provide all the food, he was good with letting her do the planning. She had promised regular meetings to update him, and he had no doubt those meetings would take place. He shook his head and headed inside.

His phone rang just as he settled himself in his big rocker in front of the television. He scowled at the screen. Mom never called just to chat. Something had to be up, and he just didn't want to deal with it.

"Hello, dear. You haven't heard from Kaitlyn, have you?"

Chris's head rolled forward and rested with his chin on his chest. What now? "Not for a few days. Why?"

"I am so exasperated with her I could just shake her. I just got home from work, and there's her cat and a note saying she's taking Olivia off on some adventure before school starts. I thought maybe you knew about it."

Chris tried to ignore the feeling of apprehension that always accompanied thoughts of Kaitlyn. "Well, I wouldn't worry too much right now. School will be starting soon, and she can't have that much vacation time built up. She only started working at that beauty shop a little while ago, didn't she?"

"She quit! I can't believe her! I called Chez Guillaume—a job I got for her, by the way—and they said she quit last Friday."

Chris sat up. This was not sounding good. "What about her apartment? Are her things still there?"

"I don't know. I'll go over and check. But let me know when you hear from her, okay? If she calls anyone, it'll be you. Bye."

Chris hung up and tried to call his sister. As usual, it went to voice mail. "Hey, Kaitlyn. What's up? Mom's really upset and you need to call her. I mean that. And hey, call me too. I need to know what's going on with you and Olivia. Stay safe. I love you."

He put his phone on the end table and paced the living room before stopping to look out the front window. The west, where Kaitlyn and Olivia ought to be, still glowed red, but darkness was fast overtaking the sky. Kaitlyn would do what she wanted to do. She'd been in and out of more scrapes than he could count, even though he did his best to keep her on the straight and narrow. But Olivia was so little, and it was so dark out there.

—◊◊◊—

Chris checked his watch for the fiftieth time since his mom had phoned. Why hadn't she called back with more information? Kaitlyn lived across town from their parents, but even so, she'd had plenty of time to go check Kaitlyn's apartment and get back to him. Finally he called his mom. She answered in a flurry of apology.

"Oh, hi, hon. Sorry I forgot to call, but everything's fine. Her apartment is just as she left it. The manager said she didn't say anything about moving out, so I guess she'll be back in a week or so. She'd better. The rent's only paid through the first of the month.

Although without a job, I don't see how she's going to pay it. And she's not getting it from me. I am done bailing her out of her messes."

Chris took a deep breath. "I've been sitting here waiting for you to call me."

"I know, and I should have. But on the way over, I got a call from a client who was ready to make an offer on a property, so after I made a real quick stop at Kaitlyn's, I swung by the office to write it up. I guess I just forgot to call. Sorry, dear."

Chris had no words, but his mother didn't seem to notice.

"But I'm excited about this offer. It's a good one on some very prime real estate, and I have a real good feeling about it being accepted. So, congratulate me! Fingers crossed, but I think I made a very lucrative sale tonight."

"Congratulations, Mom." Chris tried to put some enthusiasm in his voice. "But be sure to let me know if you hear anything, okay?"

"I certainly will. I'm submitting first thing in the morning, but it's such a good offer, they shouldn't take long to accept."

Chris shook his head as he hit End Call. *Kaitlyn, Mom. Let me know when you hear about Kaitlyn.*

—⁂—

Sarah felt pretty good when she walked through the door of the Dip 'n' Dine early the next afternoon. She had spent the morning at school laminating all the name cards she had made for her students' desks. One of the things she loved most about living in such a small town was that she not only knew who her students would be, but she knew *them*, or at least their parents.

"Don't tell me." Juanita brought over a menu but didn't put it down. "You want the special, right? Chile rellenos today. My mouth's been watering all morning just smelling them."

"Better just bring me the chef's salad, dressing on the side, and some iced tea." Sarah grinned up at her. "Something's been shrinking my jeans, and I think it's all those daily specials."

"If you say so, but you're missing a bet on those rellenos." Juanita headed back to the kitchen. "Well worth an extra notch on your belt, if you ask me."

Sarah took a deep breath. The rellenos did smell amazing, and they had tasted amazing too when she was working her way through the specials her first week back in town. But it was time to get serious. School would be starting soon, and vacation, any way you defined it, would be over.

Through the window in the kitchen, she could see Chris talking on the phone. He had his back to her, and when he hung up and turned around, she was surprised at how stern he looked. She had seen him happy, nervous, and embarrassed, but he looked almost scary serious. When he saw her, though, his face lit up and he came out into the dining room. With the casual nonchalance he so diligently tried to assume around her, Chris stopped at each table to offer a word of greeting or to ask how the diner was enjoying his meal before finally stopping at Sarah's table.

"Hey there. Nice to see you. It's been a few days."

"Not since you took the scenic tour of my neighborhood Sunday evening. What was that all about, anyway?" Sarah couldn't help it. The cooler Chris tried to act, the more she had to needle him.

"Yeah, I bet that looked funny. I, uh, thought there might be a shortcut back to the main road."

Sarah grinned. "An easy mistake. Head the opposite direction of where you want to go, and you'll find a shortcut every time."

Chris's smile began to look pasted on, and Sarah laughed out loud. People across the room looked over to see what was going on. "I'm sorry. I'm just teasing you. Being the youngest, I had to learn early to hold my own. And Gran would be the first to tell you that I may have overcompensated just a little."

Chris visibly relaxed and his smile softened. "I don't know about that, but I know backing anyone you took on would be a sucker's bet."

Sarah closed her eyes and bowed her head in a graceful nod. "And I thank you, kind sir."

Juanita appeared with the chef's salad, and Chris smiled again, a warm natural smile this time, before moving away. "Enjoy that salad. I'll talk to you later."

"Oh, Chris, wait a minute. I wanted to ask you something." Chris and Juanita both stopped and looked expectantly at Sarah. She smiled at Juanita until Juanita took the hint and, with a bit of a huff, went back to the kitchen.

Sarah watched her go before turning to Chris. "I just wondered if you might want to come over some evening, just to hang out. I know it's kind of hard when you don't know anyone."

Chris's face immediately took on the expression of a Labrador puppy being offered a treat, and Sarah wondered if she should have followed her first instincts and given Chris a wide berth. "Nothing serious, just as friends. Maybe we can heat up that chicken you brought."

"Yeah." Chris nodded and kept nodding. "Sounds good. Love to."

"Great." Sarah picked up her fork so Chris would know he could leave. "Saturday? About 7:30?"

"See you then." Chris smiled and walked away. In a second he was back. "Maybe I should get your number, in case something comes up. And I'll give you mine too."

Sarah sighed as she rummaged through her purse for pen and paper. *Oh brother, what have I done? I sure hope I don't wind up regretting this.*

8

Sarah fluffed her sofa pillows and stood back to admire the effect. She had to admit that she was looking forward to having company. If you didn't count Gran, or her parents, or the other relatives who had been by, Chris would be her first invited guest, and suddenly those faded place mats she'd snagged from her mom's linen closet just looked tacky. She glanced at the clock on her kitchen stove. She had time to get to San Ramon and back, but the thought of fighting those Saturday afternoon crowds made her shudder. Nope, these would have to do.

It wasn't till she was setting the table with her ratty place mats that it occurred to her that she might need more than just boneless chicken breast with mushrooms and artichokes to make a meal. A salad would be good, maybe some bread, and something for dessert. She sighed and went to look for her shoes. No getting around it, she was going to San Ramon.

Saturday afternoon shopping was as awful as she thought it would be. She had to circle the parking lot three times before she found a spot to park her car, but even that wasn't as bad as the crowds inside the superstore. But she persevered, and now back home, showered and wearing the new top she bought, she almost felt the trip had been worth the hassle.

The linen place mats looked terrific with the Fiesta ware, and she was glad she had decided to get the matching napkins and some cute little napkin rings. She even set a candle in the middle of the table—not tapers in candleholders, which would holler "This is a date," but a nubby glass globe with a votive candle inside. Very midcentury.

When the oven dinged, signaling it had finished preheating, she put the foil-covered casserole on a cookie sheet and popped it in the oven—just as the instructions indicated. Everything was ready for a casual, relaxing, no-biggie evening between buddies. She glanced at the fireplace, wishing again she could have a fire, but since it had been 97 degrees last time she checked, she had settled for candles, a few pillars of varying heights. Even unlit, they gave the fireplace a warm and friendly look.

The only thing left was the iced tea, and Sarah smiled to herself when she brought in the gallon jar of sun tea that had been brewing on her back porch all afternoon. "Hah! Who needs to know how to boil water?"

—⁂—

Chris locked the front door, turned off the neon Dip 'n' Dine sign, and checked his watch. He had just enough time to finish up here and get home to clean up before going to Sarah's. She had made it abundantly clear that she saw him as a friend and nothing else, but at this point, a friend would be really good.

"Well, I guess I'll go on home, unless there's something else you need." Juanita, untying her apron, came from the kitchen.

"Nope, we're good here. See you tomorrow at church." Chris glanced at his watch again.

"Well, shoot. I forgot to fill the salt and pepper shakers. Maybe I'll just get here a few minutes early Monday." She hesitated a moment and Chris was about to agree with her, but she tossed her apron on the back of a chair and reached for a tray. "Oh, I'll just do it now and get it out of the way."

"No, no. You've already put in a full day. I'll do it. You go on home." If Juanita got to talking, something as simple as filling a salt shaker could turn into a real project.

"You've had just as long a day as I have, even longer, and this is my job. It won't take a minute." She moved briskly from table to table, picking up the shakers, and Chris sneaked another look at his watch.

"Did I tell you I'm going to get another grandbaby?" Juanita stood with the salt in one hand and a shaker in the other. "This will be number six. And I would just love another girl."

"Congratulations!" Chris gave what he hoped was a sincere-looking smile and fled to the kitchen. Carlos had already started scrubbing the floor and glared at him, but he couldn't help that. As long as Juanita had someone to talk to, she'd be talking, not working.

"Customers, Chris." Juanita's voice carried over the muffled roar of motorcycle engines. "I'll take care of it."

Chris looked through the window to see two leather-clad cyclists get off their Harleys. One lifted a child off the back.

"Sorry, folks, we're closed." Juanita had unlocked the door and stuck her head out. "If you stay on this road, though, you'll be in San Ramon in about twenty minutes. Lots of places to eat there."

As if she hadn't heard, one of the cyclists took off her helmet, exposing a shock of cherry-red hair, and headed for the door. It took a moment for Chris to recognize her because the last time he saw her, her hair had been black and white, but when she saw him through the window and waved and smiled, he knew it was Kaitlyn.

Kaitlyn shoved past Juanita as if she weren't there, and Chris met her in the middle of the room, sweeping her into a bear hug. Juanita, completely unused to anyone ignoring her, much less knocking her aside, had been turned to slack-jaw stone—an event seldom, if ever, seen in Last Chance.

"Where have you been?" Chris put both his hands on her shoulders and gave a little shake. "We've been going nuts worrying about you."

Kaitlyn grinned up at him. "On the road. We decided the best way to see the country was on bikes, so I sold my car, bought the bike, and here we are."

Chris looked up. Kaitlyn's companions, Olivia and a burly guy with a three-day beard, had come in behind her. Olivia was still struggling with a helmet that was so big it made her look like a spindly space alien, but the guy shook out his damp shoulder-length hair and turned to Juanita.

"You guys got any beer? I'm spittin' dust."

Juanita sputtered to life. "We most certainly do not. And we are closed. I told you that."

"It's okay, Juanita." Chris dropped to one knee and drew Olivia to him in a hug, gently lifting the helmet from her head. When he stood, Olivia was still clinging to him with her arms and legs like a monkey. "This is my sister, Kaitlyn, and my niece, Olivia, and . . . I don't believe we've met." He shifted Olivia to his hip and extended his hand to Kaitlyn's friend.

"Jase. How's it going?"

"Everything okay, boss?" Carlos stood at the kitchen window taking in the goings-on in the dining room.

Chris turned and smiled. "Everything's fine, thanks, Carlos. My sister just got here."

Carlos nodded but never took his eyes off Jase. "Okay then, if you're sure, I'll go ahead and take off."

"See you Monday." Chris turned back to Juanita. "And you can go too, Juanita. Have a good weekend."

Juanita did not look at all eager to leave. She glanced at Jase and back to Chris. "Well, if you're sure."

"We're good." Chris turned his attention to the little girl clinging to him as Juanita left. "Hey, Liverhead! Long time no see." He gave her another squeeze and planted a noisy kiss on her cheek.

"I told you not to call me Liverhead."

Jase laughed and Olivia shot him a look that would peel paint.

Chris got the message. "Okay, Livvy it is." He leaned in to whisper, "For now."

He turned back to Kaitlyn. "I can't believe you just took off like that. Have you called Mom? She's worried sick."

Kaitlyn's laugh sounded more like a bark. "Yeah, there were all those phone messages. Oh, wait. They were from you."

"Mom called. I know she did."

"Maybe twice. And both times she just yelled. I really wanted to return those calls."

"Well, I didn't yell—much. And you didn't call me either."

"I wanted to surprise you. Aren't you surprised?"

"You could call it that." He looked at Olivia, still perched on his hip, and brushed her damp hair from her eyes. "What were you thinking, putting Livvy on a motorcycle? Do you have any conception of how dangerous that is?"

"She has a helmet."

"Kaitlyn! She's what, sixty pounds? And nothing between her and the pavement?"

Kaitlyn's face fell into the pout he knew so well. "If I'd wanted to get yelled at, I'd have called Mom. I thought you'd be glad to see us."

Chris took a deep breath to calm down. If Kaitlyn got mad, she was perfectly capable of slapping that helmet back onto Olivia's head and taking off. He put his free arm around her shoulders and gave a squeeze. "I am glad to see you. But come on, the back of a motorcycle is no place for a little girl."

Chris thought he saw a quick glance slide between Kaitlyn and Jase. He put Olivia down. "So what are your plans now? If you're heading back to Scottsdale, maybe Livvy and I can follow in my Jeep. Give the two of us a chance to catch up. I think they can manage without me here for a day or two."

"Well, our plans right this minute are about dinner." Kaitlyn's smile was back. "We're starved. Got any ideas?"

Dinner. Sarah was expecting him for dinner. Chris looked at the dusty, sweaty crew standing in his diner. If he sent them away now, even to eat, Olivia was getting back on that motorcycle. He didn't have a choice; he was going to have to cancel.

"Let's go to my place. I've got some steaks in the freezer. Just give me a minute to make a phone call." Chris walked through the kitchen and out the back door. Maybe it wouldn't be that big of a deal. After all, Sarah had stressed it was a casual, buddy dinner. And she was just heating up something he had put in her freezer. He took out the never-used number Sarah had given him and punched in the numbers.

—⚬⚬⚬—

Sarah took the foil off the casserole so it could brown and savored the aroma that enveloped her kitchen. Salad, fresh from the bag and topped with croutons fresh from the box, stood ready to be tossed with bottled French dressing. She'd pop the foil-wrapped French bread in the oven when Chris arrived, then wow him with the Sara Lee cheesecake after dinner.

"Eat your heart out, Martha Stewart, and meet the new queen of gracious living." Sarah stood back and admired her efforts. It was too bad all this perfection was only for Chris, but as Gran always said, "start as you intend to continue." And he was as good as anyone to practice on.

It wasn't till she went to light the candle on her table and the new pillars arranged in her fireplace that she realized she didn't have a single match in the house.

Who doesn't have matches? Sarah grabbed her phone to call her grandmother. *Have matches, Gran, and don't ask why I need them.*

"Of course, honey, I have a whole box full. Why do you need matches?"

Sarah rolled her eyes. "I, uh, bought some candles today, and if I ever want to use them, I'll need matches. Can I run down and get them now?"

"Certainly." Elizabeth still sounded a little puzzled. "Or I can just give them to you tomorrow when you pick me up for church."

"I'll come get them now. See you in a minute."

It took Sarah a little longer than she thought it would to get to Elizabeth's and back. If Gran thought an emergency matches run was a little odd, snatching them out of her hand at the front door and racing home without even taking the time to admire the roses or speak to Sam would likely bring Gran right down the street after her to see what was going on.

She lit the candles in the fireplace and picked up her phone to check the time as she headed for the kitchen. A New Message banner covered the screen—again.

"Just leave me alone. I don't want to talk to you." Sarah glared at the phone before she opened a kitchen drawer and shut the phone inside. "This is one party you are not invited to."

She felt the bubble of anticipation that had been building all afternoon begin to deflate, so she opened the oven to see if another whiff of chicken would kick it up again. Someday soon, she knew, she was going to have to have it out with Brandon, but not yet. She just wasn't ready. Six months ago, she thought she'd be planning a wedding by now, but at this moment, she wished she never had to speak to him again.

She inhaled the aroma that surrounded her with the puff of hot air that escaped the oven. *Go away, Brandon.* She took another deep breath. It was working. And in a few minutes, when Chris got here, Brandon would be completely banished.

At 7:30, the timer on the stove indicated the casserole was done, and Sarah took it out and covered it with the foil to keep it warm. At 7:40, she popped the French bread in the oven. Something must have come up at the last minute at the Dip 'n' Dine, but since Chris hadn't called, he should be turning up any minute.

At 8:00, with the casserole cool and shrunken, the French bread way past crispy, and the salad looking wilted even without the dressing, Sarah remembered the message she hadn't looked at. She fished her phone out of the silverware and checked. It was from Chris, of course, and she hit Play Message. *This better be good, Reed.*

"Hey, this is Chris. Listen, sorry to bail at the last minute like this, but something came up that I really need to take care of. I'll try to call later to fill you in, but meantime, that chicken ought to keep a day or so, if you want to reschedule. Talk to you soon."

Okay, so he had called before he was expected, and she had made the choice not to listen to his message. Big deal. If he thought that was going to let him off the hook, even a little bit, for standing her up, he had another think coming. She grabbed a fork, and while still leaning against the counter, dug a bite from the middle of the casserole. *Reschedule? In your dreams, Chris Reed.*

—⁓—

Chris noticed his neighbors peeking out their windows as the two big Harleys followed him up the dirt road to his house. Olivia, safely belted into the back seat of his Jeep, had been uncharacteristically quiet.

"So, tell me about this great adventure you've been on, Livvy. Have you been having fun?"

In the rearview mirror, he saw her shrug as she looked out the side window.

"That's not much of an answer. What's going on?"

The size of her exasperated sigh made him smile to himself.

"Well, Mom said we were going to take this great trip and see the Grand Canyon and maybe Disneyland and stuff. But I didn't know that Jase was coming, and I thought we were going to be in a car. All we do is ride on that motorcycle, and it's really boring."

Chris parked in his carport, and the bikes pulled up behind him. He turned around to smile over the seat at Olivia. "What if we talked your mom and Jase into going to see the Grand Canyon and then going home? We'd have to do Disneyland on another trip, though."

Olivia still did not look very happy. "Would you come?"

"Yep. And you could ride with me. No more motorcycles."

"Well, this has been a pretty lame trip so far."

"Then we'll see what we can do." Chris got out and opened the back door so Olivia could hop out. The last thing he needed to do right now was to take a few days off to go to the Grand Canyon, but Olivia clearly had her heart set on it. And frankly, Chris thought she had it coming to her.

Kaitlyn laughed when she came through the front door. "Nice place. Who's your decorator?"

Chris looked around. The room did not bear much resemblance to the home they had grown up in. Their mother had always said that their decor should reflect the quality of the homes they represented, and even the castoffs that filled Kaitlyn's apartment were of the best quality.

He grinned and shrugged. "Hey, it's home. So, do you guys want to get cleaned up while I fix us some dinner? Kaitlyn, you and Livvy can use my bathroom, and Jase can take the other one. Dinner in about half an hour?"

Chris was just whisking the vinaigrette for the salad when Olivia came running into the kitchen, comb marks still evident in her wet hair. He was pleased to notice she was in her pajamas. Good. They were at least planning to stay the night. That gave him more time to convince Kaitlyn to give up this crazy motorcycle trip of hers.

"Hey, Liverhead, feel better now?" Chris laughed as Olivia's face screwed up into a fierce scowl. She shot a look down the hall to see who else might have heard. "Nope. You're the only one out here. And I promise, as far as anyone else is concerned, you are Olivia. The Royal Princess Olivia, if you prefer."

Olivia gusted a huge sigh and rolled her eyes. "Just use my name, Uncle Chris. It's really not that hard."

"When did you get to be such an old lady?" Chris watched her climb onto a stool at the bar in his kitchen. "Here's a deal for you. I'll call you Livvy, at least when anyone else is around, and you go back to being seven. Okay?"

She gave him the look a tired schoolteacher gives an unruly class.

"Something sure smells good!" Kaitlyn, followed by Jase, headed into the kitchen.

Chris narrowed his gaze on his niece and held his fist out for a bump. "So do we have a deal, Liiiiiiv . . . ?"

"Deal!" Olivia bumped his huge fist with her tiny one.

". . . vy." Chris finished with a wink before turning his attention to the other two. "Just in time. The steaks are about ready."

"Man, is this a dry county or what?" Jase turned from the open refrigerator. "You don't have any beer either."

"Nope, afraid not." Chris finished tossing the salad and took the steaks from the broiler. "There ought to be a few bottles of water in there, though. Help yourself."

Jase looked at the bottle in his hand as if it were medicine but unscrewed the top and drained it in one swallow. As he walked past Kaitlyn, he muttered under his breath, "Man, you weren't kidding about him, were you?"

Chris ignored the comment. He knew that Kaitlyn wasn't any more impressed with his lifestyle than he was with hers, and if that didn't bother him, the good opinion of Jase wasn't even a blip on his radar.

Olivia nearly fell asleep during dinner, and Chris placed a hand on her head as he passed her chair on the way to the kitchen. "I think this girl's ready for bed. Kaitlyn, you and Livvy can have my room. I'll sleep in the room down the hall. Jase, you can take the sofa. It's pretty comfortable."

His niece wandered off to bed, scorning his suggestion that he come tuck her in, and Jase settled himself in the living room and scrolled through the TV channels. Kaitlyn started clearing the table, much to Chris's surprise. As far as he could remember, she had never willingly taken on a chore that someone else might do. Maybe she was starting to grow up after all.

He smiled at her as he turned on the tap. "I'm glad we have a minute to talk. It's been a while."

She gave him a hug. "Too long."

Chris glanced into the living room where Jase seemed to be engrossed in the images that flipped past as he pointed the remote toward the television. Chris put his hands on Kaitlyn's shoulders and looked into her face. Even now, he could see the little girl he had tried so hard, and so ineptly, to shield from anything that could hurt her. He took a deep breath while he marshaled his thoughts.

"Kaitlyn, what are you doing?" Sadness and concern, rather than anger, tinged his voice. "You have to know what a bad idea this is. You're a mom now. You need to think about what's best for Olivia."

She looked up at him and smiled the tiniest of smiles. "You're right. Taking Olivia on a cross-country motorcycle trip was a dumb move."

The happy smile that split Chris's face froze as Kaitlyn completed her thought. "So we're going to leave her here with you when we leave tomorrow. Hope that's okay."

9

W hat?" Chris knew what Kaitlyn had said; it just didn't make sense.

"You said it yourself, Chris. The back of a motorcycle is no place for Olivia. She hates it. We knew it was a mistake before we got to Tucson."

"So take her home. Better yet, I'll drive her. You can follow."

"There'd be nobody there if you did, because I'm not going back." Kaitlyn stepped away from him and crossed her arms. In the living room, Jase hit the Mute button and watched them over the back of the sofa.

"This is nuts, Kaitlyn. You can't just abandon your child. And I can't keep her, anyway. The hours I have to put in at the diner are unreal. There's no one to take care of her."

"I'm not abandoning her. It'll only be for a little while." Kaitlyn grabbed both his hands, and the look in her eyes tore at his heart. "Please. I've never done the kinds of things people my age do. There's always been Olivia. I just need to do this."

This was not the first time Kaitlyn had used premature mother-hood as a reason to do whatever she wanted to do, and Chris was about to point that out when Kaitlyn cut him off.

"Please." Her voice was an anguished whisper. "Please do this for me. Jase is done with Olivia. He's going to go on without me if I try to bring her along."

"That sounds like the best outcome possible."

Kaitlyn gripped his hands tighter, and as her eyes filled with tears, Chris felt his resolve weaken. She could get into his heart like no one else ever could.

"When does Olivia's school start?" He couldn't believe he was even discussing this.

"Two weeks from Tuesday."

"And you'll be back in plenty of time to get her home for school?"

"Promise." Kaitlyn's tears had beaded on her lashes, and an eager smile made her face shine.

"Okay, then. But you have to explain everything to Olivia before you leave in the morning. And you have to call her. Often."

Kaitlyn threw her arms around her brother. "I will. Every night. I know she'll have a great time with you, and we'll be back before you know it."

Chris was almost positive he had just made a huge mistake, and his long day, his long week, landed on him like a fifty-pound sack of flour. "I'm counting on it. Now I've got to get to bed. I'll fix you breakfast tomorrow before you leave." He started down the hall but stuck his head back around the corner. "I'll leave my door open. If you need anything, don't worry about waking me. I'm a really light sleeper."

He held Jase's gaze long enough to see understanding dawn there before he went on back to the narrow bed in the room that had been decorated for a teenage boy. It had been a long time since he had slept in something like that.

It was just dawn when the sound of his front door shutting woke him up. Pulling back the curtain, he saw Kaitlyn and Jase, back in their leathers, strapping on their helmets. Kaitlyn saw him and lifted her hand in a faint wave. As he raced down the hall, he heard the engines roar to life, and just as he threw open the door, first Jase and then Kaitlyn circled his yard and took off down the dirt road to the highway.

He stood on his porch in his sweatpants and watched the dust settle on the empty road before he walked back down the hall to check on Olivia.

She looked so tiny in her princess pajamas, even sprawled spread eagle across his bed. A pink backpack, presumably filled with her clothes, leaned against the dresser. Clearly, despite her promise, Kaitlyn had left without even saying good-bye to her daughter. Chris shook his head and backed out of the room. He'd let her sleep. There'd be time later to tell her she wasn't going on that great adventure after all.

—⁂—

By the time Sarah picked up her grandmother for church, she was ready to face Chris Reed with the nonchalant indifference he deserved. She would just smile when he apologized and assure him it was not a big deal. If he suggested rescheduling their dinner, she would confess that she had already eaten the chicken, tell him it was delicious, and sweep away, leaving him with no hope whatsoever that he would ever darken her door again. All done very graciously, of course.

Chris had not yet arrived when Sarah and Elizabeth came in, but that was okay. She could ignore him after church as easily as before. She found herself listening for his strong baritone as they sang the hymns and wondering at its absence. When the final hymn was sung and she turned around to find that Chris Reed had indeed missed church, a wave of annoyance swept over her. Leave it to Chris to mess things up again. Time was of the essence when it came to studied indifference. It had to be served up promptly. If you waited too long, it really was no big deal. So why even mention it?

Gran was busy chatting with someone, of course, but Sarah wasn't in the mood for small talk. She was almost across the parking lot when she heard someone call her name, and a young woman with a fat baby on her hip grabbed her in a one-armed hug.

"Sarah! So glad you're back." The tall brunette stood back and beamed. "I was so mad I had to miss your pounding, but this one has had the mother of all colds and I have been totally housebound." She jostled the baby on her hip for emphasis. His solemn brown eyes observed Sarah over the roundest cheeks she had ever seen. "I thought he was doing well enough to go to the nursery last Sunday, but they stopped me before I even got to the door. Green snot. It's clear now, though, isn't it, sweet boy? Oh, this is Michael. Can you say hi to Miss Sarah, Mikey?"

Mikey could not, or chose not to, and Sarah, who could not help looking at Mikey's nose, took a second before she realized her friend had stopped talking. She grinned. Megan had talked her way into detention more than once during high school, and it appeared time, marriage, and children hadn't changed her much. Sarah opened her mouth to say something, but Megan beat her to it.

"Oh, gee, there goes Danny to the car. His dad had this rule that whoever didn't beat him to the car after church could find their own way home, and Danny keeps threatening to have the same rule. Well, all I can say is, he'd better get over that idea because it's not going to fly. Not with me."

Sarah, still smiling, nodded. Megan went on.

"Tell me you're free for lunch Wednesday. Mikey spends Wednesday afternoons with his grandma so I can get some things done, and this Wednesday what I want to do is get caught up with what's been going on with you. I heard you were engaged."

"Um, no." Sarah finally got a word in. "Not engaged."

"Really? I was almost sure. Hmmph. Anyway, Wednesday, noon, Dip 'n' Dine?"

Sarah had been nodding until Megan mentioned the Dip 'n' Dine. "How about going into San Ramon? We could try something different."

"No, I need to stay close in case I have to go get Mikey." Across the parking lot an extended cab pickup began backing slowly out of its spot. Megan settled Mikey firmly on her hip and took off. "Danny! Stop that truck this minute. I mean it."

Sarah watched her friend, still fussing at her husband, throw open the back door of the pickup to strap Mikey into his car seat.

"So, how is Megan?" Gran had appeared beside her. "She sure does seem to have her hands full."

"I think she's got things under control." Sarah watched Danny's pickup pull out of the parking lot. He was staring straight ahead, and Megan's mouth was still working. "We're having lunch Wednesday."

"Are you now?" They had reached Sarah's car, and Elizabeth smiled at her over the top. "I'm glad you're spending time with other young people. I know there aren't that many in Last Chance, although, as I know I've mentioned . . ."

Sarah saw where the conversation was headed and held up a hand to stop her. "Don't go there, Gran. Really."

—⁓—

The morning was almost gone when Olivia wandered out of the bedroom rubbing one eye. "Where's Mom?"

Chris put down the *Sports Illustrated* he was reading and lifted Olivia onto his lap. "Hey, kiddo. Sleep well?"

"Uh-huh. Where's Mom?" She nestled her head against his chest and closed her eyes.

Chris laid his cheek on the top of her head. "Well, that's something we need to talk about."

Olivia twisted away and looked up into his face. All traces of sleepiness had fled. She looked as if she were bracing herself for a blow, and Chris hated, *hated*, that he had to be the one to deliver it.

"Well, your mom thought you might have more fun here with me than you'd have sitting on the back of a motorcycle all day."

"She ditched me." Olivia's voice was way too flat for a seven-year-old.

"No, she didn't ditch you." *Not much, she didn't.* "She'll be back in a couple weeks, and meanwhile, we can do some cool stuff together."

Olivia slid off his lap and curled into a corner of the couch. "She said we were going to the Grand Canyon, maybe even Disneyland. She said we were going to spend lots of time together, like she didn't get to spend with Grandma because Grandma was always too busy."

Chris tried to take her arm to pull her back, but Olivia jerked it away. He gave up and angled himself so he could face her. "Look, Olivia. I know this really stinks. I think your mom meant everything she said. She just didn't realize how hard it would be on you to ride across the country on a motorcycle. And I've got to say, it was way too dangerous anyway."

"Yeah. I heard you yesterday." Olivia's face hardened and her eyes shot sparks when she looked at him. "It's your fault she ditched me. Everything was fine till we got here. Why did you have to say anything?"

She jumped off the sofa and ran back down the hall. The flimsy bedroom door didn't give much of a slam, but it wasn't because Olivia didn't try.

Chris stretched his legs out in front of him and let his head fall back against the back of the sofa. Truth had never gotten in the way of Kaitlyn going after what she wanted, and he was beginning to believe that dropping off Olivia with him was part of the original plan. He felt like a first-class chump when he thought about how easily Kaitlyn was able, and always had been able, to manipulate him. He could almost hear her assure Jase that he could leave everything to her; her brother was a pushover.

But when he thought about the little girl who was very likely crying in the bedroom right now, a big share of the anger he was directing at himself landed right where it belonged—on his sister. Lying to him was one thing. If he was still buying what she was shoveling after all these years, that was his fault. But Olivia was seven. And Kaitlyn was her mom. A kid ought to be able to believe her mom. When you left Scottsdale, you went north to get to the Grand Canyon and west to go to Disneyland, and Olivia had trusted that that was where they were going, even as the motorcycles headed southeast to drop her off at her uncle's.

Chris jumped up and started pacing. What he really wanted to do was punch something, or tackle something, or drop-kick something, but in light of the fact that he was in a small living room and Olivia was already pretty upset, he gave up on those ideas. He flexed his arms and shoulders to try to loosen his tense muscles and thought about what to say to Kaitlyn when she called later to talk to Olivia.

He stopped and with a bitter laugh shook his head to clear it. *Do you even hear yourself, Reed? Get your head out of the sand.*

Kaitlyn's not going to call. If she even gets back here in time to get Olivia to school, it'll be the first time she's ever done what she's promised you she'd do.

There was no sound from within his bedroom when he tapped on the door. He tapped again and, after a few seconds, opened the door and stuck his head in.

"Livvy?"

She was dressed in shorts and a T-shirt and sat on the floor with her back to him. Her arms were through the straps of her backpack, and though it hadn't looked all that big when it was leaning against his dresser, he didn't see how she'd even be able to stand up with it on her back, much less carry it.

He sat on the bed across from her and leaned his forearms on his knees.

"Going somewhere?"

She turned her face away. "Maybe."

"You're kind of a long way from anyplace. You might want to think about staying awhile. Your mom'll be back."

"Yeah, right." Olivia sniffed. She *had* been crying.

Chris reached out and put his hand on Olivia's head. When she didn't pull away, he let it slip to her cheek. With his thumb, he wiped off a tear.

"Come here. Let's get this thing off." He helped her out of her backpack and lifted her onto his lap.

She curled into his arms, and he cradled her against his chest and rocked her without saying anything until there were no more tears. He brushed a strand of hair from her damp face. Olivia hiccupped.

"So, Liverhead." He smiled as something indignant was muffled against his chest. "It looks like it's you and me for a while. Got any ideas?"

10

Sarah was already sitting in a booth sipping iced tea when Megan came through the doors of the Dip 'n' Dine Wednesday at noon. She waved and got up for a hug as Megan approached the table.

"Goodness, that air-conditioning feels good." Megan returned the squeeze. "I am so sorry to keep you waiting. I was afraid you'd think I wasn't coming."

Sarah glanced at the neon clock over the counter. It was 12:03. "Nope. I knew you'd get here when you could."

Megan went right on talking. "Mikey is going through a separation anxiety phase, and it took me a few minutes to get away. Of course, it hurts my mother-in-law's feelings when he cries like that, so I had her to deal with too. She's had him every Wednesday afternoon since he was born, almost."

She paused for breath as a somber little girl with dark blonde hair caught up in a lopsided ponytail and wearing a white apron tied up under her arms appeared with two menus.

"Well, hello." Megan sat back and cocked her head. "I don't believe I know you. Whose little girl are you?"

"This is my helper, Olivia Reed. She's spending a couple weeks with her uncle Chris. Aren't you, honey?" Juanita, who had come up behind her, waited until Olivia had gone to take menus to two more customers before turning back to Megan and Sarah with the arched eyebrows and pursed lips of one in the know. She lowered her voice to what passed for a whisper with Juanita. "She came in with her mother and some long-haired guy on a motorcycle last Saturday evening just at closing, and the next thing you know, the motorcycles are gone and that child is still here. Chris couldn't just leave her at home by herself, so she's been coming in here with him every morning."

Sarah watched Olivia give her apron a hitch and head back to the kitchen. Well, now she knew what had come up that kept Chris from coming over. And if he had called her later, as he had said he would, maybe she'd have even understood. She opened her menu with a snap.

"She seems like a sweet child." Megan ripped open a packet of sweetener and stirred it into the tea Juanita had place before her.

"Well." Clearly, Juanita was struggling with her oft-stated intention never to say anything bad about anybody if she could help it. "She is a sweet child, but all I can say is, if she was a child of mine, she'd have some manners to go along with it."

"Really?" Megan was much more interested in what Juanita had to say than what was on the menu. "She doesn't seem sassy."

"Most of the time it's more what she doesn't say than what she says. Never a 'yes ma'am,' never a 'no sir,' and no matter how many times I've told her she could call me Miss Juanita, she just downright refuses."

"What does she call you? Surely not Juanita."

"She doesn't call me anything, or even look at me half the time if I talk to her. You'd think I was talking just to hear my head rattle. And more often than not, if you ask her a question, she'll just heave her shoulders up and look the other way."

"I think I'll have the BLT. And can I get a salad instead of the fries?" It was time to change the subject, and Sarah handed her menu to Juanita with a smile. Juanita had a huge heart, but she could get a little preoccupied with fixing folks.

Without even opening it, Megan handed her menu back too. "The patty melt, I guess. You know, I hate to say it, but I'm getting really bored with this menu. I mean, can't it change even a little bit? Ever?"

"Be careful what you wish for." Juanita slapped her order book shut and gave another knowing look before she left.

"What did she mean by that?" Megan watched her head to the kitchen. "I was hoping things might change a bit with the new owner, but it's just the same ol', same ol'."

"And I, for one, am glad. I don't want things to change." Sarah took a sip of her tea.

"You just wait till you've been back awhile. I'm not saying we need to bring in a slew of chain stores or put in a freeway system. But for crying out loud, would it hurt to change up the menu of the Dip 'n' Dine just a little, just for starters?"

Megan's voice had been rising with her level of exasperation, and when she got to the part about adding something new to the menu, Sarah saw Chris, who had just come from the kitchen, look over. When he saw Sarah, his expression changed from lively interest in what Megan was saying to something that looked very much like awkward embarrassment. Sarah's heart sank when, after a moment's hesitation, he came over to their table. *Do not say anything about Saturday night. All will be forgiven if you just keep your mouth shut. And I mean it.*

"Afternoon, ladies." He smiled and nodded to Megan before turning his attention to Sarah. "Sorry about Saturday. There was just nothing I could do." He tipped his head toward Olivia, who was sitting at the counter with a box of crayons, coloring on the back of place mats. "But when things settle out, I'll give you a call and maybe we can reschedule something."

The cool and careless nonchalance with which Sarah had intended to tell Chris, in so many words, to go fly a kite fled as, across the table, Megan's interest spiked, and even Juanita stopped on her way to the kitchen to pay attention. Sarah felt her face get warm.

"Sure." *Now go. Just go. Stop talking.*

"Okay, then." Chris looked a bit unsure before regrouping and turning his smile on Megan. "Enjoy your lunch. And don't give up on us. We're going to get something new on that menu yet. Wait for it."

Megan barely let Chris get across the room before she leaned across the table. "Okay, what gives?"

At least Megan knew how to whisper. Sarah took a deep breath and tried to summon her inner indifference. She smiled her best "no biggie" smile. "Nothing gives. He just brought a casserole to the pounding, and I invited him over to share it. He couldn't make it at the last minute, so I ate it myself. He's a pretty good cook."

Clearly, Megan wasn't buying what Sarah was selling. "So is this why the engagement's off?"

"No!" Sarah sat back in the booth. People across the room looked up, and Sarah lowered her voice. "There never was an engagement. And if there had been, Chris Reed sure couldn't have messed it up. He doesn't mean a thing to me. I've just met him, remember?"

Sarah thought she had been speaking softly, but she saw Chris look over at the mention of his name, and from his expression, she knew he had heard everything. Great. She felt as if she were trying to stay afloat in a vat of molasses and grasped at the first thought that floated her way. "Mikey is just as cute as he can be. How old is he?"

After that, Sarah only had to smile, nod, and look interested. Juanita brought the plates of food, reappeared periodically to refill the iced tea glasses, and finally broke into the Mikey monologue to ask about dessert before Megan even took a breath.

"Oh, my goodness. You must be bored to death." Megan shook her head as if to clear it and grinned across the table at Sarah. "Never get me started on Mikey if you have anything else to do that day. Sorry about that."

Sarah returned the smile with a feeling of genuine warmth toward her old friend. Megan could talk the paint off the barn, as Granddad used to say, but Sarah loved the way her eyes lit up when she talked of Mikey. "Don't worry about it. He sounds like a great little guy."

Megan's phone rang, and she rolled her eyes when she looked at it. "A great little guy who decided to cut a tooth, have his cold come back, and get separation anxiety all on the same day. This is my mother-in-law, and I need to take this. Sorry."

"Go right ahead." Sarah looked around the room as Megan took her call and saw Olivia still hunched over the picture she was coloring at the counter. When it looked as if Megan might be on the phone for more than just a couple minutes, she got up and walked over to take the stool next to Olivia.

"That's a great picture you're drawing."

Olivia didn't look up.

"Can you tell me about it?"

Olivia sat back a bit to view her work but still did not look at Sarah. "It's me and my mom on mules at the Grand Canyon. When she gets back, we're going to go."

"That sounds like fun. I've always wanted to do that, but I never have."

Olivia went back to her coloring without responding. Sarah tried again.

"What grade are you going to be in?"

"Second."

"Really? I'm going to be teaching second grade."

This time Olivia glanced at her before returning to her picture. But she still didn't say anything.

"When school starts, my students will call me Miss Cooley, but you can call me Sarah for now, if you'd like."

Megan, purse slung over her shoulder, appeared at her side.

"I am sorry, but I have to run. This is my treat, and I've already settled with Juanita. Mikey has a little fever and I should get him home for a nap in his own bed. We have to do this again, and next time, we talk about you." She hugged Sarah and smiled at the back of Olivia's head. "It was nice meeting you, Olivia. I hope you have a good time with your uncle."

Olivia didn't answer or even look up from her picture, and Megan shot an "I see what you mean" look at Juanita, who responded with a "Someone needs to take that child in hand" shake of her head.

As Megan pushed out the door into the hot afternoon, Sarah watched Olivia bite her lower lip in concentration as she drew. She had to agree with Juanita that Olivia fell far short in the manners department, certainly by Last Chance standards, anyway. Maybe it was that lopsided ponytail or the way her shoulders squared when Juanita, in her too-loud whisper, was discussing her poor upbringing, but something about the skinny little girl in her oversized apron touched Sarah.

"I see you two have met." Chris set a sandwich and a glass of milk in front of Olivia and smiled at Sarah.

"We have. She was just telling me about that mule ride down the Grand Canyon she and her mom are going to take."

Sarah wanted to make it plain that her interest was in Olivia only and barely glanced up, but she caught the frown that creased Chris's brow. He put his hand on Olivia's head and gave it a little shake.

"That'll be fun when it happens, Livvy. But it might need to wait a little while. School will be starting soon, you know, and I don't think there'll be time this year."

Olivia put her crayon down and stared at her uncle. Those eyes were just way too old for a seven-year-old. "So it was all just another big lie?"

"No, no one meant to lie to you, Livvy. It's just that sometimes things come up that change plans."

"Sometimes like always." Olivia jumped off her stool and ran out the front door. Chris followed, and through the window Sarah saw him catch up with the little girl and drop to one knee to talk to her eye-to-eye. She watched him put his hands on her shoulders and Olivia try to jerk away, but somehow, she wound up enveloped in a hug.

Olivia's shoulders shook as she buried her face in her uncle's shoulder. His huge hand almost covered her back as he gently rubbed it. This was a side of Chris Sarah hadn't seen and, frankly, one she'd never even suspected.

He opened the side door of his Jeep and lifted Olivia to the passenger seat before brushing an escaped strand of hair from her face and cupping her face in his hand for a moment. When he came back through the door, he saw Sarah watching and gave her a half-grin.

"She's not quite ready to come back in, but she'll be okay. She's a tough little cookie."

"So the Grand Canyon's not going to happen?"

He shook his head. "I'd be seriously surprised. My sister's great at making plans, but not all that good at seeing them through."

"The Grand Canyon's kind of an unusual thing for a seven-year-old to be obsessed with."

"I know. She was supposed to get to go to Disneyland too, but that barely even gets mentioned. I think it has something to do with the mules."

Sarah slid off her stool and smiled. "Well, looks like you have your hands full, but I like Olivia."

Chris's face relaxed into the first real smile Sarah had seen since she came in for lunch. "She's a great kid. And so smart. I just wish . . ."

His smile faded a bit as his voice trailed into silence. He shook his head as if to clear it, and his smile returned. "Well, thanks for coming in. And again, sorry about Saturday."

Sarah waved as she headed out the door. "Not a problem."

Outside, Olivia still sat in the passenger seat of the Jeep hugging her knees to her chest. She stared straight ahead when Sarah leaned in the open door.

"I really did like your picture. If you don't want to give it to your uncle, I'd love it if you saved it for me."

"It was dumb. The Grand Canyon's dumb. Mules are dumb. This whole place is dumb." She still didn't look at Sarah.

"That's a lot of dumb. But you're wrong about mules. We have a couple out at our ranch, and they're pretty smart. You'd be surprised."

Olivia actually looked at her, although her expression didn't change. "You live on a ranch?"

"I used to. But it's not far from here. Do you think you might like to go out there with me one day and see the mules?" Sarah heard herself invite Olivia to the ranch before she thought it through. She had immediate second thoughts. For one thing, she should have asked Chris first, but the eagerness that illuminated Olivia's face made taking back her invitation impossible. If Chris got the wrong idea, she would just have to set him straight.

"Can I ride the mules?" When Olivia smiled, she actually did look seven.

"You could, but I think you'd like riding the horses better. We could just visit the mules, and ride the horses. What do you think?"

"When? Now?" Olivia jumped out of the Jeep and grabbed Sarah's hand.

"I can't right now. I have some things to do. But I'll call your uncle in the next day or so and set something up. How would that be?"

The smile fell away from Olivia's face and the age returned to her eyes. She let go of Sarah's hand. "Sure."

Sarah did not have to bend over very far to look in Olivia's face. Olivia was going to be tall like her uncle, and Sarah, in a word, was not. "Olivia, don't you believe me?"

Olivia looked away without saying anything.

"Look at me, Olivia." Sarah waited in silence until Olivia met her eyes. Skepticism mixed with contempt was painted all over her face.

"Listen to me." Sarah continued. "I am going to call your uncle tonight at 8:00 and ask him when you can go to the ranch with me. You can tell him that, and when the phone rings at 8:00, you can tell him it's me. Okay?"

Olivia nodded. She still didn't look as if she fully accepted Sarah's promise, but some of the bitterness had faded.

"Okay then." Sarah smiled at her. "Until 8:00 tonight. You can count on me."

She walked to her little car and climbed in. It would have been simpler, she supposed, to just walk back into the Dip 'n' Dine with Olivia and talk to Chris now. But somehow it just seemed vital to show Olivia that someone could make a promise and then see it through. That bitter, contemptuous look should never find a place on the face of a child.

11

W hat time is it?"

Chris didn't even look up from his computer. "You know how to tell time. You tell me."

"But what if that clock is wrong?" Olivia danced from one foot to the other. "What if Miss Schooley thinks it's a different time?"

"Who?"

"Miss Schooley. She's a teacher so she makes the kids call her Miss Schooley."

Chris did look up at that. He grinned. "No, her last name is Cooley. That's Miss Cooley."

"Oh. I thought Miss Schooley was kind of a dumb name. But she said I could call her Sarah since I don't go to her school. But what if she forgets to look at her watch? Or what if she calls the restaurant? Does she even have your cell phone number?"

"She has it, and I'll just bet she calls when she said she would. Give her some time. It's not even 8:00 yet."

His phone rang at that moment, and while he tried to fish it out of his jeans pocket, Olivia danced.

"Okay, so when can I go to the ranch and ride horses? Ask her! Answer! She'll hang up!"

Chris looked at the screen and held the phone out to Olivia. "It's your mom."

All the eagerness fell from her face as she folded her arms and stepped back. "I don't want to talk to her."

"Come on, Livvy. You need to talk to her."

He continued to hold the phone out. Olivia took another step back. Just before it went to voice mail, Chris answered.

"Hey, Kaitlyn. Good to hear from you."

"I'm not going to listen to you yell at me, so don't even start. I just called to talk to Olivia. Would you put her on?"

After another unsuccessful attempt at getting Olivia to take the phone, Chris got back on. "I don't think she's feeling real chatty right now. Anything you want me to tell her?"

"Sounds like you've been telling her a lot already if she won't even talk to me."

Kaitlyn always did feel that the best defense was a good offense, and the more she had to answer for, the more belligerent she became. Right now she was ready to take down the entire team. Chris tried to keep his voice light and easy. Olivia was taking in everything he had to say.

"No, you have nothing to worry about there. We're getting along just fine. She's been a great help at the diner, and just this afternoon she wrangled an invitation to go horseback riding." He winked at Olivia, who gestured wildly at the clock.

"Oh, good." Kaitlyn's conscience had been cleared, and she was moving on. "I knew she'd have a much better time with you."

By this time Olivia was nearly frantic. It was 8:00. Chris took a deep breath. "Look, Kaitlyn. We have a lot to talk about. And believe me, we will have our conversation when the time's right. But I'll make a deal with you. You go ahead and call Olivia every day like you said you would, and I won't even pick up. I'll hand the phone to Olivia to answer, or if she's not around, you can leave a message for her."

"You mean if she refuses to talk to me, I can leave a message." Kaitlyn was moving back into self-pity.

"Give her some time, Sis. She's a good kid. She'll come around."

Chris heard a man's voice mumble something and Kaitlyn say something incomprehensible, as if she had her hand over the speaker. When she came back she was eager to hang up. "Okay, then. Give her a hug from me. Love you."

"Love you too. And take care." But from the dead sound of his voice into the phone, he knew she had hung up.

"Your mom said to give you a hug." Chris tossed his phone on the sofa next to him and smiled at Olivia.

She didn't even seem to hear him. She was near tears. "We missed it. It's past 8:00 and Miss Schooley, Sarah, tried to call and you were on the phone."

Chris pulled her to him. "You need to calm down, Liverhead. If Sarah called while I was talking to your mom, she'll call back. And listen to me." He gently caught her chin between his thumb and forefinger and tipped her head so she was looking at him. "You need to talk to your mom next time she calls, hear me? She loves you and she misses you. Got that?"

Olivia's eyes welled with tears and her lower lip jerked a few times, but when Chris tucked her under his arm, she didn't resist—until the phone on the sofa vibrated. Then she turned into a windmill of arms and legs.

"That's her." Olivia grabbed up the phone and shoved it at Chris. "Answer it."

He didn't take it. "Go ahead. You're the one she wants to talk to."

He leaned back against the sofa and watched Olivia take the call. He knew next to nothing about kids, but the range of emotions she had run through in the last half hour or so couldn't be good.

Kids' moods could turn on a dime, he knew that much, but these were more than just mood changes. She was going through some pretty serious stuff, and she was just seven. Right now he was all she had. And he didn't have a clue.

Olivia was dancing on her toes as she shoved the phone back at him. "She wants to talk to you. She wants to go tomorrow after lunch. Tell her it's okay. Tell her."

He raised his eyebrows and mouthed the words *Calm down* as he took the phone.

"Hi. Sorry I'm a few minutes late with the call." He hadn't heard her voice on the phone before, and he liked the way it sounded. "I really wanted to call at 8:00 on the nose to prove something to Olivia, but I couldn't get through."

"Well, she was waiting for you." Chris smiled into the phone. She got it. Not many people took the time to get Olivia.

"I gathered. So, tomorrow works? I could pick her up at the Dip 'n' Dine around 1:00. I'll have her back by dinner."

"Sounds good." He took a deep breath. *Go for it, Reed.* "Think you could stay for dinner? I know Olivia would love it if you would."

He heard the hesitation on the line. "Um, we'll both be pretty dirty. I think we'd probably better make it another time."

"Ah, come on. You're going to have to eat somewhere. I'll throw something on the grill and we can eat on the deck." Chris winced as he heard the wheedling in his voice. Not cool.

"Some other time." The warm tone Chris had been basking in cooled perceptively. "I'll pick her up around 1:00?"

"Sure. That would be fine." Chris willed the nonchalance back into his voice before he punched End Call. He leaned back against the sofa and closed his eyes. Briefly, he wondered if women were any easier to deal with if you could take them one at a time.

When he opened his eyes, Olivia was standing there watching him, more frozen than still. He smiled to put her mind at ease. "Looks like you're going horseback riding tomorrow. Bet you'll have fun."

A grin split her face and she tore off to her room to begin some preparation he could only guess at. Chris shook his head and reached for his computer again. If he couldn't figure everybody out at once, he was going to have to prioritize. Olivia, whether he had asked for it or not, was priority number one. She was seven, after all, and deserved to be number one in someone's life. Kaitlyn came in at number two. She and her problems, and her crises, and all her drama pretty much sucked up what was left of him. That didn't leave a whole lot of bandwidth to spend on Sarah. But if he was honest with himself, that seemed to be the way Sarah wanted it anyway.

—ᴗᴗ—

Sarah glanced at the time as she stopped her car in front of the Dip 'n' Dine. One o'clock on the nose. She looked up to see Olivia leaving her lookout spot at the window and heading for the door. For maybe the hundredth time since yesterday, she asked herself what in the world she had gotten herself into.

"I'm ready. Let's go." Olivia was at the car door yanking at the handle before Sarah was completely out of the car.

"Hang on. We have to tell your uncle that we're leaving." She watched as Olivia deflated a bit. "Come on. We can't just take off without saying good-bye. It wouldn't be polite." She held her hand out for Olivia and walked with her back into the diner. Truth be told, Sarah would have been as happy as Olivia to have her just hop in the car and take off. She didn't need more complications in her life right now, and with Chris Reed, things just got more and more complicated.

Chris, however, was all business, confusing her even more. He barely stopped on his way from table to kitchen to say good-bye and wish them a good time. Sarah had steeled herself for another offer of dinner when they returned and had what she hoped was a pleasant but firm and final refusal ready. But no such invitation was forthcoming. In fact, to watch Chris now, one would think inviting her to dinner had never occurred to him. He just asked what time she thought they'd be back, told Olivia to mind Sarah, waved, and disappeared into the kitchen.

With Chris back in the kitchen and Olivia already heading out the front door, Sarah really had nothing to do but follow her out. The people in Sarah's life tended to be pretty much the same from one time she saw them to the next, but she had yet to figure out the Reeds. They seemed pretty moody, and she wasn't quite sure what to do with that. By the time she buckled herself into the front seat, she had decided she didn't have to do anything but take the next couple weeks as they came. Pretty soon Olivia would be back home in Scottsdale and school in Last Chance would be starting. Everybody would be busy living their own lives. Meanwhile, because she liked Olivia in spite of her mercurial ways, she'd just have to figure out a way to spend time with the niece while avoiding the uncle. She drove out onto the highway and glanced into the rearview mirror. Olivia seemed to be doing an amazing amount of bouncing around for someone with a seat belt on.

"Want to pull that belt a little tighter? We want you safe." Sarah heard the commotion in the backseat calm a little. What in the world was she doing back there, anyway? "Have you been around horses much, Olivia?"

"I've been on pony rides at the fair, but I don't think it's the same."

"No, it's not the same." Sarah tried to ignore the slow, rhythmic kick on the back of her seat. "Let me tell you a little bit about horses. A lot of loud noise and fast movement around their feet can make them really nervous, and we don't want that. So I'm going to need you to stay right by me, keep your voice down, and do everything I say, okay?"

Sarah glanced in the rearview mirror again and saw Olivia's solemn nod. She caught Olivia's eyes and smiled. "Great. I can tell you're going to be a good horsewoman."

True to her word, Olivia stuck to Sarah's side and spoke barely above a whisper as they got out of the car and approached the corral. A dappled gray horse raised her head and whickered before slowly ambling over to the fence and lowering her head over the top rail for attention.

"This is Belle." Sarah scratched Belle's ear. "In a minute we'll go get her tack, but first I want you to meet her." She reached into her bag and took out a small apple. "Here. Hold this on your hand, fingers flat out, and she'll take it. She loves apples."

Even children who had grown up around horses could be uneasy the first time one ate out of their hand, and Sarah held Olivia's wrist to steady it. But Olivia didn't flinch. When Belle lipped the apple off her hand and crunched it between her teeth, Olivia smiled. "That tickled."

"Well, you're her friend now." Sarah gave Belle's cheek another pat and led the way to the barn. The tack room was large and immaculately kept. Billy, the ranch's longtime foreman, ran a tight ship. Olivia was immediately captivated by the long, glassed-in trophy case along one wall.

"Wow. There must be a hundred ribbons and stuff. What are they for?"

Sarah stopped and looked. Truthfully, she gave them no more thought when she came in the barn than she gave any piece of equipment she wasn't actually looking for at the time. But Olivia was right. There were a lot of ribbons.

"Well, these are ribbons we've brought home from shows over the years. We don't show a lot anymore, but my granddad really loved his quarter horses."

"Did Belle win any of these?"

"You know, I've never thought about that. If she did, it was a long time ago." Sarah picked up the lead rope she had come for. "Let's go ask her."

Olivia rolled her eyes as she fell in beside her. "Horses can't talk."

───※───

The shadows were stretching across the yard when Sarah finally was able to tuck Olivia into the backseat again and head down the dirt road to the highway. After an afternoon of walking and trotting around the ring with Sarah watching and calling instruction from the ground, Belle had been brushed and groomed to within an inch of her life and turned back into the corral to munch on the scoop of oats Olivia had put in her feedbox.

"I like Belle." The voice from the backseat was almost dreamy. "I think she wants me to come back and take care of her some more."

"I wouldn't be surprised." Sarah glanced in the rearview mirror and smiled. Neither the sullen, way-too-old-for-her-years little girl she met yesterday nor the overly excited, almost out of control child Olivia had become at the mention of horses was evident. All

Sarah saw was a very tired, and very dirty, seven-year-old leaning back against the seat and gazing out her side window.

"So when can I come? Tomorrow? Belle will be looking for me."

"Not tomorrow, but maybe we can make it up here another time before you go back home. School's going to be starting soon, you know, and we're both going to be really busy."

"I hate school." The voice from the backseat was matter-of-fact.

"How can you hate school?" Sarah's voice took on the cheerful, authoritative tone she had used in her term of practice teaching. "There's so much to do and to learn."

"Because the kids are mean and the teacher's mean and everybody always gets me in trouble."

"Wow, it does sound like first grade was rough." Sarah felt a flash of indignation at that first grade teacher, whoever she was. Any class could have a child like Olivia, one who needed extra time and understanding to thrive, and if the teacher was caring and conscientious, as Sarah fully intended to be, that child would *not* leave first grade hating school.

"I hated it. And sometimes my mom made me go anyway, even when I had a real bad stomachache. So, when can I come back and ride Belle?"

"We'll see."

Olivia, either satisfied with the answer or too tired to push the issue, didn't respond, and Sarah let the conversation fade to silence. The comment about Olivia's mom sometimes making her go to school anyway disturbed her. How much school had Olivia missed? The "missing school, falling behind, hating school, missing school" cycle could destroy a student's academic prospects like nothing else. And for Olivia, it was starting in first grade.

Sarah sighed as she reached the Dip 'n' Dine and turned into the parking lot. From what she had gathered, Chris seemed to be one of the few people in the little girl's life who was really concerned about her. There might not be a lot he could do from Last Chance when Olivia was in Arizona, but Sarah guessed it would be more than anyone at home did.

The diner was nearly empty when Olivia led the way inside. Juanita was talking to the last customers as she wrote up their ticket, and Chris was sitting at a booth in the back with Rita. Everyone looked up and smiled.

"Well, if it's not Annie Oakley." Juanita slapped her ticket book shut and headed behind the counter. "How would you like a glass of lemonade? You look like you're spitting dust."

Olivia just shrugged, and Juanita's mouth began to get that pinched look. Sarah nudged Olivia and muttered, "Yes, please, Miss Juanita."

Olivia looked at the floor and then out the window. "Yes . . . please." Sarah nudged her again. "Miss Juanita."

Juanita beamed. "Well then, I'd be real happy to get you one." She turned to the soda machine, and Sarah bent down to whisper in Olivia's ear.

"See? That didn't hurt at all, did it? And be sure to say thank you."

Olivia rolled her eyes. "Who's Annie Oakley, anyway?"

Juanita returned with two tall glasses of lemonade. "I brought you a glass too, Sarah. Something tells me you could use a little cooling down yourself." She raised her eyebrows and slid a knowing glance Sarah's way.

"Thanks, Juanita." Sarah smiled as if she had no idea what Juanita could be referring to. "We had a good time today, didn't we, Olivia?"

Olivia, who had muttered the barest of thanks when Juanita put the lemonade in front of her on the counter, didn't answer or even look up from her glass. After a moment Juanita sighed, shook her head, shot another meaningful look toward Sarah, and returned to the kitchen.

If Olivia noticed the exchange, she gave no sign, and Sarah felt another pang for the angry little fighter on the stool next to her. What must it be like to be seven and feel like it was you against the world? Loud, hollow slurps indicating Olivia had reached the bottom of her glass interrupted Sarah's musing, and she automatically opened her mouth to give Olivia another manners check. She gave the little girl's shoulders a quick squeeze instead. Olivia had said please, thank you, and even *Miss* Juanita. Maybe that was enough for one day.

12

Chris found it hard to keep his mind on Rita and her clipboard when Sarah and Olivia came in. What he really wanted to do was get up, cross the room, and sit down and join them for a lemonade, but after calling a brief "howdy" to the riders when they came in, Rita had returned to her plans. Chris sighed and tried to focus. It wasn't that the barbecue Rita was detailing wasn't important. It was, in fact, probably the most significant event in the life of the Dip 'n' Dine since he had arrived in Last Chance. But they had been at this for more than an hour now, with Rita doing most of the talking, and he was pretty sure they had already covered everything on Rita's list at least twice.

"This is the one thing I'm not sure about." Rita leaned back and tapped her clipboard with her pencil. "Your music. I really think your best bet is going to be country. It's what folks around here listen to mostly, and we have some local bands we could get. No reason to send all the way to Albuquerque for jazz when we've got country right here."

Chris shot another quick glance at the counter and gave up trying to end his meeting with Rita. Sarah was getting ready to leave. He lifted his hand in a wave, called "Thanks," and smiled at her "Don't mention it" before returning his attention to the matters at hand.

"I think you'll like the band I'm thinking about. They used to play in a restaurant I worked in, and they're good. I've got a CD at home I'll bring you, and if you like them as much as I think you will, I'll give Tom a call. I'll bet we could get them down here for a weekend."

"I don't know." Rita clearly was not convinced. "I had sort of thought we'd advertise it as 'A Foot-Stompin' Time at the Dip 'n' Dine.' It sort of rhymes, don't you think? I'm not sure foot-stompin' works with jazz."

"Nope, not much foot-stompin' when these guys play. But what about this?" Chris paused for effect. "Hot Chile and Cool Jazz."

He could almost hear the wheels turning in Rita's head as her pencil stopped in midtap and she looked up at him. "You know, I like that. 'Hot Chile and Cool Jazz.'" She said the words like she tasted them. "Of course, we'd have to advertise it just right, but you can leave that to me. You get me that CD, and we might just have ourselves an event."

Rita tucked her pencil back behind her ear where she kept it for easy access and picked up her clipboard. Her meetings could seem interminable, but her comings and goings were always efficient. "Now, I've got places to go and things to do. I'll swing by for the CD in the morning."

She was out the door by the time Chris got out of their booth. She must have seen someone she needed to talk to down the street, because she waved her arm over her head and took off at a brisk pace.

Chris watched her go. If he had only thought to suggest his theme a few minutes earlier, maybe he could have joined Sarah for that lemonade after all. He walked over to the counter where Olivia was drawing on a place mat what was doubtlessly meant to be a horse.

"How'd it go?"

The joy in her face as she turned to him and began to relate her afternoon in finest detail filled his heart. Olivia looked and sounded like a happy seven-year-old, and he needed to thank Sarah for that. It didn't matter that she made it clear that she wanted to keep him at arm's length. That wasn't what this was about.

—∽—

Sarah laughed to herself as she drove home. Rita was no bigger than Sarah—that is to say, about five feet tall—but she had Chris right where she wanted him in that booth, and he wasn't going anywhere until she said so. Rita just had that effect on folks. She talked. They listened. Gran was about the only one in Last Chance who could stop Rita when she was on a roll. Gran would just put her hand on Rita's arm and say, "Now, that just sounds fascinating. I'll have to hear more when I have time." Then she'd smile and walk away. Briefly, Sarah wondered how it would work if she tried that approach but decided that her old method of running when she saw Rita coming was probably the best one for her.

She was caught up in her own thoughts when she turned onto her street and didn't notice the familiar BMW parked in front of Gran's house until she was driving past it. Then she saw Gran and her guest standing on the front porch, apparently saying good-bye. Five minutes. If she hadn't been in such a rush to get out of the Dip 'n' Dine before Chris finished with Rita and had waited five more minutes, she would have missed him.

Gran and Brandon saw her and waved. Well, that was it. She'd been avoiding this conversation since she got back to Last Chance, but there was no getting out of it now. Brandon had played his trump card: Gran liked him. And if Gran still thought Sarah and Brandon were friends, or more than friends, well, that was no one's fault but Sarah's. Every time Gran had mentioned Brandon, Sarah had made a noncommittal comment and changed the subject.

She pulled into her own driveway and shut off the engine. *Good grief, Gran, you read my mind over every other thought I have. Why couldn't you have figured out that I don't want to see Brandon again? Ever.*

She rested her head on the steering wheel a moment, took a deep breath, and got out of the car. Gran and Brandon were already walking down the sidewalk to her house.

"Look what the wind blew in!" Gran was clearly delighted with her surprise, and Sarah forced a smile for her sake.

"Hey, Brandon." She tried not to stiffen as he leaned in to kiss her cheek. His cologne had once made her weak in the knees. Now it just made her want to cry. "It's been a while."

"It has." His smile tipped up on one side, and his voice was slow. Lack of confidence had never been a shortcoming of Brandon Miller. "And that's my fault. I've been so involved with getting ready for the new job and the move and everything that the time just got away."

Sarah just looked at him. *But you still managed to find time to leave a half dozen messages on my phone every day. You are such a con man.*

"Well, come on in." There was no getting around it. He was not going to go away. "You too, Gran. Come have some iced tea with us." *Please.*

"Oh, no." Gran waved a dismissive hand. "You two have a lot to catch up on, and Brandon and I have already had our visit." She turned to Brandon before heading back up the sidewalk. "Your new job sounds fascinating, darlin'. I'll be praying for you."

"Thank you, ma'am. I appreciate it."

His aw-shucks humility sounded as phony to Sarah as the blame he shouldered for not coming to see her earlier, and she huffed

121

an exasperated sigh as she headed up her walk. She did not invite Brandon to follow her, but he did anyway. She tried to let the screen door swing shut behind her, but he caught it and followed her inside.

He closed the door gently and came to where Sarah stood in the middle of the room. Placing his hands on her shoulders, he let them slide down her arms. When he slipped his arms around her waist and tried to pull her close, she stepped back.

"Seriously, Brandon? What do you think you're doing?"

His arms fell to his side and he shrugged. "Worth a try. I've missed you so much. Why haven't you returned any of my calls?"

Sarah perched on the arm of the sofa. "And say what? We went over everything a hundred times before I came home. There wasn't anything left to say."

Brandon ran a hand through his perfectly tousled brown hair. "Maybe not for you. But I have plenty to say."

"And I've heard it all. Over and over and over. Can't we just give it a rest?"

"Not till you've heard me out one more time." Brandon swung a dining chair around and straddled it.

Sarah found herself wondering if that carefully maintained two-day stubble would have to go when he started his new job. She hoped so. It really looked cheesy. She slipped off the arm of the sofa onto the seat and leaned her head back. Her eyes closed for a moment. "Then you'll leave? For good?"

"If you still want me to leave, I'll go."

"Oh, I'll want you to leave. You can pretty much count on that."

"Sarah, listen to me. I'm not here to play games or get involved in some sort of verbal sparring match. I came all the way to Last Chance just so I could talk to you. I knew from the outset that

122

you'd probably do what you're doing right now, but I had to do it anyway. So would you at least listen?"

Sarah sat up. Brandon loved recreational arguing. Whether it was politics, or religion, or just the satisfaction of having the last word, he was always up for a lively discussion, and frankly, it wore Sarah out. And often it wore her down. But this time there was something different in his tone. She looked at him and waited. Completely uncharacteristically, Brandon seemed at a loss for words. Finally, he took a deep breath and plunged ahead.

"I guess we had been dating about a year, sometime in our junior year, when I first realized that every time I thought about the future, I saw you in it with me. Every dream, every plan, you were there."

Sarah felt tears sting her eyelids. She turned away and looked out the window.

Brandon's voice wasn't as sure as it usually was. "And when you seemed to share those dreams, I really felt there wasn't a thing I couldn't accomplish."

"Please, Brandon . . ." The steely walls Sarah had built around her feelings for Brandon weren't as strong as she thought they were, and some of the pain she thought she was safe from was beginning to trickle through.

"You said you'd hear me out." Brandon caught her gaze and held it. "Just let me finish. Anyway, it did become all about my dreams, my plans. I know that. I didn't even consider that you might have a few dreams of your own."

"You wouldn't even listen." Sarah spoke barely above a whisper.

"I know. And I was wrong. I thought I would conquer the world for you, and you'd just stand there and be impressed with me."

Sarah shook her head and laughed. "Oh, Brandon, what century are you from?"

"I don't know. Not this one, that's for sure. Anyway, I've had a lot of time to think recently, and I know this: I still can't imagine a future without you in it. Can't we start over, or at least pick up where you felt like I stopped hearing you? I want to know what you want. I want to talk less and listen more. Can't you give me another chance?"

Of all the things Brandon could have said, this was what Sarah expected least. She would not have been surprised if he had trotted out his list of all the reasons why they were good together. Or if he had turned on his lady-killer charm and tried to sweep her off her feet, as if *that* would work at this point. But she had not been prepared for this humble and serious side of Brandon. She looked into the depths of his gray-green eyes, but she saw no game playing, no agenda. He really seemed to mean what he was saying.

"Okay, you want to know what I want? Well, in a few days you're leaving for that new job in Chicago. I'll tell you right now what I told you when they first started interviewing you: I don't want to live in Chicago. Not now. Not ever. I am not a city girl and I never will be."

"Fair enough. The company has branches other places. They're not out in the country, of course, but some are in smaller cities, even some here in the Southwest. And there are other companies besides the one that hired me too. How about this? Why don't we just take it slow. We can keep the door open and see if there is a future for us out there somewhere. I'll go ahead and move to Chicago for now, you stay here in Last Chance and teach, and we can email and talk on the phone, maybe even visit each other once in a while. We'll just see what happens. No pressure."

No pressure. Just having Brandon in her house was almost more pressure than Sarah could deal with. Why, oh why, hadn't she run in the house and locked the door when she saw him on Gran's porch?

Sarah looked out the window again, trying to regather the resolve that had kept her from taking any of the calls Brandon had been bombarding her with.

He must have sensed encouragement in her hesitation, because his expression changed just a bit. His smile grew just a little more confident, and he sat up a little straighter on his chair.

"All I'm saying is, let's go back to being friends and see where that takes us."

Sarah let her eyes meet Brandon's again. "I don't know. I'd like us to be friends, but I think you want us back the way we were."

"Of course I want us back together. Did I ever say otherwise? But I'm not going to push it. You're calling all the shots this time."

"And if, after all this taking it slow, all the phone calls and emails and so forth, I still just want to be friends?"

"It would kill me. I'll be honest. But I'd much rather have you in my life as a friend than not have you in my life at all."

"Oh, Brandon, what are we doing?"

Sarah spoke more to the floor than to the man sitting across from her, but it seemed to be all Brandon was waiting to hear. He jumped to his feet and stood before Sarah with his hand stretched toward her.

"Friends?" His grin was almost boyish.

Sarah hesitated but finally slipped her hand in his. "Friends. But only friends."

"I'll take it." Brandon drew her to her feet and into an embrace that even Sarah had to admit could be nothing but a buddy hug. Maybe he really did mean what he said about taking it slowly.

"Now." Brandon smiled down at her and brushed a curl from her face. "Why don't you go get ready, and we'll go out to dinner in San Ramon to celebrate being friends."

Sarah turned away from him. "No, all I want to do right now is have a bath and eat something out of the refrigerator. It's been a long day."

"That sounds good. You go take your bath, and I'll see what I can scrounge up."

Sarah put her hand on his chest. "No. I think you should go now. I have a lot to think about, and I need to be alone."

Sarah thought she saw a flash of irritation cross his face, but it was quickly covered by a tight smile. He took her shoulders and planted a kiss on her forehead. "If that's what you want, then that's what we'll do. I should probably be heading back now anyway. It's a long drive."

At the front door, he turned and took Sarah's hand again. "I'd like to see you again before I leave for Chicago."

She nodded. "Okay."

A real smile filled his face this time. "All right, then. I'll give you a call and we can set something up."

Sarah leaned against her front door after she closed it. She knew for sure now that she wasn't the same woman who had allowed Brandon to plan her life for her. She had taken the initiative to end things between them, to come back to Last Chance and to begin to build a life for herself on her terms. And she intended to continue living her life on just those terms. Surprisingly, Brandon seemed to accept that, and having him as a friend again would be nice. And if he meant what he said—if he really did want to pursue a life where the hopes and dreams and goals of each of them held equal value—then maybe they did have a future together. She would let time tell. And as Brandon said, this time she called the shots.

13

L ook what I've got!" Rita bustled into the Dip 'n' Dine waving a sheaf of papers over her head. She plopped the stack on the counter and held the top sheet up for inspection. "'Hot Chile and Cool Jazz: An Evening of Spice and Ice.' I thought that last bit just makes it perfect. What do you think?"

Chris took the flyer from her and read it, slowly nodding. "I think it's going to work. I like the 'spice and ice.'"

Rita handed another flyer to Carlos, who had appeared in the kitchen window. Since the evening party had been his idea, he had taken particular interest in the plans.

Chris handed back his flyer and Rita read it again. "I just wish the last weekend in September would have worked. When you head into October, you're flirting with a cold snap, and earlier in September just doesn't give us the time we need to do this thing right."

"Sorry, but that's the only weekend Tom can bring his band down. And we're lucky to get that since we're holding this right in the middle of hunting season."

"Just another reason why it might have been a good idea to stick with a local band, even if it wasn't jazz." Rita handed a flyer to each of the few diners finishing up a late lunch. "Here, you won't want to miss this. And tell all your friends."

"Are you kidding me?" Chris grinned. "You really think 'a foot stompin' time' is better than 'spice and ice'? This is a real winner."

"I do have a knack for slogans, if I say so myself. It just comes naturally." Rita cocked her head as she admired her own handiwork before peeling off four flyers and handing them to Chris. "One for the front door, one for the cash register, and one in each of the restrooms. Oh, and here are the tickets. The flyer says you can buy them either here or at the motel. Keep track of the number you sell and who buys them. This thing is going to sell out. Mark my words."

Chris nodded, thinking he should probably be taking notes or something.

"Well, I've got to get these flyers out. The sooner they go up everywhere, the sooner people will start talking about it and buying tickets." She stopped with her hand on the door. "Oh, what about the food? What's on the menu?"

Chris glanced at Carlos, who turned back to his kitchen with a scowl. "Well, we're still in negotiations about that. I think I've about got Carlos to agree to share the kitchen with me that night. We're thinking there'll be a choice between a traditional New Mexican combo plate and something a little more contemporary. Still haven't quite decided what."

"If he sells even five orders of that fancy Santa Fe stuff when folks can eat my cooking, I'll eat one myself." Carlos's grumble may have been intended for no one in particular, but it carried to the dining room.

"I heard that." Chris turned and pointed at Carlos through the window into the kitchen. "And you're on. I'll serve you myself, right here in this front and center booth."

"You're pushing it, boss." Carlos turned back to his stove.

With Rita gone and the diner nearly empty, Chris found some tape and set about putting up the flyers. The timing of the dinner was perfect. He could throw himself into it and not miss Olivia so much. He'd been surprised at how easily she had fit into his life, and the nearly two weeks she had been with him had flown by. But it was nearly time for school to start, and she'd soon be going home.

When the phone in his pocket vibrated, he took it and raised his eyebrows at the screen. Kaitlyn hadn't called Olivia nearly as often as she had promised, but it was often enough for Kaitlyn, he guessed. He pressed Talk.

"Hey, Sis. How's it going?"

"Just great! How are you guys doing?" Kaitlyn sounded more than cheerful, and that made Chris nervous. Usually that meant she wanted something.

"We're doing fine. I'm sorry Olivia's not here. She's out at the ranch with Sarah getting in one last ride, but she'll be home in a couple hours. Should I have her call you, or do you want to call back?"

"Oh, I'll call back. Don't worry about it. But I'm glad I got to talk to you. You usually just hand the phone to Olivia."

"I thought that was our deal."

"But you're my brother. I like talking to you too, you know."

"All right." Now he was sure of it. Kaitlyn wanted something. Probably the money to get back home.

"So, who is this Sarah that Olivia keeps talking about? Is she cute? Should I be worried about my brother?"

Chris walked through the kitchen and out the back door. Juanita and the last table of customers were following his conversation with unabashed interest, and he had a feeling the call was going to require some privacy as soon as Kaitlyn got around to why she called.

"Sarah Cooley is a teacher who's taken an interest in Olivia.

She grew up on a ranch near here and has taken Olivia riding a couple times. Now, what's this call all about, Kaitlyn? Do you need money?"

"No, I just wanted to talk to you, that's all." Kaitlyn sounded deeply hurt that Chris would question her motives. "Can't we just talk without you finding fault?"

Chris glanced at his watch. "We could and I'd love to. But I'm at work right now and I need to get back at it. Why don't you plan on spending an extra day or two here when you come back for Olivia? We could catch up then."

There was a long pause on the line, and Chris thought they might have been cut off. "Kaitlyn? Are you there?"

"I'm here."

Totally exasperated, Chris sat down on the concrete back step. "Okay. I don't have any more time for this. You called for a reason. If it's not money, what is it?"

Another long pause. "Kaitlyn?"

He heard her take a deep breath, and then the words came in a rush. "I—we've decided to spend the winter here in Florida. I'm not coming back till maybe spring, so can Olivia just stay with you?"

"Can Olivia what? What are you talking about? Of course you can't spend the winter in Florida. You have responsibilities. You have a child, for crying out loud."

"Don't I deserve some fun once in a while? I was barely more than a baby myself when Olivia came." Kaitlyn started into her old self-pitying rant, but Chris cut her off.

"Save it, Kaitlyn. I've heard it all before. You need to grow up. Olivia deserves better."

"She's got you." Chris thought he may have heard tears in Kaitlyn's voice, but he couldn't tell. The line had gone dead.

130

Muttering a curse, Chris immediately called her back, but it went straight to voice mail. Of course Kaitlyn would turn off her phone as soon as she hung up. Rage coursed through him, and his hands shook with his desire to put a fist through something. He drew back his arm to throw his phone as far into the desert as he could get it but wound up jamming it back in his pocket instead. The phone was his only link, however tenuous, to his irresponsible, immature, unreliable sister. He took a deep breath, held it as long as he could, and slowly let it hiss through his teeth. Kaitlyn had been smart to turn off her phone. He needed to cool off before he talked to anyone.

The back door opened and Juanita stuck her head out. "Everything okay?"

Chris nodded without looking at her.

"Chris, what happened? Your sister's not hurt, is she?" It was Juanita's firm and often stated belief that anyone who got near a motorcycle was bound to end up in traction, or worse.

"Nope. She's doing great." Chris jumped to his feet and headed off the step into the desert behind the diner. "I'm going for a walk. Back in a while."

—◦◦◦—

At least an hour had passed before Chris walked back up the steps and into the kitchen. And honestly? If it hadn't been for the fact that Olivia would be back and Juanita would be wanting to go home, he'd probably still be heading for that mountain in the distance.

He'd made another attempt to reach Kaitlyn but was not surprised to find the call still going straight to voice mail. A call to his mom in Arizona had been more successful, even if she was about to walk into a meeting and couldn't give him more than a few minutes.

"I can't say I'm surprised," his mom had said, "but I am so mad I could spit nails. I give, give, give to that girl and she just takes, takes, takes. She sold the car *I* gave her, quit the job *I* got her, and now I'm stuck with cleaning up her mess here. And what am I supposed to do with that cat? I just don't have time for this."

When Chris got the conversation back around to Olivia, his mom didn't see the problem. In fact, as far as she was concerned, things couldn't have worked out better for Olivia.

Carlos looked up from scrubbing his stove when Chris walked in, and even though he didn't say anything, Chris could tell from his expression that Juanita had poured out her concerns. He supposed it was too much to hope that the diner had been empty at the time.

"Well, here's your uncle Chris! We were starting to get worried." Juanita really did look more relieved at his return than annoyed at his absence, which surprised him. Maybe he had been gone a little longer than he should have been.

Olivia, on her stool at the counter, looked worried, and Chris forced a smile for her sake and tried to tousle her hair. "Sorry, kiddo. I got out there in the desert and lost track of the time. Have a good time today?"

Olivia leaned away from him and shrugged. Clearly, he was still not in her good graces. "You were gone a long time."

"Well, I'm back now." He turned to Juanita. "Sorry to have kept you. I know you need to get home. See you tomorrow."

Juanita seemed in no hurry to leave. Something was obviously amiss, maybe even gravely so, and as she often said, offering help and advice to a friend in need always took precedence in her life. "Are you sure everything's okay? I've already called Russ to tell him I might be late."

132

"No, everything is fine." Chris made his voice calm and easy and hoped his smiled matched it. "Really. You can go on home, although I do appreciate you staying with Olivia till I got back."

Juanita waved a dismissive hand. "Oh, don't mention it. We knew you'd be back when you were ready." She waited another moment, but when it became clear that Chris had said all he was going to say, she edged toward the front door. "Well, if you need anything, anything at all, you call me now, you hear?"

"Will do."

Juanita finally had nothing to do but leave. Chris watched through the front window as she walked to her car. Her brisk pace and the slam she gave the car door told him she was not a bit happy with his evasiveness. Well, too bad about that.

"So, Liverhead, what's wrong? Are you mad at me for not being here when you got here, or is something else going on?" Chris took the stool next to Olivia's.

"No, I'm not mad at you." She was busy dragging her straw through a puddle of lemonade on the counter and making squiggles.

"Then what's up?"

She was quiet for another long moment and then looked up. He was pretty sure that if it were any other seven-year-old, there'd be tears. "It's just that this was probably the last day I was going to get to ride Belle, and Sarah was going to take me on a trail ride, and then this *guy* shows up and starts bothering us."

"A guy?" Chris frowned. "What guy? Did Sarah know him?"

"Yeah. I think he was her boyfriend. They're going to go on a date or something tonight."

"Oh." Somehow, it hadn't occurred to him that Sarah might already be seeing someone. "Well, it couldn't have been too much of a bother. Did you go on your trail ride?"

"Yes, but he came too, and he kept trying to make Sarah talk to him instead of me, and we didn't ride very long, and I probably won't ever get to see Belle again, and she won't even know where I am." She looked up at him and her chin jerked a time or two, but there were still no tears.

Chris lifted her onto his knee and stroked her hair. "Ah, Liverhead, this has been a rotten day all around, hasn't it?"

She sniffed. "Not all rotten. I did get to ride Belle for a little while."

He leaned back so he could look in her face. "You know what we should do? Let's go up to San Ramon and get a pizza. What do you say?"

"Cool. I like pizza. I used to get it all the time at home."

"I'll bet." Chris set Olivia on the floor and stood up. She ran out the front door ahead of him, and Chris called a good-night to Carlos and followed her to the Jeep. He still had no idea how he was going to tell Olivia that her mom wasn't coming to get her, but he was pretty sure there wasn't enough pizza in San Ramon to make it all right.

—◈—

Chris was just getting into his Jeep when Brandon and Sarah drove by. She waved, but he must not have seen her.

"Who's that?" Brandon checked his rearview mirror to see who had her attention.

"That's Chris Reed, Olivia's uncle. He owns the Dip 'n' Dine now."

"Big guy. I wouldn't want to tangle with him. Know him well?"

Sarah shrugged. "Not really. We've talked a few times. Why?"

"Because that was either the most disagreeable kid I've ever met, or she just hated me at first sight. I could see it if she thought I was moving in on her uncle's territory."

"Don't be ridiculous. It was you and you alone that she loathed."

"Wow. Harsh. Was it something I said?"

"I think it was more like something you did. What made you turn up at the ranch, anyway? I thought you were picking me up at my place."

"What can I say? I couldn't wait." He grinned as he reached across the console for her hand. "I got into town a few hours early and got your grandma to tell me where you were."

"And look how popular it made you. You might want to call next time."

"Oh, come on, Sarah. Lighten up a little. I thought we had fun this afternoon. I'm sorry if what's-her-name didn't like it, but I'm leaving for Chicago in three days, and I wanted to spend as much time with you as I could. So sue me."

Sarah took a deep breath and looked out her side window. The summer sun was beginning to slide behind the hills, and the sky was turning every shade of pink and coral. The evening was far too beautiful to waste by being mad, and besides, she had forgotten how nice her hand felt in his.

"So, tell me." Brandon interrupted her thoughts. "Is Uncle Fry Cook going to give me any competition when I'm gone?"

Sarah slipped her hand from his. "Don't be a jerk, Brandon. Chris owns the Dip 'n' Dine, and from what I hear he's an amazing chef. And it's way too soon for you to be talking about competition, anyway."

Maybe it was the chill in her voice, or her pulling her hand away, but Brandon seemed to realize he had some damage to control.

"You're right. That was a dumb thing to say. And I'm sorry."

He kept his eyes on the road but reached for her hand again. "I'm sure he's a great guy. Maybe I can even meet him next time I'm in town. Only, it's too bad about his niece, though. I wouldn't wish her on anybody."

"Don't be mean." Sarah's laugh was light, and again she left her hand in his. "Olivia *is* attitude in tennis shoes, but I don't think she's had an easy time of it. And face it, you did turn up where you weren't invited."

"If I agree that both Chris and Olivia are terrific people and I was wrong to take shots, can we just leave them behind in Last Chance? This is the last evening I'm going to get to spend with you for I don't know how long. I don't want to spend it talking about people who aren't even important to us."

Sarah, who had lowered the visor against the setting sun, took a look in its mirror and then turned around to look over her shoulder.

"It's fine with me if we don't talk about the Reeds, but we're not leaving them behind in Last Chance. They're right behind us."

"You're kidding me." Brandon checked his rearview mirror. "Are they following us?"

"Of course not. If I had to guess, I'd say they were just going to San Ramon. Why would they be following us?"

"I don't know. That kid was awful mad at me, and her uncle is awful big. Maybe she took out a contract on me."

Sarah laughed. The silliness, the ability to make her laugh was what she found so attractive about Brandon in the first place. When was it supplanted by his need to control? And how could she bring that sense of humor back?

"I'm not taking any chances." He pressed hard on the accelerator, and Sarah watched Chris's Jeep fall farther and farther behind until they went around a curve and she lost sight of it for good. An unexpected sense of loss surprised Sarah. She loved the time she spent with Olivia; but she also had to admit that she had begun to look forward to seeing Chris when she picked Olivia up at the diner and dropped her off after their rides. And she didn't like seeing either of them disappear in the distance.

14

Olivia's dark cloud seemed to lift a bit on the way to San Ramon. Chris glanced at her in his rearview mirror as she gazed out the side window singing some nameless tune to herself. She seemed content and at peace, and it killed him that he was going to have to shatter both.

"So, Livvy. Have you thought about what kind of pizza you want?" He raised his voice a bit so she could hear him in the backseat.

"Well, I don't like pineapple, and I don't like mushrooms, and I don't like olives, and I don't like peppers."

"What *do* you like?"

"Pepperoni and cheese."

"That's it?"

"Yep. Are we almost there?"

"We are." Chris pulled into the parking lot, parked his Jeep, and turned off the engine. "Let's go eat."

Even after they had settled into their booth and ordered a pepperoni pizza, Chris couldn't think of a way to tell Olivia that her mom wouldn't be coming to get her as planned.

"Sorry your day didn't work out like you hoped it would. I know you were really looking forward to it."

Olivia just shrugged without looking up from the straw she was sipping from.

"Maybe you'll get to see Belle again after all." If there was any consolation in the news Chris was going to have to break, he was desperate to offer it.

"Nope." Olivia leaned back and shoved her nearly empty glass away. "Sarah said she had to spend all her time getting ready for school now, and Mom'll be coming for me. This was my last chance. And it got ruined."

The pizza arrived and Chris slid a piece onto the plate in front of Olivia. "Really? Ruined? I know it didn't go the way you planned, but you still spent the day riding Belle, didn't you?"

Olivia, picking her way around the hot pizza, just nodded.

"And on the trail too. Not in the arena. It doesn't sound all that ruined to me."

Olivia gave him a glare that would wither plants and, having given up on the hot cheese, picked a piece of pepperoni off the top. If she had declared her day a disaster, she clearly was in no mood for a pep talk intended to convince her otherwise. Chris gave up and turned his attention to his own plate. This was not going well.

Finally, with only one piece of pizza left on the pan, Chris knew he couldn't put off the news any longer. He slid his plate away and sat back.

"Your mom called today while you were gone."

Olivia looked up. "Is she coming to get me?"

"Well, that's the thing, Livvy. She will come back, I know you can count on that. But she won't be here as soon as she thought she would. So what do you think about starting school right here in Last Chance?"

Olivia just looked at him, and Chris felt a twisting ache take hold in the middle of his chest. He hadn't known what to expect when he told her that her mom wasn't coming back. He had been braced for anger, questions, maybe tears, but the return of that hard little nothing-can-get-me expression just sucker punched him.

"So, I was thinking." Chris picked up the check and slid out of the booth. Dinner was definitely over. "What if I took a few days off before school starts and we went to the Grand Canyon? I'll bet Miss Juanita and Carlos can hold the fort just fine."

"That's okay." He could almost see the wall that was going back up around her heart, and he wondered again that someone as small as she was could make him feel so inept and helpless.

After she was buckled into the backseat, he leaned in and waited for her to look at him. Her gaze fastened on his shirt button. "Olivia, I want you to listen to me. This is important. I'm so sorry that your mom won't be here this week to get you. But I want you to understand that the reason I'm sorry is because it makes you sad, and I hate it when you're sad. I'm not one bit sorry that you're staying longer with me, though. I love having you live at my house, and I know the two of us will do just fine."

He waited for her to say something, but when nothing came, he used his thumb to wipe the single tear that had found its way to her cheek. "I love you, Livvy. Don't you ever forget that."

He started to back out, but she threw her arms around his neck and held on. And even after the muscles in his back and neck started to complain, he stood there in a bent-double crouch gently stroking her back until she was ready to let go.

———⚌———

The stars had come out and a cool night wind swept the flag-stone patio outside the restaurant where Brandon had taken Sarah. The umbrellas that shaded tables at noon were closed and tightly bound against any gust that might catch them and lift them over the low stone railing and into the gorge below.

"How did you find this place? I've lived around here all my life and didn't know it was here." Sarah sat on the low wall and looked across the valley. Off in the distance the lights of a small town flickered against the darkness.

"Oh, I have my ways." Brandon tried to sound mysterious, but Sarah had known him too long.

"Seriously."

He shrugged. "Internet research, what else? Actually, it hasn't been here all that long—the restaurant, that is. It used to be a ranch house. I think the whole ranch is going to be developed into a retirement community."

Sarah wished he hadn't said that. More change. Visions of bull-dozers and cul-de-sacs and golf courses thrust the gentle night aside. She took a deep breath. Nope. She wasn't going to let an uncertain future spoil the here and now.

"Let's take a walk before we head back." She held out her hand, and Brandon tugged her to her feet.

Brandon kept her hand, and as they walked down the road, Sarah had to admit to herself that her hand felt right in his. After all, that was where it had been for most of their college years. When they reached the end of the road and turned to head back to the car, Brandon put both hands on her shoulders and looked down into her face. She knew he was going to kiss her and stepped back. This was not taking it slow, as he had promised. But before she could say a word, he bent over her and lightly, almost imperceptibly, brushed her lips with his.

"Something to remember me by." He smiled down at her and took her hand again.

They walked back to the car without saying anything else, and even the drive back to Last Chance was quiet. Sarah was glad Brandon was leaving for Chicago in the morning. That kiss, more than anything Brandon could have done, had turned her thoughts upside down.

Over her protest, he insisted on walking her to her front door, but he didn't try to kiss her again. And when she didn't invite him in, he accepted it without a word.

"Thanks." Sarah smiled up at him. "I really enjoyed tonight."

"You sound surprised."

"Well, I didn't know what to expect. But this was fun. I'd do it again—most of it, anyway." The corner of his mouth and one eyebrow tipped up, and Sarah changed the subject. "When do you leave tomorrow?"

"I'll hit the road before dawn. I want to get to Oklahoma City tomorrow and then on into Chicago the next night."

"Wow. Those are some long days."

He shrugged. "I'll take the scenic route next time. I'm anxious to get there and get started."

"Drive safe." Sarah put her hand on his arm. "Be sure to stop when you get tired. And let me know when you get there safely."

Brandon covered the hand on his arm with his own and moved it to his chest. "You could still come, you know. Just for the ride and to see where I'm going to be."

Sarah took her hand back and reached for the doorknob. "Good *night*, Brandon. I do wish you all the very best with your new life. I hope it's everything you want it to be."

She slipped into the house and closed the door behind her. After a minute, she heard his BMW purr to life and glide down the street until the sound was swallowed by silence. As smooth and tasteful as Brandon himself.

"Oh, Brandon." Sarah slipped out of her shoes and wandered into the kitchen to put the kettle on. "Why do you need to complicate everything?"

It had not been easy to reclaim her life when she saw it disappear into Brandon's plans, but she had done it. And now, when she was finally getting everything arranged the way *she* liked, here he came again.

By the time the whistle on her teakettle blew, she had changed into an oversized New Mexico State T-shirt and some gym shorts. She took her mug of tea onto the front porch and tucked one bare leg up under her as she settled into the rocker. Except for the whisper of the night wind through the cottonwoods, the night was silent. Even the crickets seemed to have gone to bed. Pushing the rocker into motion with the foot that still touched the porch, she took a sip of tea and offered a quick prayer of thanks that Brandon would be on his way tomorrow. She had been so sure of the way her life would go until he had turned up on her doorstep, and even now, she knew teaching here in Last Chance was what she really wanted to do. But Brandon had this way of stirring everything up and making it all murky again. She had promised him she'd keep an open mind and let things unfold as they would, but oh, she was glad he was going to be in Chicago.

Sarah glanced at her watch. Nearly midnight, and the town had pretty much rolled up the sidewalks. How different from Chicago where the city never slept. Or was that New York? The only light on her silent street came from the glow of Elizabeth's front room. Gran must still be up. On impulse, Sarah got up and padded down the street in her bare feet, still clutching her mug of tea.

The curtain drew aside and Elizabeth's concerned face appeared at the window at Sarah's tap, followed almost immediately by the unlatching of the front door.

"Sarah, what in the world? What's wrong?"

"Nothing, Gran." Sarah smiled as she came in. "I was on my porch and saw your light and thought I'd come say hi."

Elizabeth did not look at all reassured. "But you're in your nightclothes."

Sarah looked down at herself. "They're only nightclothes because I wear them to bed. They can be day clothes too, you know."

Elizabeth just stood in her quilted bathrobe and fuzzy slippers looking at her, and Sarah realized Gran was not going to buy the "zany visit in the middle of the night" story.

"Okay, I've got a lot on my mind, and I was hoping we could talk." She held out her mug. "More?"

Elizabeth was a self-proclaimed night owl anyway, but even if she had begun to flag a bit, nothing could energize her quite like the promise of a heart-to-heart.

"Of course, honey. Let me just cut that television off and I'll put the kettle on."

Sarah followed her grandmother into the kitchen, and when Elizabeth turned from the stove, Sarah was already sitting at the kitchen table. Elizabeth got a box of cookies from the cupboard and joined her.

"Now, what's got you running barefooted up and down the street in the middle of the night?"

By the time the kettle boiled, Sarah had told her story, ending with Brandon driving off to Chicago.

"I knew we hadn't seen much of Brandon since you got home this summer, but I just assumed it was because you were both so busy." Elizabeth poured boiling water over the leaves and set the teapot on the table. "I have to admit I was surprised, though. In my day, when you were in love, you looked for every possible excuse to be together. I just figured things must have changed there too, like they have everywhere else."

"Nope, things haven't changed all that much in that department. Which is why I tried to put distance between us."

"Well, I'm just as sorry as I can be that I messed things up for you. If I had known you weren't seeing him anymore, I would never have invited him in for a visit. And I certainly would not have walked him down to your house."

"I know, Gran." Sarah patted her grandmother's hand. "I should have said something. But maybe it was for the best. Brandon says he's changed and that I can have all the time I need to see that for myself. Maybe he is the one, and I would never have known it if you hadn't brought him down."

"Well, I'd be the last one to say a person can't change. I've seen it too many times." Elizabeth refilled Sarah's mug and poured a cup for herself. "But it usually takes a lot more than want-to. What's Brandon's relationship with the Lord?"

"I don't know. He went to church with me, and I do have to say he's a good person, but it's not something we've really talked about. Faith was just a given."

"Faith is never just a given, sweetie. You haven't asked for any advice, but I'm going to give you some anyway. When you do start talking about the future, start with that. Because with a shared faith, even a Chicago city mouse and a New Mexico country mouse can make a nest. And I should know."

Sarah smiled. "That's right. You've been here so long I sometimes forget that you came from Chicago. And you made it work."

"It wasn't always easy, especially at first. We were as different as chalk and cheese, and without our shared faith, oh my, I likely would have been on the first eastbound train."

Sarah squeezed her hand, the one with the thin gold band almost embedded in her fourth finger. "I'm glad you stayed."

"Oh, I am too. I wouldn't have missed the life I've lived for anything."

"I guess I should go. It's awful late." Sarah picked up her mug and got to her feet. "Thanks for the tea. And the talk."

"Anytime, honey. That's what I'm here for." Elizabeth picked up her cup too. "I think I'll just take my tea into the front room. *Hawaii Five-0* is fixing to come on. They have the best shows on late at night."

The sidewalk still felt warm against her bare feet as Sarah headed back home, though the night had turned cool. The days of August and early September could be among the warmest of the year, but the nights tended to whisper that summer was almost over and fall was on the way. Soon school would be starting and she'd be far too busy, she hoped, for all this emotional hand-wringing over Brandon. As if he sensed she was thinking about him, the phone in her pocket signaled a text: "DFILY." *Don't forget I love you.* It was a shorthand message they sent each other as texts, or left on untended computers, or even murmured when they parted all through college. Brandon was really pulling out all the stops. She almost smiled as she slipped her phone back into her pocket, but she didn't respond.

———ꝏ———

Across Last Chance, in the yellow-and-white singlewide, Chris shut down his computer and stretched. It was way too late and that alarm clock was going to go off way too early, but he couldn't help that. Olivia had had a rough night, and even going online shopping with her and letting her pick out a new bedspread and curtains for the bedroom that was now hers didn't help all that much.

She was a tough little cookie, careful not to let anyone see her feelings, but good-nights were eventually said, the lights were turned out, and Chris had to leave her alone. After she went to bed, he tried again a few times to reach Kaitlyn, but his calls, no surprise, went straight to voice mail. Finally, fighting the urge to throw his phone through the front window, he took a deep breath and willed the calm into his voice. "Call your daughter. She deserves that." Not trusting himself to say another word, he hung up and shoved his phone back in his pocket.

On his way to his room, he thought he heard sniffling as he passed her door and stepped in her room to check on her. She lay still and her eyes were closed, but her stiff little shoulders and the scowl on her face told him she was not asleep. He brushed the hair from her face and stooped to kiss her damp cheek.

"It's going to be okay, Livvy. We're going to be fine." His voice was low, barely above a whisper, and though his words were meant to reassure his niece, he found himself repeating them after he had gently closed her door and gone to his own room. *Everything's going to be okay. We'll be fine.* Just before he turned out his light, he put his face in his hands. *Lord, if ever I needed your guidance, it's now. I don't know what I'm doing. Please don't let me ruin that little girl's life.*

15

There are no secrets in Last Chance. Chris had heard the words almost from the day he arrived, but he was still astounded at how many people who came into the Dip 'n' Dine already knew that Olivia would be staying. It had barely been three days, for crying out loud. Even Sarah had swept into the diner and carried Olivia off to the ranch for the afternoon. She seemed to think that an afternoon on horseback could help any situation, and from the way Olivia's face had lit up, so did she.

"Well, have you heard anything more from you-know-who?" Juanita, who prided herself on discretion, kept her voice low.

Chris glanced around the dining room. Juanita's whispers had a way of permeating every corner of any room she was in, but this time all the diners seemed intent on their own conversations.

He had intended to deliver just the barest of facts—that Kaitlyn was going to be delayed and that Olivia would be starting school in Last Chance—but he hadn't reckoned on Juanita's ability to get to the bottom of things, another trait she prided herself in, and before he knew it, she had the whole story.

"She's talked to Olivia a time or two, but not to me." Chris tried to keep moving so he wouldn't have to talk about it, but when Juanita just raised her voice so he could hear her, he stopped to let her catch up.

"Chris, you know I'm the last person to go around butting into other people's business, but have you thought about taking legal steps?" This time she caught him by the sleeve and hauled him into the kitchen. And if she had actually lowered her voice, they might even have found some privacy there. "I know she's your sister and all, but my goodness, Chris, our dog's a better mother, and we had to lock her in the shed with those pups to make her feed them."

Chris just glared down at Juanita. He was getting accustomed to Juanita's proprietary attitude toward any information she might come across, but she had stepped over the line here. Big time. He tried to push past her without answering.

"Now, you just get off your high horse, mister." Juanita blocked his way. "I'm sorry if I stepped on anyone's toes, but you know as well as I do that if someone doesn't take hold real quick, that child is headed for a world of trouble. She's half wild right now, and it's only going to get worse the older she gets."

"Excuse me. I need to get by." Chris was head and shoulders taller than Juanita and his voice was like granite, but Juanita, not a bit intimidated, stood her ground. Faced with either shoving her aside or talking to her, Chris gave up.

"No, I'm not going to take legal steps, at least not for the time being. Olivia doesn't need more upheaval in her life right now."

"And if her mother turned up tomorrow and wanted to take her, you'd just hand her over?"

"She's her mother."

"Good night, nurse, Chris! If that's not upheaval, I don't know what is. You need to get legal custody of that child and see that she's raised right. And you need to do it right now."

Chris smiled a half smile. "And you think a bachelor uncle is the one to raise her right?"

"Well, if you were still in the city, I'd probably have to say no. But it's different here in Last Chance. You'll have all the help you need."

"I'm sure you're right about that." Olivia had only been with him about two weeks, and he'd already had way more help than he could appreciate, most of it in the way of advice offered by the woman standing in front of him. "But I still think the best thing for Olivia would be to be with her mom, and for her mom to be the one to raise her right."

"And I think it would be a good thing if the sky rained chocolate kisses. But I don't think I can count on it."

Chris looked past Juanita to the dining room. He really did not want to talk about this anymore. "We've got a room full of people to take care of, Juanita. We need to put this aside for now."

Juanita gave him a look that said that he wasn't fooling her one bit and that she had every intention of returning to the subject.

"Wait, Juanita. There is something you could help me with." Juanita had just turned away when Chris stopped her. "School's starting pretty soon and I'll need someone to watch Olivia after school. Do you have any ideas?"

"Let me think on that. I'm sure I can come up with someone." She headed out the kitchen door and almost immediately stuck her head back in. "I think I know just the one. Sue Anderson. She has a little girl about Olivia's age and that child is just the sweetest, politest, most helpful child you'll ever hope to meet. Just between you and me, I think she might be just the influence Olivia needs. I'll give her a call for you."

"No, there's no need for that. I'll call her later."

"Don't be silly, Chris. She doesn't know you from Adam, except that you bought the Dip 'n' Dine from Fayette. And it's not like she's advertising for children to take in after school. Let me call her first."

She was already reaching for the phone, and Chris gave up and let her call. Any other place and he would ask around, get references, and interview people. But this was Last Chance. Apparently things were done differently here.

"They're on their way to the dentist in San Ramon right now, but Sue said they'd stop by on their way home." Juanita hung up the phone and turned around. "Do you think Olivia will be back by then? She wants to meet her before she makes up her mind."

"Did you tell her I was offering her the job?" This whole thing was moving a little fast for Chris. After all, he was the one hiring.

"It's not like you have a whole lot of options, Chris. And truthfully, if results are anything to go by, you can't do better than Sue Anderson. Wait till you meet Emma. You'll just love her."

⁓

Chris wasn't sure he could say he loved Emma when she and her mother stopped by on the way home from the dentist, but he certainly had to admit her manners were flawless. And she was very clean to boot.

"Well, look who's here!" Juanita met them at the door. "Chris, come meet the Andersons."

Chris stepped in from the kitchen and shook Sue Anderson's hand. She stepped back so she could look at him without craning her neck and smiled, while placing protective hands on her daughter's shoulders. "So nice to meet you. This is my daughter, Emma. This is Mr. Reed, Emma."

"How do you do, Mr. Reed?" Emma extended her own hand.

"Hi, Emma." Chris took her hand and bent down to smile at her. "But you can call me Chris. I don't think anyone has ever called me Mr. Reed."

"Mr. Reed has a niece about your age, Emma." Sue Anderson's message was clear. There would be no first-naming. She turned to Chris. "Is she here? We'd love to meet her."

"We're expecting her any minute. She's been out at the Cooley ranch with Sarah." Juanita led them to a table. "Meanwhile, why don't I bring you a dish of ice cream and a soda? It is hot out there today."

"No, thank you." Emma slid into the booth and folded her hands.

"No ice cream?" Juanita stopped on her way back to the kitchen. "Would you rather have pie?"

"We don't eat a lot of sugar." Sue slipped her sunglasses into her purse. "And it's getting toward dinner anyway. Do you suppose we could just have a glass of ice water? It *is* hot out there."

"What about a diet soda then? It's sugar free." Juanita wasn't going to give up.

Sue wrinkled her nose. "But there are way too many chemicals. Really, water is fine."

"Okay, water it is." Juanita placed two glasses on the table. "How about some fruit? Carlos has been using watermelon slices to garnish today. I could bring you some of those."

"No, thank you. We don't want to spoil our appetite, do we Emma?" Sue took a sip of her water and glanced at her watch. "Do you think Olivia will be along soon? We really should be getting home."

On cue, Sarah's car turned off the highway into the parking lot. Sarah stopped her car and waved through the windshield as Olivia got out and ran into the Dip 'n' Dine.

"Sarah said to say hi, but she couldn't come in." Olivia didn't acknowledge the Andersons in the booth by the window as she climbed onto a stool at the counter. "Can I have some lemonade? I'm about to croak, it's so hot."

152

The contrast between Emma in her white sandals and crisp sundress and Olivia in dusty jeans and the lopsided ponytail she insisted on putting up herself couldn't have been greater. Chris felt a surge of protective love well up for his motherless waif as Olivia's gaze found Emma's and the two girls sized each other up.

"Olivia, come over here. There are some people I want you to meet. This is Mrs. Anderson and her daughter Emma. I think Emma's going to be in your class when school starts." Chris lifted Olivia off her stool and led her across the room. From Sue's expression, he thought he'd better hold off a while before mentioning the after-school arrangement.

Olivia yanked her hand from his and sauntered alongside him. Sue was smiling expectantly, but Olivia ignored her. "I'm going to be in Sarah's class," she said to Emma. "She takes me to ride her horses all the time. Whose class are you going to be in?"

Sue's smile had faded, but when she took charge of the conversation it was back, even if it did look a bit pasted on. "Hello, Olivia." She reached for Olivia's hand and shook it. "Emma's going to be in Miss Cooley's class too, so I imagine you'll be friends."

"And you're going to get to go over to her house every day after school. Won't that be fun?" Juanita wasn't about to let the fact that this was all her idea go unacknowledged.

Olivia's head whipped around and she glared at her uncle. "That's what you think."

Both he and Sue jumped to amend Juanita's statement.

"We're just talking about it," Chris said.

"We just stopped by to meet you since you're going to be in Emma's class," Sue said, opening her purse and fishing out her sunglasses. "You'll have to come over and play sometime."

Olivia, still staring at Chris in undisguised outrage, did not even look at Sue, much less answer her. Emma, who hadn't said anything anyway, followed her mother out the door.

Juanita watched them go. "That went well. I have absolutely no idea who we can get to watch Olivia after school now." She grabbed up the two nearly untouched glasses of ice water and took them back to the kitchen.

"I'm not going over to her house after school every day." Olivia found her voice.

"No, it doesn't look like you are. But we do have to think of something. You can't spend all your time in here."

"Why?"

"Because it's not good for you, that's why. You need to spend time playing outside, or just doing things kids do."

"I don't want to play with kids. I hate them and they hate me. I just want to stay in here with you."

Chris propped himself on a stool and lifted Olivia onto the stool next to him. "Kiddo, we've got to get that worked out. And it's not going to happen with you just hanging out with me all the time. I'll bet if you let them get to know you better, the kids would like you just fine. And you might even like them."

"Yeah, right." Olivia slid off the stool. "I'm going to go hunt for lizards."

"Stay where I can see you."

Olivia gave him another withering look as she threw her weight against the heavy front door.

Chris stretched his legs out in front of him and leaned his elbows on the counter. Kids should come with an operating manual. No two ways about it.

"Chris, I've been thinking, and so far I haven't come up with anyone who Olivia could stay with after school." Juanita was back.

"You can see what I mean about Sue being just the one to help polish some of those rough edges Olivia has, but I think that bridge has burned to the ground."

She waited for Chris to say something, but he went right on watching Olivia through the front window. "You can't think Olivia made a good impression this afternoon."

Chris's laugh sounded more like a bark. "No, I can't say that."

"Well, for pity's sake, why didn't you do something? You heard how Sue did it. Never once did she say, 'Now, Emma, you need to do it this way,' but Emma got the message anyway." Juanita was clearly exasperated with him, and truth be told, he was exasperated with himself, though not for the same reasons.

He stood up and put his hand on her shoulder. "I thank you, I really do, for trying to help me. It doesn't take a genius to see that I am in way, way over my head. But I'm doing the best I can."

He gave another glance at Olivia, who was wandering around the vacant lot next to his parking lot hitting at bushes with a stick she had found. He had no idea what he was doing, but he was going to have to figure it out.

—⁂—

Sarah sat on her front porch and pulled off her boots before padding inside in her stocking feet. She had actually planned to go inside the diner and brag a bit on what a horsewoman Olivia was becoming. And since she didn't think it would be a good idea to single out one student for so much out-of-class attention once school started, she had found another place Chris could take Olivia for riding lessons. She needed to talk to him about that too.

But seeing Sue and Emma Anderson sitting in the window of the Dip 'n' Dine when she drove up had changed her mind. She wasn't exactly avoiding Sue Anderson. Sue was a parent, after all, and deserved the time and attention of her child's teacher. But Sue had already taken the time to express her misgivings at Emma having a first-year teacher. Oh, she was nice enough about it, but if she had pointed the first two fingers of her right hand at her own eyes, then at Sarah's, her message couldn't have been clearer. *I'm watching.*

She checked her phone again for messages—no voice mail, no text. Understandable, she supposed, since it was his first week at the new job. But Brandon had texted her whenever he stopped for gas on his trip east, and he had called her nightly. At first she had been apprehensive when her phone signaled another communiqué from him, but all the messages had been breezy and the phone conversations light and friendly. "DFILY" had not made another appearance, and she found she actually looked forward to hearing from him.

When the phone did ring a few minutes later, she snatched it from the table where she had left it. But it was only Gran.

"Hi, darlin'. I just saw you drive by. How did it go this afternoon?"

Sarah settled into her chair. She had no doubt that Gran had a reason for calling, and she had just as little doubt that Gran would get around to it in her own sweet time. Finally, after discussions about the welfare of folks at the ranch, Olivia's equestrian progress, and Sarah's readiness for school to start, she did.

"At church last Sunday I invited Chris and Olivia over for a light supper tonight. Why don't you come join us?"

Sarah took a deep breath, but before she could say a word, Elizabeth jumped back in. "I know, I know. You think I'm matchmaking, but I'm not. I know how things stand with you and Brandon. I just want a little party, that's all. And it's only dinner."

"Sure. Why not? What time should I come?" Sarah had answered before she realized it and surprised herself.

She was not the only one surprised. A long silence followed. "Well. How does 7:00 sound? It's a little late, I know, but that's about as early as they can get here."

"Okay, see you then. Can I bring anything?"

"Just your own sweet self." Pleasure had replaced the surprise in Elizabeth's voice. Sarah smiled as she headed off to the shower. It didn't take much to please her grandmother. Just do whatever she said.

—⁓—

Two things occurred to Sarah as she sat down to dinner across the table from Chris and right next to Olivia. One, Gran had absolutely no concept of a light supper, and two, if Gran had read even one of the missives put out by nutritionists in the last thirty years, she had immediately dismissed it as nonsense. The table held fried chicken, mashed potatoes with cream gravy, green beans long-simmered with bacon, and piles of fluffy white biscuits with homemade plum jam. A cake, plenty tall enough for three layers and covered with white frosting and coconut, waited on the sideboard.

"This tastes so much better than the stuff you fix." Olivia, with one elbow firmly planted on the table, waved her drumstick at her uncle. "Why don't you cook this?"

Chris tried to catch her eye while making subtle signs with his own elbow. If Olivia saw it, she ignored it.

"I'm just so happy you like it." Elizabeth smiled. "Here, let me pass those biscuits to you so you don't have to reach."

"I see you met Emma this afternoon." Sarah moved the mashed potatoes a little closer to Olivia. If Gran could ignore the manners of a guest, so could she. "She's going to be in our class too."

157

"She told me." Olivia turned her attention to her plate, clearly disinterested in the direction the conversation was headed.

Sarah raised an inquisitive eyebrow at Chris, who shrugged. "I've been considering after-school options for Livvy, and Juanita thought Sue Anderson might . . ." His voice trailed away.

"I'm *not* going there after school. And you can't make me." Olivia put down her fork and glowered at her uncle.

Sarah shot a look at her grandmother, expecting crashes of thunder, flashes of lightning, and the earth to open up. *No one* talked back in Gran's house. It had never happened. But Gran acted as if she didn't even notice.

"No, I can see how that might not be the best plan. But what about here?" She looked at Chris. "Why doesn't Olivia come here after school and spend the afternoon with me? You can pick her up on the way home after you close up."

Neither Sarah nor Chris said a word, but Olivia brightened. "That would be cool. You said I couldn't hang around the restaurant all the time. I can come here."

Finally Chris found his voice. "I don't know, Miss Elizabeth. She's such a handful."

"That's right, Gran." Sarah chimed in. "This would be a huge undertaking. Don't you need some time to think this through?"

"Oh, shoot, you two. You're just trying to figure out a way to remind me how old I am. Well, you don't think I know how old I am? And I say Olivia and I will get along just fine." She turned to the little girl who was following the conversation like a spectator at a tennis match. "Won't we, Olivia?"

Olivia nodded and her face split in a grin, but Chris still looked as if he had his doubts.

"Tell you what, Chris." Elizabeth got up to pour more iced tea.

"Let's give it a month. You can keep looking if you want, and then if Olivia isn't happy or it does turn out to be more than I can handle, well, we can just reconsider the whole thing. What do you say?"

Chris looked from Elizabeth to Olivia, who was nodding like a dashboard cocker spaniel. "Well, I guess I say, let's give it a try."

16

Sarah knew one thing as she brushed her teeth and got ready for bed. She and Chris were going to have a talk. When he and Olivia had said good-bye shortly after dinner, he did not have the look of a man who still had a huge problem—namely, who was going to look after his niece after school. In fact, he looked happy and relieved. And Sarah intended to impress upon him just how unsuitable the arrangement was and to remind him that he needed to keep right on looking.

She punched her pillows as she propped them up against her headboard before climbing into bed with her book. She felt bad for Chris. She really did. He hadn't asked for this. And she felt bad for Olivia as well. But her concern was for Gran. Sarah found her place in the book and snuggled back against her pillows. She'd stop by the Dip 'n' Dine tomorrow and offer her help in finding someone. After all, other than Chris himself, she knew Olivia better than anyone in Last Chance. And unlike Chris, she knew the rest of the folks in town too. There had to be someone besides Gran in Last Chance who could see a diamond in this little lump of coal. They just had to find her, that's all.

The book and the soft night wind ruffling her curtains had pretty much done their work a half hour later and Sarah was beginning to nod over the page when her ringing phone snapped her to wakeful-ness. She smiled as she answered.

"Hey, you. What are you doing up so late?"

"Is it late? I just got home, and I wanted to tell you good night."

Sarah glanced at her watch. "It's nearly 1:00 where you are. That's pretty late for someone who has to get up early tomorrow. What have you been up to?"

She winced. Did she sound friendly and interested, or nosy and possessive? She certainly was not ready for Brandon to read any-thing more than casual friendship into their conversations.

"Some of my co-workers took me out for dinner, sort of a wel-come to the team. We finished up with drinks someplace else. I guess time just got away."

"How do you like your co-workers? It's nice that they took you out."

"There are some really sharp people in the company. I'm not the smart kid in class anymore, that's for sure. I just got there, but I think I'm going to love it."

"Tell me." Sarah put her book down and snuggled back into her pillows as Brandon described his first day on the job and the people he had spent the evening with. She caught the names of at least a couple women and was surprised that they would jump out at her like that. Of course Brandon would be working with women. That's just the way things are—and should be, for that matter.

"Anyway, the restaurant where we ate was incredible." Brandon was finishing his account of the evening. "I guarantee that you've never seen anything like it in your life. And I can't wait to take you there when you come. Which brings me to the question: When *are* you coming to see me?"

"Wow, Brandon, I don't know. I guess I won't really have any time off until Thanksgiving."

"Can't you take some time? Isn't that what subs are for?"

"I can't just get a substitute and go flying off to Chicago my first month of teaching. Get real, Brandon."

"Well then, I guess I'll just have to come to you." Brandon sounded cheerful, maybe even a bit tipsy. "Lemme check."

Sarah heard him humming to himself for a minute or two, and then he was back. "How's the first weekend of October sound? I'll fly out Thursday night, take a personal day Friday, and then take the red-eye back Sunday night."

Sarah smiled into the phone. "Perfect. That's the weekend Chris is having that jazz and chile night at the Dip 'n' Dine. I'll get us tickets."

There was a long pause on Brandon's end. "Sounds . . . great. Just what I had in mind."

"Oh, come on. Don't be that way. It will be fun. There's a jazz band coming down from Albuquerque, and Chris always has great food. Everyone's coming."

"And the kid's gone home, I take it."

"Olivia? No, actually she's staying. In fact, just this evening Gran said she'd watch her after school."

Sarah tugged her covers up to her chin and prepared to fill Brandon in on what had been going on in Last Chance since last they talked, but he spoke first.

"Well, she'll have her hands full. Listen, it is awful late. And I do have work in the morning. You take care, and I'll call you soon."

She looked at the "Call Ended" message on her screen a moment before turning out the light. Brandon was right. It was awfully late, especially where he was. He needed to get to bed. Otherwise, he would have remembered to ask about *her* day. She was almost sure of it.

—⁓—

"I had a long talk with Sue Anderson last night." Juanita was talking before she got completely through the front door the next morning. "And we just may have your problems solved."

Chris indicated with a tip of his head that Olivia, who was eating scrambled eggs and biscuits at the counter, could hear her, but that did not slow Juanita for a moment.

"No, Olivia needs to hear this too. And we should probably talk about it before the customers start coming in."

"What do we need to talk about, Juanita?" Chris's voice was cool, but Juanita didn't seem to notice.

"What we talked about all day yesterday." Juanita plopped down on a counter stool next to Olivia. "Where this child is going in the afternoons after school."

Olivia glared at Juanita and stabbed her sausage patty with a fork like it was trying to get away. She held it up and tore off a portion with her teeth.

Chris shot her a warning glance before turning his attention to Juanita. "Actually, we got that all taken care of last night. But thanks anyway."

If Juanita even heard him, she gave no indication of it. "Sue's still not at all sure it's going to work, but I did manage to talk her into giving Olivia a trial run. But . . ." She paused for emphasis. "She only agreed to a trial, and she does have some conditions."

"Juanita . . ." Chris tried again.

"First, you and she have to agree on some form of discipline. She does, and always has, run a tight ship. You can tell that just by being around Emma for five minutes. Second, if Olivia is to spend time at their house, she's going to have to learn some basic manners. We all know it's not Olivia's fault that she's had no upbringing, but that's no reason to leave things as they are. Sue's willing to take that on herself, but she needs to know you'll back her up. Now, third . . ."

"Juanita." Chris looked grim as he held up his hand. "Stop."

Juanita did stop. Her mouth got a pinched look when she shut it, and she seemed to swell up. Clearly, she did not appreciate being interrupted. Her eyebrows said, "Well?"

"We have this covered."

Juanita waited.

"Elizabeth Cooley has offered to have Olivia come to her house after school. So thank Sue for me, but we've made other arrangements."

It took a second, but Juanita found her voice. "Elizabeth? Do you have any idea how old that poor thing is? She's eighty-five if she's a day. There's no way she's up to riding herd on a child like Olivia."

Olivia was staring at her food, but Chris had no trouble reading her expression. It was time to end this conversation. "She and Olivia get along great. Thanks anyway."

"Do Joe Jr. and Nancy Jo know about this? You know they're going to have a fit."

"Who?"

"Elizabeth's son and daughter-in-law. Sarah's parents."

"I have no idea. That's between them." He gestured with his chin at a car that had just parked out front. "Customers. We need to shelve this conversation."

Olivia slid off her stool and ran through the kitchen and out the back door. Chris followed her, calling over his shoulder as he left the dining room, "And we need to keep it just between you and me."

Chris found Olivia sitting on the back step, elbows on knees, chin in hand. She wasn't crying, but her face was as sad as he'd ever seen it. When he sat down next to her and tried to pull her close, it was like trying to cuddle a broom handle.

"I want to go home." Her voice was so low he had to bend to hear it.

"I bet you do, Livvy. And you will someday. But right now you are going to be staying here with me. Is that so bad?"

She shrugged and didn't look up. "Mom said she'd call me every day, and she's only called three times."

"I'm sorry about that, Livvy. I know you miss her, but I'm glad you're here. And I bet Belle is too." Her stiff little shoulders relaxed a bit, and he went on. "It's obvious that Miss Elizabeth is glad you're here, or she wouldn't have invited you to come over after school every day. And Miss Cooley's your friend too."

Olivia shot him a look. "You mean Sarah?"

He laughed. "Better get used to Miss Cooley, kiddo. School starts in just a little over a week, and you know you're not going to call her Sarah then."

She sighed as if the world had rolled onto her shoulders. "This is not going to be easy."

"Maybe not, but you've got it nailed."

The back door opened and Carlos stuck his head out. "Rita's out there looking for you."

Chris stood up and squeezed Olivia's shoulder as he headed back into the kitchen. "Hang in there, Livvy. We're going to be fine."

We're going to be fine. It seemed every time he opened his mouth he was telling Olivia that things were going to be fine. He shook his head. *Who am I trying to convince here?*

"Hey, boss." Carlos slid a pan of biscuits in the oven and turned to face Chris as he passed through. "It's none of my business, but she's a good kid. You're doing all right."

That was the most encouraging thing anyone had said to him since Kaitlyn and Jase had driven their Harleys into his parking lot. It didn't change a thing, but it helped. A lot. He cleared his throat. "Thanks, man. Appreciate it."

Through the window, Chris could see Rita sitting in a booth riffling through a sheaf of papers. Rita turned out a flawless event. She was known for it. However, she also could turn the most trivial detail into an hour-long meeting, and usually the sight of her bustling in the front door made him want to take off out the back. But thanks to an offhand remark by his cook, he felt he could even take on Rita. He smiled as he pushed through the door into the dining room.

"'Morning, Rita. You're up and at 'em early. What can I do for you?"

Rita took the pencil out from behind her ear and tapped the list in front of her as Chris slid into the booth across from her. "I really wish you'd reconsider using those little salt and pepper packets instead of the shakers. They cost next to nothing, and you don't have enough shakers anyway."

Chris signaled to Juanita to bring coffee and began to explain his vision for "Hot Chile and Cool Jazz" . . . one more time.

———

It took a while, but Rita finally seemed satisfied that Chris had the salt and pepper shaker situation under control. She gathered her papers together and slid from the booth.

"Okay, I guess this is it for now. If I think of anything else, I'll give you a call."

"You know where to find me." Chris waved away her attempt to pay for the coffee and walked her to the door. "And I do appreciate all you're doing."

"Well, this was a terrific idea, Chris." Rita stopped at the door, and for a minute Chris was afraid she might decide to sit back down. "I've been trying for years to find a way to get this town on the map, but Russ Sheppard and the town council keep shooting down every blessed thing I try to do. But this! This is going to be good. I know it started out with you wanting to do something a little different here at the Dip 'n' Dine, but it's going to be great for Last Chance. You wait and see."

"Hope so." Chris managed to usher her out and turned to check the clock over the counter. True to form, she had been in the diner for well over an hour, leaving Juanita to handle the bulk of the breakfast crowd herself. And Juanita did not look happy.

"I did not appreciate that comment about Russ one bit." Several tables of diners had doubtless heard Rita's criticism of the town council, and Juanita's comments, though spoken to Chris, were doubtlessly directed toward them. "If I've heard him say it once, I've heard him say it a thousand times. 'A little advertising is fine and good, but bankrupting the town to promote it is sheer tomfoolery.'"

Whether it was Rita's comment about Russ or the fact that she had to call Sue Anderson back to tell her Chris had made plans of his own for Olivia's after-school care, Juanita's mood for the rest of the morning made Chris decide that owner or not, staying out of her way was the better part of valor.

A little past noon, Sarah and Elizabeth came in for lunch, and Olivia, who had been sitting at the counter drawing, saw them drive up and met them at the door.

"Well, hello there, sweet girl." Elizabeth put her arm around

Olivia's shoulders and gave her a squeeze as they walked to a booth. "What are you up to this afternoon?"

"Drawing." Olivia stood by the table, but when Elizabeth scooted over in the booth to make room, she grinned and climbed in beside her.

"Olivia, we need to let Miss Elizabeth and Miss Sarah eat their lunch now." Juanita, still a portrait of irritation, set down two glasses of water and held out her hand. "Come on."

Olivia returned the glare and pressed closer to Elizabeth. Juanita, as she often said, could tolerate just about anything but outright defiance, especially from a child. Her smile was fixed and never reached her eyes as she stood by the booth with her hand outstretched.

"Oh, we don't mind a bit." Elizabeth was unperturbed. "In fact, we'd love to have Olivia join us for lunch. Do you think that would be all right with Chris?"

"I'm sure I don't know." Juanita put the menus on the table, turned on her heel, and stalked off toward the kitchen.

Sarah watched her go. "So is she going to ask Chris, or what? What's with her, anyway?"

"I wouldn't worry about it. It'll all sort itself out." Elizabeth reached for the drawing Olivia had brought with her. "What do you have here, Olivia?"

Across the table, Sarah watched the white curls and skewed ponytail bend over the place mat while Olivia launched into a detailed description of her artwork. Gran was such a natural with kids. They instantly loved her. And truth be told, Gran was never happier than when she had a child or two at her elbow. Maybe this after-school arrangement wasn't a totally bad idea. But Sarah still intended to keep an eye on things.

"Olivia, you're not being a pest, are you?" Chris had appeared at the table.

"Not at all. She's just telling me all about her picture. Have you seen this?" Elizabeth held up the drawing and smiled at him. "She's quite the little artist."

"I've got lots more. I'll go get them." Olivia slid out of the booth and ran off.

Chris stepped back to let her go. "You're sure she's not a bother?"

Before Elizabeth could do more than shake her head and say, "Not at all," Olivia was back with a sheaf of drawings that spoke of far too many hours spent entertaining herself in the diner while her uncle worked. She scooted back in and began explaining each one in detail.

"Okay, then. Enjoy your lunch." Chris hesitated a moment before turning away, but Elizabeth and Olivia were already engrossed in her drawings and didn't look up. Only Sarah smiled her thanks and watched him go. Why had she been so quick to mark him as arrogant and overbearing? She was beginning to think he might be one of the most caring men she had ever known.

"Olivia, these are just amazing." Elizabeth sat back and looked at the earnest little girl sitting next to her. "You know, Sarah's cousin is a real artist, and he's going to be here for a visit in a few weeks. I want you to show these to him."

"Ray's coming?" This was the first Sarah had heard of it. "When?"

"They're coming down for this chile-jazz thing in October. I thought I mentioned it."

"Lainie's coming, too?" Juanita had appeared to take their order and seemed as delighted as Sarah was with the news. "I just love that girl. You know, Russ and I were in here having breakfast that first morning she came in. In fact, it was my idea that she stay with you, Elizabeth. Of course, I didn't know at the time she'd be staying for a year. We were thinking two or three days at the most."

"It was a good year in so many ways." Elizabeth smiled. "I came to love her like she was one of my own. And since she married my grandson, well, I guess she *is* one of my own now."

"Did you ever hear Lainie sing, Sarah?" Juanita seemed entirely recovered from her earlier fit of pique. "She has the voice of an angel."

Olivia had frowned when Juanita interrupted them, and the longer she claimed the attention of Elizabeth and Sarah, the deeper Olivia's scowl etched itself across her face. Finally, she turned herself in the booth so her back was to Juanita.

"Which picture do you like best?" She shoved the stack toward Elizabeth and raised her voice to drown out Juanita's.

The surprised silence that fell over the group was broken by Elizabeth's calm voice. "We'll talk about this in just a minute. Right now we need to order our lunch, and you may not realize it, but you interrupted Miss Juanita. So after you say excuse me, you can tell her what you'd like."

Olivia heaved a sigh that bespoke a burden heavier than one person should be called to bear. "Excuse me. I want a grilled cheese."

She looked back at Elizabeth, who only smiled and waited. Olivia sighed again. "Can I have a grilled cheese . . . please?"

17

Sarah released the last of her second graders into the custody of the last hurrying parent and allowed herself to collapse at her desk for just a moment before she got up to straighten the room. Exactly six weeks ago today she had faced her class of second graders for the first time, and just this morning the calendar monitor had placed the last pasteboard apple on September 30.

The weeks had flown by, and she had discovered two things she hadn't realized about teaching. One, she didn't know half as much as she thought she did, and two, she *loved* teaching. She knew it was what she wanted to do when she went to college, and she had enjoyed her student teaching, but she had not been prepared for the sheer joy she felt when she and her very own class were engaged in learning. Maybe it had something to do with their age. Seven- and eight-year-olds seemed hardwired to love their teacher, if not everything she wanted them to do.

Her eyes fell on one desk, a little cockeyed from the others in the row, and she sighed. Olivia was not having an easy time of it. She was way behind the others academically, for one thing, but that wasn't the real problem. Gran was working with her every day after school, and she'd soon catch up. It was that chip on her shoulder that was causing the real problem. She had come into the classroom with the attitude that no one was going to like her and she didn't expect to like them either. Of course, it was becoming a self-fulfilling prophecy.

Sarah got up and went to take the big September calendar down. She picked all the pasteboard apples off the numbered squares and put them back in their box. Tomorrow the new calendar monitor, Emma Anderson, would put the first pumpkin on October 1. Emma, who never got dirty, who never spoke out of turn, who was always offering to help, and who, quite frankly, really got on Sarah's nerves.

For one thing, she was pretty sure that Emma was behind most of the animosity directed toward Olivia, not that Olivia didn't help it along. Sarah had overheard Emma warning a group of kids not to play with Olivia because her mother said they'd learn too many bad things from her. Sarah had followed with a talk to the class about being kind and welcoming to everyone, and Emma had sat on the front row nodding at everything Sarah said. But it still seemed to be Olivia against the world.

"Hi. Are you busy?" Chris stuck his head in the door.

"Just turning September into October. Come on in."

"Ah, so you're the one who's doing it, huh? I'd noticed it was happening." He paused. "I wonder if you have a minute to talk."

"Sure. I'd ask you to sit down, but . . ." Sarah gestured around the room of child-sized chairs.

"It's okay. I'm not staying long. I'm just on my way back to work." Concern marked his face. "How's Olivia settling in?"

Sarah hesitated. "What does Olivia say?"

"Well, that's why I stopped by. When I pick her up, she seems pretty happy, until I try to find out how her day went. Then she stops talking altogether unless it's to say how much she hates everyone. But when she gets out of the car at your grandmother's, she's happy again. Do you know what's going on?"

"It hasn't been a real easy adjustment. It's always hard being the new kid in class, especially when everyone else has known each other all their lives." Sarah wished she could be more reassuring. "But I'm keeping an eye on things, and if a real problem develops, of course I'll tell you."

"Yeah, well, she's not had it easy." He took a deep breath, held it for a moment, and then blew it out in a gust. "Well, I'd better get back. It's pretty much a madhouse over there. We've been getting deliveries all day."

"How's it going?"

"I know we'll be ready by Saturday night. Rita says so, and I hear she's never wrong about these things. But I have to say, I'm sure having to take her word for it. I know the food is under control, but that's the only thing I know."

"If Rita says you're good, you're good." Sarah laughed. "Just run your kitchen and leave the rest to her. Did you sell a lot of tickets?"

"We've been sold out for nearly two weeks—and not just to local folks either."

"I know. My friend Brandon is coming all the way from Chicago for this."

"Yeah, right." Chris grinned. "That's exactly why he's coming." He headed for the door, stopping just before he stepped through it. "You'll keep me posted about Livvy, right?"

"Absolutely."

Chris threw her a grateful smile and closed the door behind him. Not for the first time, Sarah wished she had about five minutes to explain a few things to Chris's sister. That woman had no idea what she was just tossing away. And Sarah wasn't just thinking of Olivia either.

—⚬—

Chris could have put in at least a couple hours more work at the Dip 'n' Dine when he locked the door and got in his Jeep. Elizabeth had assured him that he need not be concerned about those nights when he would be unavoidably detained, but he wanted to make them as few as possible. Olivia seemed truly happy and relaxed when he picked her up at Elizabeth's, and he did not want to mess that up.

Olivia must have seen him pull up, because she came flying out the door as he opened the gate. "Come inside. I made some cookies all by myself. Miss Elizabeth didn't do one thing."

"Not one thing?" Chris let her grab his hand and tug him up the steps.

"No, sir." Elizabeth met them at the front door with a smile and a plate of cookies. "I stood by with some advice, but Livvy did all the measuring, mixing, scooping, and baking by herself."

"And I didn't burn myself either, like you always say I will." Olivia looked up at him, and the pride in her face touched his heart.

Why hadn't he thought to cook with Olivia? He supposed he was either too busy at work or too tired afterward. Whoever said that being a single parent wasn't for the faint of heart knew what they were talking about, that's for sure.

"Here, have one." Olivia took the plate from Elizabeth and held it up to her uncle.

Chris chose one and took a bite. "Livvy, these are amazing. Are you sure you did this all by yourself?"

"Ask her." Olivia gestured toward Elizabeth with the plate, causing the cookies to come precariously close to sliding off the edge.

"Well, if Miss Elizabeth says so, it has to be true. But I have to say these are incredible. Good job, Livvy."

"Have some more." She held the plate up to him again.

"You don't want your uncle to spoil his dinner, Olivia." Elizabeth took the plate back and handed her a brown paper bag. "I saved some cookies for us to have when you get home from school tomorrow, but you can take the rest home with you. And don't forget, I want you to show your uncle how well you can read too. So, five pages before you go to bed, okay?"

She looked at Chris for confirmation and he nodded. "Sounds great. Cookies, milk, and a good book. I can't wait."

Olivia skipped next to him as they walked to the car, and she was humming a little bit when he made sure her seat belt was fastened in the backseat. He knew asking the wrong question could easily bring on the sullen silence Olivia hid behind when she felt cornered, but she was in such a good mood that he took the risk.

"Livvy?" He glanced at her in the rearview mirror. "How was school today?"

She shrugged. "Sort of okay. Mostly I hate it."

"Why? Miss Cooley is nice, isn't she?"

"She's not as nice as when she took me to ride her horses, but she's still sort of nice."

"I'm glad to hear it. So why do you hate it?"

"Because the kids are dumb. And they're mean."

"All of them?"

"Yep. Especially Emma A."

"Emma Anderson? The girl I met? I thought she seemed like a nice girl."

"Well, she's not. She's mean and she makes all the other kids be mean too."

"Does Miss Cooley know?" Chris had stopped under the carport of his singlewide and turned around to look at Olivia in the backseat.

She shrugged and looked away. Chris saw the light fade from her face and knew he was in danger of losing her to that dark place she hid in when life overwhelmed. He retreated.

"Okay. I want to go get dinner over with so I can eat some more of those cookies. What shall we fix?"

Olivia hopped out of the backseat, still clutching her brown paper bag. "Macaroni and cheese with hot dogs in it." She didn't hesitate. "The kind from the box. Not that kind you make."

Chris followed her inside. There was a time, and fairly recently too, when boxed macaroni and cheese, not to mention hot dogs, would never have been found anywhere near his house. But he had learned.

—⁓—

There was something in the air the next morning that Sarah couldn't quite put her finger on, but she felt a little uneasy. The class was a little harder to settle, but that could be attributed to the excitement that rippled through the room when she told them they would be going on a field trip to a pumpkin patch later on in the month. But there was more. More whispering, more giggling, more shoving in line. For the first time, she found herself exasperated with the entire class and not just a rowdy one or two.

It all came to a head during recess. Sarah didn't have yard duty, so she was using the time to prepare for the next segment of the day when she heard the eruption of noise on the playground. She raised her head and listened briefly before returning to her task. The playground was well monitored, and all would be taken care of.

Suddenly Anthony Montoya and Ethan Casey charged through her doorway. "Teacher! Teacher!"

"Miss Cooley," Sarah corrected automatically as she got to her feet. *Now what?*

"Miss Cooley! Olivia is beating up Emma A.!"

By the time Sarah got to the playground, the girls had been separated and the playground monitor was trying to establish what had happened. Both girls were crying and neither would answer any questions, but the group of students who had gathered around all vied with each other to be heard. Sarah raised her hands to quiet everyone.

"What is going on here? Emma? Olivia? What in the world happened?"

Olivia, still sniveling, shot a murderous glare toward Emma but said nothing. When Sarah pressed her, she looked at the ground and refused to talk. She wiped her eyes with her fist and her nose with the back of her hand.

Emma, however, was sobbing and ready to tell all. "She pushed me down, and I'm bleeding." She showed Sarah a skinned knee and elbow that were indeed bleeding before she noticed further outrage. "And my dress is torn! It was new too." She could not continue her narrative, so great was her grief.

Sarah took a deep breath. This was going nowhere. She looked at the crowd gathered around. "Did anyone see exactly what happened?"

Again they all erupted in explanation, and Sarah could gather nothing. "Okay, you and you." She designated two of her second graders who she knew to be fairly serious. "You come with Emma and Olivia and me. We're going to the principal's office."

Stopping long enough to ask an aide to stay with her class until she got back, Sarah marched a sullen Olivia, a loudly sobbing Emma, and two witnesses, grave with the importance of their task, off to the principal's office to see if *she* could figure out what had actually happened.

—⟋⟍⟍—

Late that night, when Sarah took her mug of tea and her book and crawled into bed, she could only be thankful that at least the day was behind her. It had been a disaster. Mrs. Martinez, the principal, was much more adept at getting to the bottom of things and had it all sorted out in about two minutes. Sadly, it appeared that the physical attack, anyway, had been entirely one-sided. And Emma had gone down like a roped calf.

It still wasn't entirely clear what had provoked the attack. Emma had said she had just asked Olivia where her mother was. Olivia hadn't refuted Emma's account. She had not, in fact, said a word in her own defense the entire time she had been in the principal's office. Sarah knew there had to be more to it than that, but rules were rules. Violence definitely violated those rules; asking questions did not.

Sue Anderson and Chris Reed had been summoned to the school. Sue, quite understandably, was outraged. After all, it was her child with the bloodied knee and the torn dress. She pointed out that it was the school's responsibility to protect children from bullies, that Olivia was twice the size of Emma even if they were the same age, and that she herself had warned Miss Cooley that Olivia bore watching.

In the end, Olivia had been suspended for three days. Sue thought the punishment far too lax, but Mrs. Martinez told her—and warned Olivia—that three days' suspension was the penalty for a first infraction. It went up from there.

Chris apologized to Sue Anderson and Mrs. Martinez, offered to pay for the ruined dress, and took Olivia away. He looked so defeated and Olivia looked so hostile that Sarah's heart broke. Just yesterday she had assured him that she had everything under control and that she would let him know if any problems developed. Today he was taking Olivia out of school in disgrace. She followed him outside and caught up with him in the parking lot.

"Chris." He turned to wait for her to catch up. She only hoped that the anger in his eyes was not directed toward her. "Take her to Gran."

He put his hands on Olivia's shoulders and started to shake his head, but Sarah interrupted before he could say a word.

"Seriously. You both need some space. Gran's is absolutely the best place for Olivia right now. I'll call and tell her you're coming. You can explain why when you get there."

He didn't say anything for a long moment, and his face, usually so warm and open, was closed and grim. Finally, he nodded and walked away with Olivia. As his friend, and as someone who had come to truly care for Olivia, there was so much she wanted to say. She wanted to apologize for allowing the situation to escalate like it did; she wanted to say that she knew this wasn't all Olivia's fault and that Emma had played more of a part than she was getting credit for. She wanted to call out that Chris was doing an amazing job and that Olivia was a terrific little girl. But as Miss Cooley, second grade teacher, she could only watch him go, then turn and walk back to her classroom.

Sarah snuggled back against her pillows and tugged her covers up under her chin. She took a deep breath, held it as long as she could, and then released it in a long, gentle hiss. Time to let the day go. There were plenty more coming up she'd have to deal with.

She smiled to herself as she let her thoughts go to the upcoming weekend. Brandon was landing in El Paso Friday morning and would be in Last Chance by the time she got out of school Friday afternoon. She had to admit that while she originally hadn't been wild about his idea of flying in for the weekend, she had come to really look forward to it. They were going out for dinner somewhere Friday night. He wouldn't say where, but she knew it would involve a drive. Saturday they were going for a long ride at the ranch. Brandon wasn't crazy about horses, but he was a good enough rider. And Saturday night there was "Hot Chile and Cool Jazz." She was really excited about that, even if Brandon did keep teasing her about having a low threshold for excitement.

When the phone on her bedside table rang, she didn't even have to look to see who it was. He was putting in long hours at work, and it was always after midnight in Chicago when he called.

"Hey there. I was just thinking about you." Sarah smiled into the room.

"Really? That sounds promising. What were you thinking?"

"Oh, just about the stuff we're going to do this weekend."

"Oh?" His voice was low and almost purred. "And what kind of stuff is that?"

Sarah sat up and made her voice matter-of-fact. It was time to bring Brandon back to reality. "Dinner, horseback riding, the chile and jazz thing at the Dip 'n' Dine. You know, the things we talked about."

"Ah. And that brings me to the reason I called."

"What?" Sarah did not like the sound of this. At all.

"Well, babe, I'm afraid I'm going to have to beg off this weekend."

"You're what?"

"Things have just gotten crazy. I'm going to have to work all weekend. I hate it that I'm not going to get to see you, but hey, you're coming Thanksgiving, right? It'll be here before we know it."

"Then what was all that stuff about wanting to know what we were going to do this weekend?"

There was a pause on the line, and Sarah could almost see him shrug. "I don't know. Just hoping I'd hear something I liked, I guess."

It was Sarah's turn to let the line go silent a moment. "Well, that really stinks."

"Yeah, well, I hate it too, babe, but it can't be helped." He waited for a moment and then continued. "Listen, I still have a boatload of work tonight, so I'd better get to it."

"All right. Bye."

"Bye-bye. Call you soon."

Sarah let her phone drop on the bed beside her. The chief drawback of cell phones, other than their occasional bent for self-drowning, was that you could not slam down the receiver. And if ever there were a time to slam a receiver, it was now.

She got out of bed and padded to the kitchen to put the kettle on. Her tea was cold and she was way too mad to sleep.

18

Saturday morning Chris was at the Dip 'n' Dine even earlier than usual. Saturday was always busy, and he couldn't afford to close it up for the day just to get ready for his big night. He felt bad about hauling Olivia out of bed hours before sunup, but with his Jeep parked right out front where he could keep an eye on it, she was curled up in the back with her pillow and blanket, still asleep.

He flipped on the kitchen light and took a clipboard off a hook by his desk. Rita had presented it to him with a checklist attached, and he had to admit it was a system that worked. He leaned against the desk as he went over it. They were closing off the parking lot at noon, and shortly after that, the canopy that would cover it and the stage for the band would go up. They were bringing the tables over from the church fellowship hall sometime this afternoon. Rita had a crew coming in to set tables and decorate, and Carlos had a crew of nieces and nephews coming in to serve. Now all Chris and Carlos had to do was keep the food coming.

Chris looked up and smiled as the back door opened and Carlos came in. At least the kitchen would have a team of pros, even if they did spend the whole evening jostling for elbow space.

"Hey, boss. You're here early." Carlos hung his hat by the door and reached for an apron.

"Big day." Chris tossed the clipboard on his desk and headed for the dining room.

"I don't see Olivia."

Chris stopped at the door. "She's still sleeping out in the Jeep. I'll get her up just before we open. And Elizabeth Cooley invited her to spend the day, so I'll run her over there after breakfast."

"How's she doing with all this school stuff?"

Chris shrugged. "Olivia? Well, we've got two days gone and Monday to go. She's not looking forward to going back, I can tell you that."

"No, I can't imagine she is." Carlos shook his head. "I think it's pretty rough, kicking a little kid like that out of school, especially just for pushing somebody down. I used to get in fights every other day when I was a kid. They'd just pull us apart and make us sit on a bench till recess was over."

"Yeah, well, times have changed, Carlos. They have a thing they call 'zero tolerance' when it comes to any kind of physical violence. No second chances." Chris pushed on into the dining room. Behind him, he could hear Carlos muttering something about "zero sense." It didn't change anything, but it felt good to have an ally, anyway.

The breakfast crowd swelled to capacity around midmorning, then ebbed until lunchtime, and the diner stayed pretty full for the rest of the afternoon. Juanita usually didn't work Saturdays, but she had come in so Chris could spend more time in the kitchen. Things had been pretty cool between Chris and Juanita since the incident at the school Wednesday. Chris didn't blame Juanita for what happened. That was all on Olivia. But he sure wished Juanita had just minded her own business for once and let Olivia and Emma meet at school on their own terms.

"Chris, I need to say something. And I need for you to listen to me." Juanita had come into the kitchen behind him and stood with her arms crossed. He automatically checked behind her to see who in the dining room might be able to hear her thunderous whisper, but for once it was full enough and loud enough that he did not think she would be overheard.

"All right. Here I am, listening."

"Well, the first thing is, I couldn't be sorrier about Olivia getting suspended and all. She's got a lot of rough edges, I think anyone can see that, but she did not deserve to be suspended and Emma Anderson not even get a slap on the wrist."

Chris didn't know what he had expected Juanita to say, but it wasn't this. He shrugged. "Well, those are the rules. Any student who lays a hand on another student is automatically suspended."

"I still don't think it's right. And I intend to tell Sarah Cooley that the next time I see her."

"No. Don't." Chris held up his hand. "It's not her rule. It's not even Mrs. Martinez's rule. This came from the school board."

Juanita shook her head at the injustice of it all, and just when Chris thought she had nothing more to say and was about to turn away, she stopped him with a hand on his arm. "One more thing. I haven't seen Olivia since Wednesday, but would you give her a great big hug and tell her it's from Miss Juanita? And tell her from me that she's not the first child to be suspended from that school, and she won't be the last, but she needs to march back in there on Tuesday with her head held high, determined to get with the program and not let anyone throw her off track. Would you tell her that for me?"

"I'll do that." He was going to have to figure out exactly what she meant, but he would do his best to pass on Juanita's message.

"Good." She patted his arm. "Now, I'm going to go out there

and start putting checks on tables. These folks need to get on with their day so you can get on with yours."

The last part of the plan fell into place about four in the afternoon when the door opened and Rita led a group of five men into the Dip 'n' Dine.

"Lookie who I found." Rita seemed as pleased as if she alone were responsible for the band turning up.

"Tom!" Chris crossed the room and clasped the hand of the leader. "Hey guys, I can't thank you enough for coming all the way down for this." He shook the hands of the rest of the band in turn.

"Wouldn't miss it." Tom grinned through his Yosemite Sam mustache. "'Hot Chile and Cool Jazz,' huh? Nice."

"You guys hungry?"

"Nah. Thanks anyway. We found a Blake's on the way down and had a burger. We just thought we'd stop by and look things over before we checked in at the motel."

"I'm going to run them over and check them in right now." Rita was clearly ready to get the schedule back on track. "I'll be back in ten minutes, tops."

"Be sure to be back in time to eat before you go on. I've got something really special I'm introducing tonight. Chicken breast in a green mole sauce." Chris walked the band to the door.

"Or you can have the best enchiladas and rellenos you've ever put in your mouth." Carlos had appeared in the window to the kitchen and jerked his chin in greeting. "Hi. I'm Carlos. Glad you made it."

Tom paused in the doorway to look from Chris to Carlos and back. Finally he grinned. "Chris, I'm sure your mole is truly outstanding. But Carlos has me where I live. See you in a couple hours."

He raised his hand in a wave and followed Rita and the rest of the band outside. Chris glared at Carlos, who gave a "don't blame me" shrug and turned back to his stove.

———

The last half hour before the dinner was to begin was the hardest. Everything was done. The kitchen was organized with the precision of a military operation. Tiny lights twinkled up in the canopy that covered the parking lot, while underneath it long, family style tables decorated with chile ristras and votive candles stretched in rows from one end to the other. The band had finished eating and gone out to set up. Chris's stomach was tied up in such knots that he thought he might be sick. This was it. This was what could turn the Dip 'n' Dine from Fayette's diner to his own restaurant. And Carlos was even on board.

He went out the back door of the kitchen and sat on the step. The day had been unseasonably warm for early October, and as the sun went down, a light breeze had sprung up. The night was going to be perfect. He closed his eyes and held his face up to the cooling breeze. *Deep breath. It's all going to be good.*

The back door opened and Carlos stuck his head out. "Showtime, boss."

Once guests started arriving, Chris had no more time to worry. He and Carlos were spinning like windmills just to keep up with the orders, which ran about three to one in favor of Carlos's enchiladas. When he did have a minute to catch his breath, he took that time to go out and walk between the tables visiting with the diners.

Olivia had come with Elizabeth Cooley and her family and was sandwiched between Elizabeth and Lainie Braden, who sat next to her husband, Ray, who sat next to Sarah. Chris was delighted to see Lainie again. As hard as it had been to get his feet on the ground at the Dip 'n' Dine, he didn't know if he'd have been able to do it at all without Lainie. She had run the place for Fayette when Fayette was in Albuquerque with her son in the hospital. Then, after Chris bought the diner, Lainie had stayed on for the transition.

"Chris, this is amazing!" Lainie gestured with her fork at the mole chicken. "Have you added it to the menu?"

"Not yet." Chris noted with satisfaction that everyone in the Cooley-Braden party had ordered his mole chicken, even if someone had scraped all the sauce off Olivia's portion and put the chicken on a clean plate. "Maybe if there's enough popular demand."

"Well, where do I sign the petition? This is terrific."

"Thanks." Chris got Lainie's promise that she'd come into the diner for a meal before she and Ray headed back to Santa Fe, dropped his hand on Olivia's head, and moved on down the table. It didn't escape him that Olivia hadn't looked up the entire time he had been standing next to her.

Finally, a party of diners left and there wasn't another waiting to take their spot. The tables gradually began to empty. With just a few diners left lingering over their flan and coffee, Tom and the band played their last number and started to pack up.

"Chris, we did it!" Rita came inside and held up her hand for a high five.

For Chris, who towered head and shoulders over the motel-owning mayor, it was more of a medium-five, but he accepted her congratulations with a wide smile.

"I mean it," Rita continued. "There hasn't been anything this big in Last Chance for I don't know how long. Not since I've been mayor, anyway." She turned to the band, who had come in behind her. "And you gentlemen were a big, big part of it. I know people out there tonight who don't even think 'The Star-Spangled Banner' is done right unless Waylon Jennings or somebody sings it, and you just had them eating out of your hands."

"Yeah, you guys were great. I can't thank you enough for taking your weekend and coming down for this." Chris shook hands with each of them.

"There's something I haven't told you." Rita looked from Chris to Carlos, pausing to build suspense. "I contacted the food editor for *Western Home and Garden* magazine, and he came. He was out there, and he was having a good time too. I could tell."

"Why didn't you say something? I would have stopped to talk to him."

"You did talk to him. You made him feel as welcome as you made everyone else feel. He had to leave, but he said he'd call you in a few days if he had any questions."

"What did he eat?" Carlos had joined the conversation.

"Sorry, Carlos, but I think he had the chicken."

"Aw, man." Carlos turned back to the kitchen. "Now *Western Home and Garden*'s gonna think we don't even know what color mole's supposed to be."

"Chris? Sorry to interrupt." Sarah stuck her head in the door. "We're getting ready to leave, and Gran wonders if you'd like her to take Olivia home with her. It's getting late, and you could pick her up on your way home."

"No, I appreciate the offer, but you all have done way more than your bit today." Chris smiled his thanks. "I won't be much longer. Just send her on in."

"She's not in here?"

Chris looked around. "No. The last time I saw her was when I stopped by your table."

Sarah looked over her shoulder into the nearly deserted dining area under the canopy and back at Chris. Her face was twisted with apprehension. "She got antsy about half an hour ago and said she was going to come inside and color. You haven't seen her?"

Chris stood stone still a moment, trying to make sense of what she was saying, then pushed past her as he ran out the front door. "Livvy? Olivia?" His voice grew more frantic as only silence answered him. "Olivia! Olivia!"

His shouts caught the attention of a few diners walking to their cars, and they turned back to see what the problem was. Carlos went out the back door, Sarah checked the restrooms, and soon everyone had fanned out calling for Olivia.

Finally Elizabeth stated the obvious. "She's not here. I'm calling the sheriff."

A few minutes later, she turned from the phone. "Ben wants to talk to you."

Ben Apodaca's questions were terse and few. When was the last time anyone had seen Olivia? What was her exact height and weight? And most gut-wrenching of all: Had Chris, or anyone, noticed anyone watching Olivia or talking to her? Finally, he told Chris to just sit tight. He'd get this information out there and be right over.

"You know, nine times out of ten in cases like this we find the kid has just found a good spot and gone to sleep," Ben said. "You check every inch of the diner, and I'll swing by your place to make sure she hasn't got herself home somehow. I'll see you in about fifteen minutes."

Nine times out of ten, Ben had said. But what about that tenth time? Chris headed for the door.

"Chris, wait, I'm coming with you." Sarah ran to catch up with him. She put her hand on his arm and looked up into his face. "We're going to find her, and she's going to be all right. Have faith."

Someone had come up with flashlights and he could see their beams sweeping over the vacant lots and reflecting off the darkened windows of closed stores. Ever so often, he heard Olivia's name called off in the distance, but there was never an indication of any answer.

Ben pulled up in his patrol car about ten minutes later, and Chris met him when he opened his door. Ben just shook his head. "Let's go inside."

Once they did, he continued. "Okay, we need to know who was here tonight. Do you have a list or something?"

"Yeah, I've got a reservation list. I'll go get it." While Chris went into the kitchen for his list, he could hear Rita talking to Ben.

"I made a point of talking to every single guest. I wanted to find out how they heard about us and why they decided to come. I bet I can come up with their names too, if I see that reservation list."

Chris handed her the list, and while she and Ben went over it, he went and stood in the doorway and looked out into the night. It was so dark. And Olivia was so little. Where was she?

As if she could read his mind, Elizabeth stood beside him. "You know, Chris, wherever Olivia is right this minute, God has his eye and his hand on her. She's not lost. We just need to pray for her protection." Chris nodded soundlessly, and Elizabeth prayed.

Time just seemed to stop. Chris could not have said whether minutes or hours had passed. Ben left, saying he'd stay in touch. One by one the flashlights went out as it became painfully clear that wherever Olivia was, it wasn't here. Lainie prepared a big pot of coffee and made sandwiches as if she had never left the Dip 'n' Dine. And Chris paced. Then he sat on the edge of a chair and bent his head over fists clasped so tightly his knuckles were white. Sarah sat next to him, hand lightly rubbing his back, praying with him.

The phone rang just before midnight. Chris, pacing by the front door again, froze. Carlos, who was closest to the phone, answered it. He listened for a few minutes, said a word or two, and then hung up. He smiled at Chris and gave a big thumbs-up. "They found her. She's okay. She hid in the backseat of some folks who came over from Deming. They didn't even know she was there till they got home. She about gave 'em a heart attack when she sat up. Ben has gone to get her. He'll bring her to your place, so I guess we can all go home now."

Without realizing he was even doing so, Chris looked for Sarah, and when his eyes found hers, he opened his arms and she walked into them. She all but disappeared in his embrace, and while he struggled to control his tears, Sarah didn't even try, and he could feel her sobbing in his arms.

19

Chris was waiting on the porch of his mobile home with his hands in his pockets when Ben stopped his patrol car in the drive. He ran down the steps as Ben got out and opened the back door for Olivia. As soon as her feet touched the gravel, Chris snatched her up in his arms, holding her head against his shoulder with one hand and inhaling the sweet, soapy, sweaty fragrance that was Olivia.

"Don't you ever, ever do that again," he murmured into her hair. "Never. Do you hear me? Never."

"She's in pretty good shape for a stowaway." Ben slammed the back door of his car and leaned against it. "By the time she'd gotten herself to Deming, she was rethinking the whole operation and was ready to come home. We had us a good talk on the way back, didn't we, girl?"

Olivia nodded against Chris's shoulder and sniffed. She had grabbed his neck in a vice-like grip and had yet to let go.

Shifting Olivia's weight to his left arm, Chris reached past her to grip Ben's hand. "Thanks. I just . . . Thanks."

He stopped to clear his throat, and Ben just waved as he walked around the car and got back in. "Glad it worked out like it did. You stick close to home from now on. You hear me, Olivia?"

She nodded again without looking around, and Chris stood in the drive until Ben's taillights faded into the distance before carrying Olivia inside. He sat down on the sofa with Olivia in his lap and tenderly pried her hands from around his neck. When she still would not meet his eyes, he gently raised her face until she was looking at him.

"What were you thinking about, running off like that?"

She just shrugged and looked away.

"Where were you going?"

"Florida."

"Oh, Livvy." He held her close and gently rocked her in silence for a few minutes. Finally, he spoke. "You know, I think that the moment that I knew you were gone was absolutely the worst moment of my life. I was so afraid."

She leaned back so she could look up at him. "You were afraid?"

"Honey, I've never been so scared. All of the bad things that could have happened to you just filled my head all at once. I couldn't think. I could hardly talk. All I knew was that you were gone, and I didn't know where you were."

"I'm sorry." Her voice was tiny.

"Just promise me that you'll never, never do that again, okay?"

"Okay."

"Were you going to Florida so you wouldn't have to go back to school Tuesday?"

She nodded against his chest.

"Well, it's not going to be easy, I'll give you that. But I have a message from Miss Juanita for you."

"I know. She said I needed to be good, like Emma A."

"No, that's not what she said at all. First she said to give you a big hug, so here's a hug from her. Then she said, I think, that you should just go in there with your head held high, and not let anybody get you down, and decide you're just going to be good like Olivia."

She looked up at him again. "Really?"

"Really. At least I think that's what she said. It's kind of hard to know just what she means sometimes."

"Yeah, I know." She leaned against his chest again.

He rocked her in his arms, feeling her body gradually relax against him, and listened as her breath slowed to a measured rhythm. When he was sure she was asleep, he carried her back to her room and laid her on her bed. She didn't wake up when he took off her shoes, and for a long time he sat next to her watching her sleep. In repose, she had no anger in her face, no defiance, no suspicion. She was just a seven-year-old, like any other. He ran a finger over her cheek and kissed her forehead before quietly stepping out and closing the door behind him. If only there were a way to see that expression of childish innocence and vulnerability when Olivia was awake—but he was afraid it was gone for good.

—⁓—

Chris leaned against the counter in his kitchen cradling a mug of coffee in his hands and watching the sun crest the mountains in the distance and flood the desert around his mobile home with light. Last night, when Olivia was still gone, he had given himself until dawn to find her before he called her mom in Florida. He hadn't even been able to articulate the unthinkable to himself. What in the world would he have said to his sister? But it was dawn now. And Olivia was asleep in her own room. *Thank you, God.*

"I'm still dressed." Olivia wandered down the hall, frowning down at her jeans and T-shirt as if she'd never seen them before.

"Well, you fell asleep before you got your pajamas on. Want some orange juice?"

She shook her head, curled up in a corner of the sofa, and closed her eyes again.

"Come on, Livvy." Chris poured the juice anyway and set it on the counter. "You need to wake up. You have to shower and have breakfast and get ready for church."

She gave a whimper of protest and flipped so her face was buried in the back of the sofa.

"Liv, come on." He walked over and gave her a light swat on the seat of her jeans. "Get up."

She sat up and brushed her hair from her face. "Is everybody going to be mad at me?"

"Nobody's going to be mad. In fact, I'm pretty sure everyone's going to be very glad to see you. We were all really worried."

She didn't say anything, and he sat in a chair across from her and leaned his elbows on his knees. "Why'd you do it, Livvy?"

She wouldn't look at him. "I was trying to find my mom."

"Florida's a pretty big place. Finding her might have been hard. Do you think we should talk to her and tell her you want to come live with her?" Sending Olivia to live with her mom and that Jase guy under who knows what circumstances would all but kill him, but keeping a little girl from her mom might be even worse. What did he know, anyway?

Olivia looked up and met his eyes. "But I don't want to live in Florida. I want her to live here with us. I was going to go get her. But not Jase."

Chris nodded. Maybe Olivia had something there. Although if Last Chance wasn't ready for a simple menu change, he was pretty sure it wasn't ready for Kaitlyn Reed. "Well, you can ask her about that when you talk to her next time." He reached for her hand and tugged her to her feet. "You know we're going to have to tell her about your little trip to Deming, don't you?"

"Why?" Olivia slumped into a chair at the kitchen table.

"Because she's your mom. And she cares what happens to you."

Olivia didn't say anything. She didn't have to. The cynicism in her face said it all. Chris opened his mouth to contradict her but closed it again. What would be the point?

He set a skillet on the stove. "So, scrambled eggs sound okay for breakfast?"

———

They ran into Elizabeth Cooley and her family in the church parking lot, and Olivia was passed from one to the other for gentle scoldings and hugs. Olivia bore it all with the slightly jaded expression Chris had learned she used to cover the discomfort of too much attention. But when Elizabeth held her at arm's length and just looked at her, Olivia's face crumpled, and Elizabeth enveloped her in a big hug and whispered something in her ear. Olivia stood with arms at her side until Elizabeth let her go, then slipped her arm around Elizabeth's waist.

As they walked toward the front door of the church with their arms around each other's waists, Sarah and Chris fell in behind them.

Sarah let Elizabeth and Olivia get far enough ahead to be out of earshot. "So, did you find out what this was all about?"

"Yeah. She was going to find her mom."

"Poor kid. Was she running away because of the suspension?"

"Well, actually, she was going to get her mom to come back with her and yell at everybody."

"What?" Sarah laughed.

"I heard the whole story over breakfast. It seems no matter what trouble Olivia ever got into, her mom took her side. Teachers, neighbors, other kids' moms, Kaitlyn took them all on. And knowing Kaitlyn like I do, I can see her doing it."

"You know, that does explain a lot."

"Yeah, well, the plan was for Kaitlyn to come yell at Emma and Sue Anderson, Mrs. Martinez, and even you."

"Me?"

"Yes, for taking her to the principal's office in the first place, but since you had been so nice to her, Olivia was planning on sticking up for you."

"Good, I guess."

Elizabeth and Olivia as well as Lainie and Ray had already gone inside by the time Sarah and Chris reached the church steps. He stopped and looked down at her. "I am so out of my league here. Did I let Olivia down by not standing up for her more? I mean, my feeling was that she had broken the rules and had to suffer the consequences. Should I have done something different?"

"Nope, I can't think of a thing. You don't need to stick up for someone to stand by them. And as far as I can see, you are right there with her—no shame, no blame." She took his arm as they mounted the steps. "And for my part, Tuesday I'm starting a unit on verbal bullying called 'Words Can Hurt.' Think that will get me off the hook with Kaitlyn? I really hate getting yelled at."

The pianist had just begun the introduction to the first hymn when Sarah and Chris entered the sanctuary. Down front, in the third pew on the left, Olivia sat between Elizabeth and Lainie. Sarah slipped into a spot near the back and Chris followed her. He found he liked standing next to her in church, and when she found the page in the hymnbook, he found he liked holding one side while she held the other. He really liked the fragrance of the curly dark hair at his shoulder, and when they sat down, he found he even liked her absorbed expression as she listened to Brother Parker.

Even those who had arrived at church not knowing about Olivia's midnight trip had learned of it by the time the service started, and a small group gathered around Elizabeth and Olivia after the benediction had been pronounced. Chris could see the top of Elizabeth's head, and before she was blocked from his view, he could see Olivia standing next to her, Elizabeth's arm around her shoulders.

"Makes me think of *my* first Sunday." Lainie and Ray had worked their way though the crowd and had joined them in the back.

"Yeah, as I heard it, you had quite a little crowd gathered around you too." Ray grinned.

"Why?" Sarah stepped out of the aisle so people could get by.

"Well, I hadn't been to church in, like, ever, and I was mad that Elizabeth was making me go, so I thought if I put on some really short shorts, she'd let me stay home."

Sarah laughed. "Wrong."

"Yes, well, I found that out the hard way. But Elizabeth did just what she's doing now. She stood beside me, just as pleasant and sweet as she could be, introducing me to people. She didn't say a word about what I was wearing and almost dared anyone else to. She is one amazing lady."

"See?" Sarah turned to Chris. "That's what I mean about standing by someone without excusing conduct. Gran has made it an art form."

"Here you all are. I wondered where you had gone." Elizabeth, her arm still around Olivia's shoulders, joined them. "Chris, why don't you and Olivia come have dinner with us? We have plenty, and we'd love to have you."

Chris looked down at Olivia, who had left Elizabeth's side and come to lean on him. Her eyes drooped. He smiled and shook his head. "I'm afraid I need to get Livvy home. I think a nice quiet afternoon, with maybe a nap, is what we both need. I thank you, though."

"Another time, then." Elizabeth patted Olivia's back. "But you're probably right. It doesn't cure everything, but there's not a whole lot that doesn't look better after a Sunday nap."

———

Sarah was considering a nap of her own when there was a tap at her front door, and she opened it to find Lainie on her front porch.

"Hi. Are you busy?"

"Lainie." Sarah smiled as she opened the screen door. "I'm not a bit busy. Come on in."

"Elizabeth's taking her nap, and Ray's gone to check on his studio at the ranch, so I thought I'd pop over and see if anyone else in town was awake. I'd almost forgotten how quiet things can get in Last Chance on a Sunday afternoon."

"I'm glad you did." Sarah led the way to the kitchen. "Want some tea? I was just about to make a cup."

"Love some." Lainie followed and slid into a chair at the kitchen table. "I really love how you've done your house. It's so bright and happy."

"Thanks. Bright and happy was what I was going for." Sarah looked around her kitchen in satisfaction. Her newest find, a black cat clock with a pendulum tail and eyes that moved from side to side with each tick, hung on the wall over the table. "I'm afraid most people around here think it's just odd."

"Well, I like it. We're still coming to a meeting of the minds at our house. If Ray had his way, our place would look like a museum. You know, old carvings, pottery, weavings and stuff." She rolled her eyes. "But my heart just sings when I go into the housewares section of Target. Everything is so cheerful and colorful, and you can decorate the whole house for what one of those carvings Ray loves would cost. I know. That makes me pitiful."

Sarah laughed and put a plate of cookies on the table. "No, it doesn't. I like Target too. But I can see the problem."

"Well, right now the problem is being solved by finances. Ray's paintings are doing well, but not so well yet that we could afford to buy one."

"And you? What are you doing these days?" The teakettle whistled, and Sarah got up to brew the tea.

"I'm working part-time at a restaurant near the plaza. And I'm going back to school."

"Are you? Well, good for you."

"Yep. I had more or less promised Elizabeth I would last winter. That idea had to be shelved when I had to run the Dip 'n' Dine for Fayette, but now, if I can keep up with the program, I'll be a high school graduate within two years."

Sarah held up her hand for a high five. "Couldn't be prouder, cuz."

"Thanks. So, what about you? Do you love teaching as much as you thought you would?"

"I sure don't have all the answers like I thought I did, but I do love it. The kids are great, most of the time, anyway."

"Yeah, when they're not pounding the stuffing out of other kids on the playground." Lainie smiled.

"Oh, Olivia. Well, that was a onetime thing, and I hope it stays that way. For all our sakes."

"Hey, I love Olivia. I *was* Olivia. I can't tell you the number of fights I got into. It sure wasn't a onetime thing with me." Lainie sipped her tea. "Of course, I didn't have an uncle like Chris either."

"Ah, Chris. Yes, he's good for Olivia, all right. He really cares about her." Sarah tried to keep her face expressionless as she changed the subject. "Tell me more about your classes. What are you taking?"

It didn't work. "No, you tell me more about Chris. What's going on between you two?"

"Nothing's going on. We share a concern for Olivia, but that's all."

"Come on, Sarah. I've only been in town three days, and even I can see that you're way more than just his niece's teacher to him. You really don't see that?"

Sarah sighed. "Well, it's complicated. He took some getting used to, but, yeah, he's nice. Really nice. But there's Brandon."

"Brandon? Is he still in the picture? I thought he was moving back east somewhere."

"Chicago. He's there now, although he was supposed to be here this weekend. As for whether he's still in the picture, I don't know. Maybe. I guess we're trying to figure that out. At least, I told him that I'd give it another try."

Lainie was quiet for a few minutes while she considered all Sarah had said. Finally, she shook her head. "Well, it's your life."

"That sounds ominous."

"Sorry. I didn't mean to sound all voice-of-doom-ish." Lainie grinned. "I really don't know either of them that well. But Chris seems like such a nice guy. He really, really cares about that little girl. I can tell he cares about you. And he can cook. You can't beat that."

"Brandon has his good qualities too, you know."

"Really. So tell me about Brandon's good qualities. I just met him once at the ranch last Thanksgiving, and to tell the truth, they didn't exactly shine forth. He seemed a little standoffish, like nobody was quite up to his standards. But maybe he's shy and just comes across that way."

Sarah laughed. "Brandon shy? Uh, no. I don't think I've ever known anyone more confident or sure of what he wants. And he likes my family and all. He just doesn't think he has a whole lot in common with them."

"Has it occurred to him that if you guys do get married, your family will be his family, like for the rest of your lives? That's a whole lot of Christmases and Thanksgivings spent playing solitaire on his phone while everybody else has a good time."

"Well, I'm sure things would change with time."

"Oh, Sarah, you don't plan a life with someone hoping things will change with time. Even I know that."

Sarah avoided answering by refilling their mugs of tea.

"Okay, I'll mind my own business." Lainie sat back in her chair. "But I want to say one thing first. Last Thanksgiving was the first time I met you too. And, sorry, but I thought you were timid and a little short on personality. It wasn't until I saw you without Brandon around that I realized those were the last words to describe you. I'm just saying don't do anything without putting a whole lot of prayer into it. This is not something you want to mess up."

"You thought I was timid?" Sarah stopped in midpour.

"Well, let's just say awfully concerned about whether Brandon was enjoying himself or not. Any time he blinked twice, you were there to see what he wanted, laughing at any lame comment he made as if it were the wittiest thing anyone had said all day."

"You make me sound pathetic."

"Not pathetic. Just worried about making him happy. And truthfully? He seemed to think that's the way things should be."

"Well, we've talked about it and he recognizes that he was a bit controlling. He's asked me to give him a chance to prove himself, and that's all I've done—given him a chance."

Lainie swirled the tea in her mug and stared into it. Finally she looked up at Sarah. "I know control. I lived with it. And even though Brandon and Nick, the guy I tried to leave behind in California, are miles apart in every other way, I see that same need to hold the strings. And what I see is you here in Last Chance doing things the way Brandon, who is in Chicago, wants you to do them." She smiled, as if to soften her words. "I started out by saying I was going to mind my own business, didn't I? Sorry. So I'll just repeat what I said earlier. Pray and keep praying. Marriage lasts a long, long time. And frankly, you don't do timid all that well." Lainie looked at her watch and got to her feet. "I'll bet Elizabeth is awake and wondering where I am. Are you coming over for waffles this evening?"

"Of course. The edict was issued today after church." Sarah tried to smile as she walked Lainie to the door, but she was feeling more than a little shaken. Timid? Short on personality? Was that how people saw her when she was with Brandon?

"Good. But you should know that Elizabeth has talked Chris into coming and bringing Olivia so she can show Ray her drawings."

"Oh, I'm so glad that Ray's going to look at her pictures." Sarah couldn't help smiling. "She's so proud of them. And they're good too. I hope he encourages her. I know Chris does, but Ray's the artist. It will mean so much coming from him."

"I'm sure he will." Lainie leaned over and gave Sarah a hug. "And I have just one more observation before I really start minding my own business. We talked a whole lot about Brandon, but the first time your face lit up was when I mentioned Chris and told you Ray was going to look at Olivia's pictures. Think about that a little bit."

Sarah watched Lainie head back down the sidewalk to Elizabeth's. Her face didn't light up when Chris's name was mentioned. She would know if it did. If Lainie noticed anything, it was just Sarah being pleased that Ray was looking at Olivia's pictures. That's all it was.

—⚮—

When her phone rang late that night as Sarah was getting ready for bed, she was almost surprised. She and Brandon had not ended his last call last Wednesday on the best of terms, and she had not heard from him since.

"So am I out of the doghouse yet?" She could hear the coaxing smile in his voice.

"Is that where you've been?"

"It sure feels like it, and it's not my favorite place, I'll tell you that. But I did get a lot done this weekend."

"So it was all worth it?" Sarah wasn't quite ready to let him off the hook.

"Short term? Not even close. There's no place I'd rather be than with you. You know that."

"Then why weren't you? You had the plane tickets."

"Because I've got the long term to think about." Brandon's voice went from gently teasing to serious. Sarah could almost see the intense, eager expression he always wore when he talked about the future, their future. "Sarah, the level of commitment you have to have to get anywhere in this company is unreal. I was ready to work hard, but these guys are something else. I don't think they know what a weekend is."

Sarah gave up with a sigh. She'd been trying to get her feet on the ground in a new job too. It wasn't easy. "Well, you were missed."

"I'll make it up to you at Thanksgiving. Promise. I'll work so hard between now and then that they'll be ordering me to take some time off." Brandon sounded as if he were trying to inject some enthusiasm into his voice, but mostly what Sarah heard was exhaustion.

"Well, don't kill yourself. We'll have plenty of opportunities."

This time there was no mistaking the relief Sarah heard. "That we will. So, other than you, what did I miss? How did the chile-jazz thing work out?"

Sarah sat cross-legged on the bed. "It was amazing. Of course, things got really exciting, terrifying actually, when Olivia went missing. But, thankfully, she was found safe in Deming, of all places, after just a few hours . . ."

As she went on, Brandon's comments became fewer and shorter, and finally she realized he wasn't responding at all.

"Brandon?"

Silence.

With a half smile, Sarah hit End. She couldn't blame Brandon for falling asleep. It was past midnight where he was, and he had worked hard all weekend, so he said. But one of these times, she was going to tell about her day first, just so she could finish.

20

Well, I have to say, 'Hot Chile and Cool Jazz' was a huge hit. Beyond my wildest dreams. Everybody's talking about it." Rita bustled through the door of the Dip 'n' Dine midmorning Monday. "Congratulations, everybody!"

"Thanks." Chris smiled. Now that Olivia was home and his heart rate had returned to normal, he could take the time to think about how the night had gone, and he had to admit it had gone well. He doubted that it had exceeded Rita's wildest dreams, though. The woman could dream, especially when it came to Last Chance.

"Now." Rita plopped her clipboard on an empty table and took her pencil from behind her ear. "Do you have a minute? I have some thoughts I want to run by you."

"Rita, I really don't. We had to put the day-to-day business of the place on the back burner while we got ready for Saturday, and I need to spend the day getting things back on track. Could we set a time for later in the week?"

"Not even five minutes?" When Rita was on a mission, she was hard to put off. The problem was, she was always on a mission.

Chris gave up and sat down across from her. "Okay, five minutes, but that really is all the time I have today."

"Fine." Rita had already gone to her clipboard. "First, it's getting a little cool now, but I'd love to see us do this once a month once it warms up again—maybe May through September. What do you think?"

What Chris thought must have been evident on his face, because Rita just flapped a hand at him and went right on. "The first one's always the hardest. Once you get going, it flows like cream. Trust me on this. It's going to be great. Now, if this takes off like I think it will, you might have to go to two seatings, so be thinking about how we're going to do that."

Truthfully, Chris had come into the diner that morning just glad "Hot Chile and Cool Jazz" was behind him. Jumping right into planning a whole season of such events was a little more than he wanted to deal with at the moment.

"Rita, that's just more than I can get my head around right now. As I said, we're just trying to get back to normal around here this morning." He got to his feet and extended his hand. "But it does sound interesting, I'll give you that. We need to schedule that meeting and go over this a little more carefully."

Rita ignored the hand and swept in for a quick hug. "Don't worry about a thing. We've got more than six months before the next one, and as I said, it'll be a piece of cake. Just leave it to me."

She was almost out the door and Chris was just drawing a deep breath when she paused. "I just thought of our next theme. I don't know how these things come to me, but what do you think of 'Red Chile and Blues'?"

She was gone before Chris could respond, but he had to admit to himself that it did sound pretty good. He had no idea where Rita got her ideas either, but she surely had no shortage of them.

It was a slow morning, and for once, that was just fine with Chris. Juanita, when she came in, didn't have a lot to say once she asked how Olivia was. And in the kitchen, Carlos just seemed pleased to have his domain back under his control.

Just before noon, a car parked just outside the front door, and a man Chris didn't recognize got out and came in. He let Juanita show him to a booth by the window and accepted a menu before asking to speak to the owner. Chris, sitting at his desk in the kitchen, heard him and met Juanita on his way into the dining room.

"I have no idea who he is," she said in her distinctive whisper. "I've never seen him before. But he does drive a nice car."

Chris had noticed. Most of the vehicles that parked at the Dip 'n' Dine were pickups or SUVs, and the few sedans tended to be a bit worse for the wear. But you didn't see many hybrids.

"Chris Reed." He smiled as he crossed the room and extended his hand. "What can I do for you?"

"Nate Silverman." The man handed Chris a card as he shook his hand. "I'm the food editor for *Western Home and Garden* magazine. I didn't get to talk to you Saturday night and took a chance on swinging by on my way back to El Paso to catch my plane. Can you give me a few minutes?" He gestured at the seat across the table.

"Sure, glad to." Chris slid into the opposite side of the booth. "I hope you enjoyed yourself Saturday. It was the first time we'd done anything like it, so there were probably some rough patches."

"Everyone really seemed to be having a good time. That band was something else. Local boys?"

"No, they came down from Albuquerque. Everything else was local, though. Carlos, our cook, makes his red and green chile sauces from scratch from chile grown in this area." Juanita edged closer to the table, and Chris smiled up at her. "In fact, Juanita

Sheppard here and her husband own the chile farm just outside of town that supplies most of it."

Nate smiled, nodded, shook Juanita's hand, and returned to his menu. "What do you recommend?"

"The special today is green chile stew, and you can't go wrong with that. We serve it with either homemade tortillas or sopaipillas. But I'll stand by anything on the menu."

Chris fought the temptation to fill the silence with babbling while Nate took his time with the menu. *So what did you think of the chicken with mole verde, Mr. Food Editor? I'm glad you liked the band, but what about the food?* Finally, Nate handed his menu to Juanita.

"I'll have a bowl of the stew, and I'll have the same combination plate you served Saturday if you don't mind my just taking a taste or two and leaving the rest. If I ate everything I wanted to, I'd be as big as a house."

Chris sat with Nate Silverman while he ate, telling him about the history of the Dip 'n' Dine, his part in it, and what he hoped its future was. And while Mr. Silverman ate every bite of his green chile stew and a good deal more than just a taste or two of the combination plate, he said not a word about how he liked it. Finally, after stopping in the kitchen to meet Carlos and asking for a menu to take with him, he took his leave.

"You've got a nice little place here." He shook Chris's hand at the door. "One of the things I like best about my job is discovering these little gems off the interstate. As soon as you get the schedule worked out for those food and music nights you're going to be having next summer, you let me know, okay?"

He waved as he got in his car, and they all watched him drive away.

"Well, what do you know? He called us a gem, and we've been

discovered." Juanita brought a bin of dirty dishes into the kitchen where Chris had returned to his desk.

"Yeah, like Columbus discovered America." Carlos turned back to his stove. "How long have we been here? I know I've been here twenty years."

"What did he say, Chris? Is he going to put us in his magazine?"

"I have no idea what he's going to do. He didn't say. He just ate, asked a ton of questions, and left." Truth be told, Chris was a little annoyed with Nate Silverman. He could have at least mentioned the chicken mole he ate at the "Hot Chile and Cool Jazz" night. He didn't have to say he loved it, or even that he liked it, but he could have said *something*.

—⚭—

Sarah checked her watch as she climbed in her car after school. Now that the school year was well under way, it was next to impossible to meet Megan for lunch on Mikey's afternoons with his grandma, so they had settled on after-school coffee—with Mikey in tow. And she was about ten minutes late.

Megan was already in the booth at the Dip 'n' Dine when Sarah drove up, and Mikey was in a high chair eating Cheerios.

"I'm so sorry I'm late. I had a parent want to talk a few minutes when she picked her daughter up." Sarah slid in the booth across from Megan.

"Don't think a thing about it. Mikey's just up from his nap, so he's in a good mood, and I was talking Juanita's ear off."

"So what can I get you?" Juanita, who was indeed standing right by the table, took out her order pad.

"Just some decaf coffee, thanks." Sarah smiled at her and turned to Megan.

"Oh, aren't you going to have any pie or anything?" Megan's face fell. "I was going to have just a tiny little piece, but if you don't have anything . . ."

"You go ahead. I'm just not real hungry."

Megan sighed. "Okay, I guess I'll just have coffee too."

She looked so sad that Sarah changed her mind. "What if we split something? You choose."

"Perfect!" This was all Megan was waiting for. "Let's have pecan, warmed up with a scoop of ice cream."

"Got it." Juanita put pencil to pad. "And two cups of decaf."

"Not mine." Megan sprinkled a few more Cheerios on Mikey's tray. "Full strength for me."

"Don't you have trouble sleeping if you drink caffeinated coffee this late in the day?" Truthfully, after her long day, Sarah could have used the little pick-me-up caffeine offered too. But she knew she'd be regretting it long after midnight.

"Are you kidding me? Nothing keeps me awake but this guy, but if he's asleep, I'm out too."

Sarah smiled at Mikey, opened her hand for the Cheerio offered her, and held her palm flat as he took it back again and put it in his mouth. "How is he doing? He's growing like a weed."

That was all Sarah had to say, and Megan was off and running. She didn't pause for breath, even when Juanita brought the pie and coffee, finally finishing up a half hour later with, "And that's why I give him a jar of prunes every day."

She sat back, and it took Sarah a moment to realize she had finished and was waiting for Sarah to say something. Sarah reached for the first thing that came to mind. "Well, he certainly must keep you busy."

Megan rolled her eyes. "That's the understatement of the year."

She took another bite of pecan pie. "So, what's going on with you? Are you dating anyone?"

A little wave of irritation rippled through Sarah. There was so much going on in her life. Why would whether or not she was dating be the first thing Megan would want to hear about? "No, I'm not, as it happens. My class keeps me totally busy, and then there's Gran. I like to kind of keep an eye on her, but don't tell her I said so."

"That sounds like you." Megan scooped up the last bite of ice cream and smiled at her. "Always looking after someone else. But don't forget about you. You need some good times in your life too. What about . . . ?" She lowered her voice and jerked her head toward the kitchen.

"Carlos? He's married, and for a long time too. I thought you knew that." Sarah grinned at her friend.

"No, I do not mean Carlos." Megan bit off each word in an exasperated whisper. "I mean Chris. He's good-looking. He's single. He's a strong Christian. And he owns his own business. What's not to like? Well, I guess there is the little girl, but she won't be here forever."

Chris had come out of the kitchen and was doing something behind the counter. When he looked up and saw both women looking at him, he smiled. "Everything okay? Need anything?"

"Everything's great. That pie is out of this world." Megan smiled back.

"Good." He went back to whatever he was doing.

"See? And he's tall too." Megan went back to her whisper.

"And I'm not. What's your point? Chris and I are just friends. And as for the little girl, I love Olivia. I'll miss her like crazy if she has to go back with her mom. So let's talk about something else. Tell me more about Mikey."

212

"Nice try, but it's not going to work this time. You get to do the talking now. If not Chris, what about that guy you used to be engaged to? Is he completely out of the picture?"

"I was never engaged." Sarah was about ready to plead papers to grade and head for the door. "But to answer your question, Miss Nosy, he's not completely out of the picture. He's working in Chicago, but we talk on the phone."

"Really? Oh, Chicago is so far away. Do you think you'll move there?"

"Megan. No. And I don't have anything more to say about this. Can we change the subject? Please?"

Megan must have realized that the topic had played itself out, and Mikey must have become bored with the whole discussion, because he started fussing. She sighed. "Okay. Don't be mad. I just worry about you, that's all."

"You don't need to. I'm okay, promise. In fact, I really like my life."

Sarah smiled and reached across the table to put her hand on her friend's arm, and Megan smiled back at her. Mikey, however, went from fussy to crying in earnest.

"I need to get this boy home." Megan dipped her paper napkin in her water glass and tried to wipe his face. That just made Mikey madder, and he howled his protest. In a moment, Megan had extracted him from his chair, gathered the paraphernalia that accompanied them everywhere, and left with promises to call soon. Sarah just sat a minute listening to the quiet Megan had left in her wake.

"How about another cup of coffee?" Chris appeared at the table with the carafe. He smiled down at her, and she noticed the fine lines at the corner of his eyes.

"If you have one with me. You look like you could use a break too."

Chris looked around the room. There was only one other table with diners, and they were almost finished. "I think I can take a few minutes. Let me go get another cup and I'll be right with you."

"Watch out for the Cheerios," Sarah called after him. "They're everywhere."

When he got back, Sarah noticed two things. One, he seemed to fill the whole other side of the booth, and two, he really did look tired. Whether it was the stress of putting on "Hot Chile and Cool Jazz" or the worry Olivia seemed intent on putting him through on a daily basis, he looked beat.

"I haven't had a chance to tell you, but Saturday night was really amazing. The mole verde was incredible." She smiled at him and couldn't help noticing the way he brightened when she did.

"Thanks. I'm glad you liked it. I didn't see your friend, though, the one who was coming in from Chicago. Did I just miss him or what?"

"No, he didn't make it." Sarah shook her head and shrugged. "Something came up at work. His loss, though. It was a great evening—at least until our little traveler took off."

"Yeah, Livvy. She keeps things exciting." He paused for a long moment, and when he did speak, he almost blurted his question. "I know it's none of my business, but this guy Brandon, is anything going on between you two?"

Sarah leaned back and laughed. "That is a really good question. And if I knew, I'd tell you."

Chris just raised his eyebrows and waited.

"Well, we were together most of the time we were in college. Then we weren't. And now, I don't know. We're just seeing how things go."

"So if I asked you out to dinner, I wouldn't be stepping out of line?"

That came out of left field, and Sarah had to take a minute to process it. It wasn't that the idea of going out with Chris had never come up. In fact, nearly everyone in Last Chance seemed to think it was a brilliant idea. It was just that until now the idea had never come from either of the two people most involved.

"I'm just talking about dinner. We eat. We talk. We come home. You never know, you might even have a good time." He grinned and wiggled his eyebrows.

Sarah laughed again. She'd forgotten what fun it was to be with someone who made her laugh. "Sure. Why not? In fact, I'd love to—as long as we're clear that it's just dinner."

"Great! Just dinner it is. Next Sunday evening?"

"Sounds good."

"There's one more thing." He leaned forward, and Sarah had never seen him look more serious. "I need to ask you a question I never thought I'd ask, at least not for a long, long time."

Uh oh.

"Could you recommend a good babysitter?"

21

Sarah had tried on and rejected three different outfits, and fussed at herself for doing so, by the time Chris picked her up Sunday evening. She had also told Brandon about the dinner, and he had not been happy.

"It's only dinner," she had told him. "Just a chance to get out for the evening with a friend."

"Don't you have any women friends?"

"Married women friends, with small children. And Last Chance is just not a girls' night out kind of place. Families sort of pull in their sidewalks in the evening. What kind of question is that, anyway? I'm only allowed to have women friends?"

He had gone silent, and she tried to coax a better mood.

"We're just going as friends. Promise. Besides, he knows all about you and that I'm coming to see you next month. I told him."

"And he decided to try to move in anyway. Is that supposed to make me feel better?"

"Brandon, I'm going to ask you something, and I want you to be completely truthful."

He didn't say anything, and Sarah took that as agreement.

"In all the time you've been away, have you never had a dinner or a lunch or a cup of coffee with another woman? Not even once?"

"Well, yeah, co-workers."

"And the difference would be?"

"They don't mean anything to me, at least not like you do. They're someone to talk to so I don't always have to eat alone, and that's how they feel about me too."

"And that's exactly how it is with Chris and me. Just friends."

There was a long silence on the phone before Brandon finally broke it.

"You know, when you say you just see this guy as a friend, I believe you. I know you, and if there were something more, you'd tell me."

Sarah had been pleased at his trust and was about to say so when Brandon went on. "But I don't trust this Chris guy any farther than I can throw him. If I were there, I'd knock his teeth in for him."

"If you were here, Brandon, I wouldn't be going to dinner with Chris." *And I'd like to see you try to knock Chris Reed's teeth in.* Sarah had been suddenly so done with the conversation.

"All I'm saying is be careful."

"Good-bye, Brandon."

"Call me as soon as you get home."

"Bye."

After she had hung up from talking to Brandon, Sarah had almost called Chris to cancel. Truth be told, she felt a tiny twinge of guilt at Brandon's confidence that she would tell him if she felt anything more than friendship for Chris. Yes, Chris was just a friend. And yes, they had agreed that this was to be a dinner between friends, and friends only. And yes, she was as committed as ever to seeing where things went with Brandon. But being honest with herself, she knew she would never have tried on three different outfits to have dinner with Megan.

She finally decided on some dark jeans, a crisp white shirt, and a leather jacket—nicely casual and yet sharp too. She was tying a red scarf into her dark curls when the doorbell rang and she found Chris standing on her doorstep holding a pie.

"Come in." She opened the door for him and accepted his gift. "A pie. How nice. Thank you."

"Hey, if there were a florist within forty miles of here open on Sunday, I'd have brought flowers." Chris gave her shoulders a quick one-armed squeeze. "I guess I could have brought candy. I think Manny has a few packages clipped to a rack down at Otero Gas and Oil. But I went for the pie. I hope you like it. Just made it this afternoon."

Sarah laughed. "It looks delicious, although why you'd want to spend your only afternoon off cooking is beyond me."

Chris shrugged and followed her into the kitchen to put the pie away. "It relaxes me. I put on some jazz, make a huge mess in the kitchen, and before I know it, I've forgotten what was bothering me."

"So what was bothering you?"

He shrugged again. "I don't know. I've forgotten."

Telling herself that the surge of joy she felt was because she was going out for dinner for a change, and because Chris made her laugh, and because it was good to have a friend, Sarah led the way out the door and to the Jeep parked at the curb.

Elizabeth hadn't drawn her drapes against the evening yet, and when they drove by they could see her sitting in her recliner with Olivia leaning over the arm.

"I sure appreciate your grandmother letting Olivia come over this evening. I really hesitated asking since she has Livvy all week after school."

"Gran's the one who volunteered, remember? She loves Livvy.

And despite my earlier misgivings, I think Livvy's really good for her too. They're a couple of buddies. I think she said they're going to make waffles and then crochet."

"Yeah, Livvy showed me this crochet chain she's been working on. It's about ten feet long and growing, but she's really proud of it."

"I can see it now—the two of them sitting side by side crocheting the evenings away."

"We'll have to bring in another recliner."

Sarah smiled and let the highway disappear beneath them a while before talking. The October sun was just slipping below the horizon, and soft jazz came from the radio. It felt good to just be.

"So, where are we going?" Sarah broke the silence. "You never told me."

Chris glanced at her before looking back at the road. "I guess I should have checked with you, huh? I should have warned you that with me it's way more about the food than the atmosphere, so sometimes the places I go might be a little short on charm, but the food is always outstanding."

"Well, that sounds promising. At least I'm not underdressed."

"You look incredible. Didn't I mention that? I meant to."

Sarah smiled. "Thanks. But you still haven't told me where we're going."

"It's called Papa's. Have you heard of it?"

"No. Where is it?"

"About forty miles from here, up in the mountains. They do steaks over mesquite coals, and that's about all they do. But the steaks are supposed to be out of this world. And there's live music on the weekends."

"Sounds perfect."

The conversation comfortably drifted after that, slipping from the food editor's visit to the Dip 'n' Dine, to Sarah's second graders, to Olivia and her new riding teacher. It had been a long time since conversation had been so easy, and Sarah was almost disappointed when Chris turned off the road and brought his Jeep to a stop next to the pickups in the gravel parking lot.

The smell of wood smoke permeated the cool air, and they could hear that the band had already begun. Papa's had a wide porch across the front and half doors that opened on a large room paneled with varnished pine and filled with well-scrubbed wooden tables. Cattle brands had been burned into a border around the top of the room.

Chris bent down to whisper in Sarah's ear when they walked in. "I warned you. Not much charm, but we can still hope the food measures up."

"Are you kidding me? This place is loaded with charm. I love it." Suddenly she grabbed Chris's arm and pointed to the border. "Look! There's the Rocking JC, our brand. I wonder how it got here."

She asked when the hostess came to show them to their table, and the hostess, who looked as if she could have been there the day Papa's first opened, stopped and looked up. "Well, the first few years we were open, we let ranchers bring in their branding iron. We'd heat it up in the coals and let them brand the wall. Can't do it now. Blamed fire marshal made us quit."

"That's our brand right up there. The Rocking JC." Sarah was still excited.

The hostess nodded and led them to their table. "Every now and then someone comes in and recognizes their brand. It's good to see some things are carrying on."

"Sounds like you've been here awhile yourself." Chris smiled at her as he held Sarah's chair for her.

"Oh, yes, honey. I'm Mama." She handed them their menus. "Just a word about the steaks. You can get them any way you want them, but anything doner than medium has no guarantee whatsoever."

"Oh, Chris, I like this place. I can't believe it's been here all this time and I've never heard of it."

Chris looked up at the brands circling the room. "I wonder who brought your brand up here? Your dad maybe? Or your granddad?"

"One of the hands, more likely. They were the ones who liked going out on the town, such as it was. My parents and grandparents always stuck pretty close to home."

The steaks, ordered medium rare, lived up to Papa's reputation, and the sides—beans, slaw, and biscuits—were the perfect accompaniments. Finally, Sarah leaned back from the table and her completely empty plate.

"That had to be the best steak I've ever had. I am so full I'm about to pop."

"I have to say I am in awe." Chris grinned at her. "For such a tiny thing, you can really pack it in."

"You all about ready for dessert?" Their waitress appeared at the table. "We've got peach cobbler, berry cobbler, and chocolate cake."

Sarah groaned and Chris shook his head. "I think we're about done here, thanks. We really enjoyed the meal, though."

"I can see that." She put the check on the table and picked up the empty plates. "Well, I hope you all come back soon, and try to be hungry next time, you hear?"

"Well, that's embarrassing." Sarah slipped her jacket over her shoulders and headed for the door with Chris's hand gently resting in the small of her back. "Even the staff is commenting on what a pig I made of myself."

"No greater compliment than having someone scrape the design off the plate. And I speak as a professional." Chris took her jacket off her shoulders and held it so she could slip her arms into the sleeves.

She shivered when they went back into the mountain night, and he put his arm around her and held her close. "I'll get the heater on and we'll be warm in no time."

The ride back home seemed so much shorter than the ride to Papa's, and the conversation was even easier. Sarah watched Chris's profile, gently lit by the lights from the dashboard. She was glad they could be friends. She still had no idea what the final outcome with Brandon would be, but she had promised to see that through, and she intended to do just that. She hoped that didn't mean giving up this new friendship. Brandon had seemed to think that's exactly what it meant, but Sarah was sure once he knew Chris, he'd have to like him too. After all, what was there not to like?

As if he could feel her looking at him, Chris glanced over. He grinned. "What are you thinking?"

"Oh, lots of things. I was thinking that life can get so complicated when all you want is simple. I was thinking that someone a long time ago took a branding iron from the ranch and burned our brand into the wall, and I was trying to picture that night. And I was thinking that my jeans are about to cut me in two, and if you will kindly keep your eyes forward, I'm going to unsnap them so I can breathe."

A little later, when they stood on Sarah's front porch, she found that she wasn't quite ready for the evening to end.

"Can you come in for a cup of coffee?" She smiled up at him. "I've got pie."

Chris shook his head. "It's getting late, and I need to go rescue your grandma. Maybe next time."

"Gran's a real night owl. She's never in bed before midnight." Chris's comment about "next time" had not gone unnoticed. "Why don't we get the pie and take it down to her house? I can't wait to tell her about Papa's and the brand."

——∞——

Despite everything Sarah thought of to prolong it, the evening had finally come to a close. Chris lifted a pajama-clad Olivia from the bed in Elizabeth's guest room and draped her over his shoulder.

"You know, it would be the easiest thing in the world to just let her sleep." Elizabeth took the purple and lavender afghan from the back of the sofa and handed it to him to drape around Olivia. "I could give her some breakfast and she could ride to school with Sarah."

"I need to get her home." Chris smiled down at Elizabeth over his purple and lavender bundle. "But I can't thank you enough for letting her come over tonight. I think she was more excited than I was, and that's saying something." He winked at Sarah.

Sarah walked with him back down the street to his Jeep and stood next to the car while he propped Olivia up in a corner of the backseat and fastened the seat belt around her. When he straightened up and turned to her, she knew he was going to kiss her. She could read it in his eyes.

"No, Chris." She placed her hands on his chest when he took her in his arms. "I can't. You know that."

He took a deep breath, and she watched his face change. "Yeah, that was the deal, wasn't it? Sorry if I stepped out of line."

"No, listen." She couldn't let him leave thinking even one thing had gone wrong with the evening. "This was the nicest time I've had since I don't know when. I loved every minute of it. Really. I hope we can do this again."

"Sure. I'll give you a call."

Chris had changed. Sarah saw it in an instant. He waited by his car door until she reached her porch, and when she stopped to give him a last wave, he waved back and then drove away.

Not knowing whether she should be mad at herself, or Brandon, or even Chris, Sarah let herself in the front door. She just knew that what had started out as the world's most perfect evening had somehow gone south. Fishing her silenced phone out of her bag, she saw there were three missed calls and two messages, all from Brandon, and the first had come in at about 9:30.

"Nine-thirty, Brandon? For crying out loud." She carried the phone back to her room with her and tossed it on the bed. "You can just wait till tomorrow. It's late."

She heard the phone while she was brushing her teeth, and by the time she got back to her room, it had gone to voice mail. That would make message number three. She had a feeling that those messages would just keep coming all night till she took a call, so she stabbed at her phone with one finger and waited.

"Where are you?" Sarah couldn't tell if Brandon sounded mad or just worried.

"Right here, Brandon, at home. And it's past midnight. Why are we talking?"

"You said you'd call when you got home."

"No, I don't think I did."

There was a long pause, and Sarah was just about to say good night when Brandon spoke up again. He seemed to have decided to drop the attack.

"So, did you have a good time?"

"I had a great time. We ate at this little steak place up in the mountains that I didn't even know was there."

"Tell me about it." Brandon's cheerful interest sounded forced and also plain weird for 12:30 in the morning, actually 1:30 his time.

"Another time. I have school tomorrow and I need to get to sleep."

"Shall I call you tomorrow night?"

"Yes, do. I think we have a lot to talk about."

There was another long pause. "Okay. Sleep well, and I'll talk to you tomorrow."

Sarah had turned off the light and snuggled under the covers when her phone signaled an incoming text. As she groped for the phone and turned it over, the glow of the tiny screen lit the room. "DFILY." *Don't forget I love you.*

—⁓—

When Chris saw Sarah wave good-bye and go inside, he would have kicked himself if he could have managed to do that and drive too.

You couldn't leave a perfect evening alone, could you, Reed? She laid all her cards on the table before she even said she'd go out with you, and you agreed to it. Then you had to go and ruin everything.

He tried to picture this Brandon she was trying to work things out with. Smooth and sophisticated, no doubt. Made for the city. A man with a brilliant career and a bright future, and ready to lay it all at her feet.

A loud snort from the backseat drew his eyes to the rearview mirror. Olivia was slumped in the corner with her head thrown back, mouth hanging open, and a trickle of drool finding its way down her chin.

And what did Chris have to offer? A diner that made its way from month to precarious month while consuming his every waking hour and, at least for the time being, a wounded little girl who owned his heart and beat people up on the playground.

Some contest. He parked in the carport next to the yellow-and-white singlewide and opened the back door of his Jeep to carry Olivia inside.

22

Sarah kicked off her shoes at the door when she got home Monday afternoon and went to put the kettle on for tea. Sometime between now and the time she went to bed, Brandon would call, and she needed to think about what she was going to say to him. It would be so helpful to have someone to talk to, but her options in Last Chance were pretty slim. Chris was a great listener but hardly the right person for this conversation. She liked Megan, but Megan always did a whole lot more talking than listening. And then there was Gran—warm, wise, never judgmental . . . and her grandmother, for crying out loud. Who went to their grandmother for advice about men?

Me, I guess. Sarah sighed and dug for her phone.

"Hey, Gran." She tried to make her voice light and casual. Gran could spot a problem at a quarter mile. "Say, I thought I might come over after dinner for a little while, if it's okay with you. Maybe have some more of that pie, if you and Olivia haven't finished it off."

"Sure, honey. What's wrong?"

"Nothing's wrong." She laughed lightly. She tossed her hair too, for effect, but of course Gran couldn't see that. "I just wanted to come over for a bit."

"You can come right now if you want. Olivia's busy with her homework, but we can go out on the porch if you need some privacy."

"Gran, I don't need privacy." *Well, yes I do. Olivia's the last one I'd want to overhear me, which is why I'm not coming till after she goes home.* "I just want to visit. Now that school is taking up so much of my time and Olivia is taking up so much of yours, I don't get to see you as much as I'd like."

Sarah was starting to feel uncomfortable. What had begun as hedging was turning into outright fibbing, and fibbing to Gran had never been a good idea.

But Gran was ready to let her off the hook. "Okay, dear. I'll save you a piece of pie and see you after dinner. We'll have us a talk."

—∞—

After scrounging around in her refrigerator for something to call dinner and eating it while leaning against the counter, Sarah walked down the street. Gran was in her recliner watching one of her old detective reruns and crocheting. She smiled when Sarah came in.

"Hello, sweet girl. I've been waiting for you."

Sarah collapsed onto the sofa. "Oh, Gran, things are in such a mess."

Elizabeth rested her hands on the afghan in her lap. "Cut that television off for me, will you, darlin'? And then why don't you tell me what's in such a mess. I bet we can get something figured out."

Sarah did as she was asked and then plopped back on the sofa. She tucked her bare feet up under her and blew a gusty sigh. "I had such a good time last night."

Elizabeth just nodded.

"We just went as friends, of course." Sarah stroked Sam, who had jumped up next to her when she sat down. "But I think Chris would like for there to be something more."

"And what do you want?"

"That's just it. I don't know. I mean, I told you that when Brandon came over that time, I promised him I'd give things another try, just taking it a day at a time. I'm going to go see him Thanksgiving." She shot a quick look at her grandmother. "Don't worry, Gran. I'm staying in a hotel."

"It never occurred to me that you'd do otherwise."

"But now," Sarah went on, "I don't know what to do. Chris is such a great guy, and I have such a good time with him. I think I want to see where things go with him too."

"Do both men know about each other?"

Sarah nodded, feeling miserable.

"And what do they think?"

"Well, Chris accepts that I've made a commitment of sorts to Brandon, and he says he's willing to just go out as friends. But Brandon hates that I went to dinner with Chris last night. He called five or six times before I got home, and we sort of argued about that. He's going to call again tonight so we can talk things over some more. And really, Gran, I'm about ready to tell him I don't think we have any future together and he should stop calling."

The silence in the room grew until Sarah broke it. "So what do I do, Gran?"

Elizabeth picked up her crocheting again. "Well, you didn't ask who I thought was the better man for you, so I'm not going to say anything about that. But as for the predicament you did mention, as I see it there are several different issues. First, you made a commitment to Brandon. I'm not saying it's carved in stone, but the first thing you need to decide is what you're going to do about it. If you're sure Brandon's not the man God has for you, then tell him so plainly and let him get on with his life while you get on with yours."

"But that's just it, Gran. He might be the one. I'm just not sure yet."

"Well then, find out. Talk on the phone, write letters, go see him, and encourage him to come spend time with your family. Do a lot of praying on it. You thought he was the one at one point. And if you find his faith is real and not just a given like you said, maybe he is."

"But what about Chris?"

Elizabeth sat back and looked at her. "Honey, I just don't see how you can have it both ways. Brandon wants to marry you, and you have given him reason to think that might happen someday. So going around with Chris and pretending to yourself he's just a friend isn't right. It's not fair to Chris, and it's not fair to Brandon, and it's sure not fair to you. It's just tearing you up. So here's my advice, for what it's worth: go ahead and talk to Brandon tonight. If you decide to continue with him, then give it everything you've got until you know. That's the only honorable thing you can do. And that means no more dates with Chris Reed until you've decided one way or the other. If you decide to end things once and for all with Brandon, why, I can't think of a finer man to spend time with than Chris. Oh, shoot, I said I wasn't going to tell you which man I favored, and then I went and did it."

"Don't worry, Gran." Sarah's smile was sad. "It didn't come as a complete surprise."

Elizabeth went back to her crocheting. Sam laid a paw on Sarah's leg and hooked a claw in her jeans to remind her of her petting duties. After rubbing under his chin and scratching his ears for a few silent minutes, Sarah sighed again and got to her feet. "I just wish life didn't have to be so complicated."

Elizabeth just shook her head. "Well, it is, darlin'. And there you have it."

Sarah leaned over her grandmother's recliner and kissed the

cheek Elizabeth turned up to her. "I think I'll go on home. I need to do a lot of thinking before I talk to Brandon."

"Don't you want any pie?"

"No, I guess not. I'm just not in the mood for pie."

"Okay then, sweetie. Just be sure to spend some of that thinking time praying."

"I will."

"And don't forget, I'm right here if you need me."

Sarah stopped with her hand on the door latch and smiled at her grandmother. "You always are."

—⁂—

"Are we having macaroni and cheese for dinner?" Olivia wandered into the kitchen and leaned against the counter.

"Nope." Chris didn't look up from his cutting board.

"Awww. Why?"

"You know our rule. Macaroni and cheese once a week, and it's not due till Thursday."

"Mom let me have it any time I wanted it. Every night, even."

"Yeah, well . . ." Chris let his thought fade away without finishing it. "Why don't you set the table for us? Dinner will be ready in a minute."

"I want to eat on the coffee table and watch television."

"What's with you tonight, Livvy? We eat at the table, you know that." He turned toward the refrigerator and waited an instant for Olivia to move out of his way. She just stood there, looking at the floor.

"Livvy? Something wrong?" She sniffed, and Chris saw her shoulders heave. He squatted on his heels and waited for her to look at him. "What is it, honey?"

Her eyes were squeezed shut against tears that were finding their way out anyway, and her face was a mask of misery. At his touch, the floodgates opened. "I miss my mom."

Chris drew her into his arms and held her while she buried her face in his shirt and sobbed. After a couple minutes, he became aware that he was either going to have to stand up or going to fall over, so he picked her up and they moved to the sofa. Olivia hardly ever cried, and when she did, it never lasted, so it wasn't long before she was resting quietly against his chest, sniffing. Chris handed her a tissue.

It was the most natural thing in the world that a little girl would want her mother, and Olivia's stay with him had never been intended to be permanent. In fact, when Kaitlyn first took off, he'd found the arrangement to be inconvenient at best, as much as he loved Olivia, and heading downhill from there. But the two of them had done just fine, hadn't they? There had been a few rough spots, sure, most notably the fight at school, but things were looking up. She was doing better in school, loving her riding lessons, even making friends. She was happy, or least Chris had thought she was.

He leaned his head back against the sofa. *What do you know anyway, Reed? In less than twenty-four hours, you've managed to get both Sarah and Livvy heading for the hills. The only thing you haven't fouled up is the diner, but give it time. There's always tomorrow.* He straightened up and shook his head to clear it. *But you are pretty good at feeing sorry for yourself, I'll give you that.*

Olivia looked up at him to see what was going on, and he gave a straggly lock of her hair a little tug. "So you think we need to tell your mom it's time for her to come home?"

She nodded.

"Okay, here's what we're going to do. Just this once, we're going to have our dinner on the coffee table and watch television. But you need to set it with place mats and everything."

"And have macaroni and cheese?"

"No. Don't push it, kid. And then, after dinner, we'll try to call your mom. But you have to remember that she's already told us she's not coming back till spring. So she'll very likely say no. Got that?"

"Yep." Olivia jumped off his lap and ran for the place mats, as if hurrying dinner would hurry her mom's return.

Chris watched her go. He realized he hated the thought that Kaitlyn was going to return and take Olivia back home to Scottsdale. Kaitlyn was immature, selfish, and careless, but she did love her daughter, in her way, and would eventually want her with her. He didn't want to think about what that would mean for Olivia, both in the near and distant future. And if he were honest, he didn't want to think about what that would mean to him either.

—⁂—

When her phone rang at 11:00, Sarah was ready. She had thought, considering the way they left things the night before, that he might call earlier, but Brandon was not a random kind of guy. He called at 11:00.

Unless you're checking up on me. Sarah picked up her phone and curled up in a corner of the sofa. "Hi, Brandon."

"Hi." There was a long pause. Sarah waited. "I guess first I need to say sorry for all the phone calls last night."

"Well, that's a good place to start."

"I really thought you'd be home by 9:00 or so, since it wasn't a date or anything."

Was Brandon apologizing or taking shots?

"Anyway, when you didn't pick up, I thought maybe you were

just busy or saying good-bye to Chris or something, so I called again, and when you still didn't pick up, things just got a little out of hand."

"I'll say they did. What did you do? Hit Redial every time you hung up?"

"I guess that's how it seems. But it wasn't quite that bad. Anyway, I am sorry for the whole thing—the jealous jackass I was before you left, and all those pathetic phone calls while you were gone. That isn't me. And I give you my word that it's not someone you'll ever see again. Will you forgive me?"

"Of course I forgive you, Brandon." Sarah took a deep breath. This was not going to be easy. "But I've been doing a lot of thinking today, and praying, and I just don't think this is working. We're just in such different places in our lives—literally, figuratively, spiritually, any way you can think of."

"No. No, I don't think we are." Brandon cut her off. "Well, we're in different places physically, obviously, but that's the only problem I can see. The rest, no, I just don't agree with you at all."

"Brandon . . ."

"Let me finish. Please. These last few weeks have been hard on us both. We're both starting new jobs, new careers actually, and I don't know about you, but I'm finding I don't know a fraction of what I thought I did."

Sarah almost smiled. That was quite an admission coming from Brandon, but she had to admit to herself that she knew what he was talking about.

"And we live so far apart," he continued. "Things that we might not even notice, or that we could talk over, get blown way out of proportion because we can't be together—things like your dinner with a friend, or my having to change plans because of work."

"That's just what I'm talking about, Brandon. This long-distance thing just isn't working."

"And I say it can, if we give it a chance."

Sarah closed her eyes. "Brandon . . ."

"Look, when I get married, and I hope it's to you, it's going to be for keeps. That means that every single problem that comes up is going to have to be met head-on and dealt with. You can't run from them. Even I know that much. So, as I see it, this is just the first hurdle. I think we can clear it, and I don't want to give up until we know for sure."

"What if I think I already know?"

"Do you know, Sarah? For sure? I don't. Look, you've already made plans to come here for Thanksgiving. Let's give it till then. That's only about six weeks. If you still want to end things between us then, it'll kill me, but I'll know you gave it everything you had."

Sarah felt a twinge of conscience. Had she really given it everything she had? Or had she sort of taken Brandon's attentiveness for granted while she kept her options open?

She took a deep breath. "Until Thanksgiving?"

Sarah heard relief, maybe it was even joy, flood Brandon's voice. "Until Thanksgiving, that's all I ask."

Really, Brandon? That's all? It sure sounds to me like you're asking for a lot more than that.

"All right, then." Sarah smiled into the phone and willed her voice to catch up. "If, as you say, this is just the first of a lifetime of hurdles we're going to clear, then we should know by Thanksgiving."

"We're going to make it. Wait and see. This is going to be one of those 'you kids today have it easy' stories we tell our grandchildren."

Sarah laughed. Brandon's mood was infectious. "By then fifteen hundred miles will seem like nothing. Their long-distance romances will be between planets."

"Long-distance romance. I like the way you say that."

"Is it the long distance you like, or the romance?"

"You know the answer to that without my saying. I hate the long-distance part. And I want you to know that as of, well, last night, I'm butting out of your social life in Last Chance. I trust you implicitly, and that means if you want to go to dinner with Chris, go for it."

"Oh, I don't know." Sarah kept it breezy. "We had fun, but it was probably a onetime thing."

There was just a beat of silence before Brandon picked up the conversation again. "Well, okay, but it's totally up to you."

"Thanks, Brandon. Your confidence means a lot." She looked at her cat clock in the kitchen. "You know what? It is way late, even in Last Chance, and I need to get to bed. We'll talk again soon."

"Oh, one more thing. I was going to surprise you, but all things considered, I'd better let you know. I have a meeting in LA next Monday, and I thought I'd fly into El Paso Friday night and then go on to LA late Sunday. Are you free this weekend?"

"Oh, yes. I think we need a little face time."

"My thoughts exactly."

Sarah laughed. "That's not what I meant."

"We'll just see." Sarah could almost hear his grin. "I'll keep you posted on my flight times. Call you tomorrow at 11:00?"

"I'll be waiting." She heard him blow a kiss as she hung up.

Sarah sat for a moment holding her phone. This was not how she thought the call would go, but she was okay with it. In fact, she found she was actually looking forward to the weekend and having Brandon in Last Chance.

Turning out the light, she headed back to her room. On the way, her phone signaled a text. It was from Brandon: "DFILY." *Don't forget I love you.*

She hesitated a long moment before she sent her own text: "DFILY."

—⁂—

Chris turned off the television and tossed the remote on the coffee table. He had told Olivia she could wait up for her mom to return her call if she put on her pajamas and curled up on the sofa under a blanket. Olivia had been asleep since 9:00, and, of course, Kaitlyn had never called.

He turned out the light and scooped Olivia off the sofa, blanket and all. The princess movie he had put in for Olivia hadn't really captured his attention, and he'd had plenty of time to think things over as the evening went on. He had come to a couple of conclusions. First, as much as he loved his sister, she was beyond rotten as a mother, and he was going to do everything he could to keep Olivia. He didn't think Livvy stood a chance otherwise. And second, he wasn't all that crazy about this Brandon guy either. Chris had been around women in love, and to tell the truth, all of them seemed a lot happier about it than Sarah did. He was done worrying about stepping on some other guy's turf. If Brandon won the day, it would be because he was the better man. But it would not be because Chris hadn't given him the fight of his life.

He strode down the hall with Olivia in his arms and her blanket trailing behind. He had learned a long time ago that if something was worth having, it was worth fighting for.

23

Friday night was, hands down, Sarah's favorite time of the week. The school week was over, the weekend stretched out in front of her, and with the added ritual of frozen pizza for dinner and a good, scary movie, what was there not to love? Some Fridays, between the pizza and the DVD, she went to a football game at Last Chance High, which made the night perfect. Tonight the team was away, so it was just pizza, *Whisperer in the Wood*, and, of course, Brandon. But he wouldn't be getting in until late. And truthfully? That was okay with Sarah. She needed a little decompression time between school and Brandon.

She was into her second piece of pizza—and the part in the movie where the first girl, for some unfathomable reason, decides to wander through the woods by herself at night—when the doorbell rang. Sarah jumped about a foot, hit the Pause button on the remote, and opened the front door to find Rita on her porch.

"Sorry for just barging in like this. I tried to call a couple times, but you didn't answer."

Sarah looked around the room as she opened the door for Rita. "I guess my phone's still in my bag. Sorry. What's up?"

Rita held up a key hooked to a large red plastic tag with a seven on it. "I was hoping I could drop off Brandon's key. Other than him, my last guest has checked in, and I would love it if I could just go back to my apartment and turn in early."

"Sure." Sarah held out her hand for the key. "He's planning on stopping by to let me know he's here anyway."

"I thought he probably would. Good night, nurse, Sarah, what are you watching?" Rita's attention had been caught by the television, where the girl's face was frozen into a mask of sheer, addle-brained terror and her arm was thrust out to protect herself from some unseen horror.

"Oh, Rita, you caught me. Scary moves are my secret vice, developed young to prove to my brothers that I was as tough as they were."

Rita gazed at the screen a moment longer before shaking her head. "Well, as secret vices go, I suppose that's not a particularly bad one. But I have to say it's not one I would have thought about you having."

"Well, now you know." Sarah grinned. "What about you, Rita? Any secret vices you want to confess?"

"Now, if I did that, they wouldn't be secret, would they?" Rita headed for the door. "Be sure to give Brandon a big 'Welcome to Last Chance' from me, will you? And ask him to stop by the office in the morning so we can get him checked in."

"I'll do that." Sarah tossed the key on the mantel and went back to her sofa. She picked up the remote, hit Play, and jumped another foot as the scream ripped through her living room.

She had finished the movie and most of the pizza and had dozed off on the sofa when a tap on her front door brought her to her feet almost before she knew she was awake. She stood swaying next to the sofa, trying to figure out what was happening. Another tap. Brandon.

It hadn't taken very long, maybe five minutes, after she hung up from talking to Brandon Monday night to wonder if she hadn't just made a big mistake, and she hadn't repeated the DFILY text despite the fact that one had appeared on her phone every night since within seconds of Brandon saying good night.

But now that he stood before her in his rumpled suit pants and dress shirt with the sleeves rolled up, she realized to her surprise that she *had* missed him and that she really was glad to see him.

"Hey there! I thought you were going to call once you got on the road out of El Paso." Sarah returned his warm hug but turned her head just a bit so his kiss fell on the corner of her mouth.

"I tried to." If Brandon was disappointed with his reception, he gave no sign. "You didn't pick up."

"Oops, I never did get my phone." Sarah dug through her bag and held up her phone. "Silenced too, of course. Sorry."

She couldn't help taking a quick look at the call log. Only one message. Maybe Brandon was ready to stop hovering after all.

"Come sit down." Sarah pointed toward the sofa. "Are you hungry? I could heat up that pizza."

"No, thanks, I bought a sandwich on the plane." Brandon sat down and picked up the DVD case. "Another action-packed Friday night, I see."

"Hey, it's how I know it's Friday. Would you rather I had been out looking for a party? Not that I would have found one." She laughed as she sat down beside him. "Stubble's gone, I see."

Brandon rubbed his jaw and made a face. "Yeah, the company likes a clean look, so I just shave like everyone else now."

"Well, I'm glad. I think you look a lot more handsome this way." She leaned over to kiss his cheek, but when he turned to her, she moved away.

"I'm sorry. I really am glad you're here. But I'm just not ready to . . ." She searched for words. "To pick up as if nothing had ever changed between us. I still need more time."

"I see. Well, I noticed you only answered one of my texts. I was hoping you weren't getting cold feet again." His smile looked a little weary as he took both her hands. "But listen, that's why I'm here. I love you and I believe you love me too. And if you need a little time to figure that out for yourself, then time's what you've got."

"Thank you." It had never been a question of loving Brandon. It was all about whether they could be happy together, but Sarah was just too tired to go into all that now. "Rita brought over your key, but she wants you to swing by the office tomorrow to check in. I'll bet you're beat."

Brandon took the hint and got to his feet. "It *is* late, but I'd like to take you and your grandmother out for breakfast tomorrow. Can I pick you up about 9:00?"

"Sure. I'd like that. And I'm sure Gran would too, but if you want her to come with us, you'd better make it 10:00. She likes a bit of a slow morning."

"Okay, 10:00 it is. Is this the key?" He took it off the mantel and stopped at the door. His smile was tender. "Good night, sweet Sarah. Sleep well, and I'll see you in the morning."

Sarah crossed the room, and without quite knowing how it happened, she found herself in his arms. He bent his head and brushed her lips with the lightest of kisses, and this time she didn't turn away.

———

"So, Carlos, when are you going to eat a plate of mole verde like you promised?"

The Dip 'n' Dine was nearly full, but a busy room always energized Chris.

"What?" Carlos ladled green chile sauce over three plates of huevos rancheros simultaneously without spilling a drop. "Don't know what you're talking about."

"Yeah, you do. You said if we had even five orders for the mole, you'd eat a plate yourself, right in the front window. Well, I had more than ten times that, so when's it going to be?"

"Oh. I already had some." Carlos never even looked up from his work.

"You did? When?"

"Took some home that night."

"And?"

"Not bad."

Coming from Carlos, that was high tribute. He never bragged about his cooking; he didn't have to. Everyone else did it for him. But then he never praised anyone else's either. That would be false humility.

Chris hid his smile as he went back into the dining room. He'd get something new on that menu yet. The smile did a pretty good job of hiding itself, though, when he got out there. The Saturday waitress was showing a party of three to a booth—Elizabeth, Sarah, and some smooth-looking guy who could only be Brandon. Elizabeth had mentioned that Brandon was coming for the weekend when Chris had picked Olivia up after school Wednesday. He tried to figure out how Elizabeth felt about it, but she had been pretty noncommittal about the whole thing. And here he was—Brandon himself. Chris busied himself with something or other until they had their menus and water and then went over to their booth.

"Good morning, Elizabeth, Sarah. Good to see you." He smiled at Brandon, and an unspoken *And you are?* hung in the air. Chris knew, all right, but Brandon didn't have to know that.

"Chris, this is Brandon Miller. I know I've told you about him. Brandon, this is Chris Reed."

"Pleased to meet you." Chris extended his hand. "Are you in town long?" *Came in last night, going on to LA Sunday night.*

"Just for the weekend. Leaving tomorrow night." Brandon shook Chris's hand. He had a strong grip, but then, Chris may have put a little extra muscle behind his handshake too.

"That's a long way to come for a short visit." *But don't prolong your stay on my account.*

"Ah, she's worth it." Brandon rested his arm along the back of the booth and smiled at Sarah. "Besides, we've always been able to pack a lot into a short time, haven't we?"

Before Sarah could answer, Brandon went on. "Which reminds me, Sarah told me all about that steak place you went to last week. Sounds like kind of a fun place, so I thought we'd go back tonight." He grinned. "That way she'll have something to compare those great Chicago steaks to when she comes to see me next month. Can you tell me how to find it? She said it was out in the boonies."

"Yeah, it pretty much is, but it's not hard to find. I'll write out the directions for you."

"Outstanding." Brandon picked up his menu with his free hand and started looking at it. "Say, can we get some coffee? And I take cream."

"Sure thing. I'll get it right over." Chris walked away. *Score: Brandon 1, Chris 0.* He stopped the waitress and told her that table 4 needed coffee and might be ready to order.

The Dip 'n' Dine stayed busy, and it wasn't too hard for Chris to be elsewhere in the diner and yet not look as if he were actually

243

avoiding Sarah's table. Finally, though, he could see they were getting ready to leave, so he thought he'd better stop by.

"How was your breakfast? Everything okay?"

"Delicious, Chris. It always is." Elizabeth smiled up at him. "Tell Carlos I said so, would you, please?"

"I surely will." He handed Brandon a hand-drawn map. "Here are the directions to Papa's. How long did it take us to get there, Sarah? An hour, maybe?"

Brandon made no move to take the slip of paper. "I guess we're not going to need it, after all. Sarah said she'd rather go somewhere else." He shrugged and started to slide out of the booth. "Any other suggestions?"

Chris thought a minute and then shook his head. "Sorry, can't think of a thing. Oh, wait, I think an all-you-can-eat buffet just opened in San Ramon. I haven't tried it myself, though." *You're on your own on this one, Miller. Sorry, but I'm not planning your romantic evening for you.*

"Well, when you two figure out where I want to have dinner, be sure to let me know." Sarah had followed Brandon out of the booth. "Or here's a thought. You could ask *me*."

Brandon laughed and gave her shoulders a one-armed squeeze. "Sorry. Any place you want to go. Just name it."

He turned to Chris and extended his hand again. "Chris, it was a pleasure. I always like coming into the Dip 'n' Dine when I'm in the area, so I imagine I'll see you again."

"I hope so."

Chris took his hand, and again the grip was a little too strong and lasted a shade too long. There was not a doubt in Chris's mind that if he chose to, he could bring Brandon Miller to his knees with his handshake. But in the end, it was Brandon who was offering his arm to Elizabeth and leaving with Sarah. All Chris could do was watch them go.

—⁓—

"We've got the whole day in front of us. What shall we do?" Brandon got back in the car after seeing Elizabeth to her door and started the engine.

"I hadn't thought about it." Sarah raised an eyebrow. "I just assumed you had the whole day planned. That's been your style."

"That was then. This is now. The day is yours. Anything you want to do, we'll do."

"I don't know." Sarah was exasperated, more with herself than with Brandon. How many times had she seethed because he always had everything planned and just assumed she'd like it? Now here he was, just waiting for her instructions, and she couldn't think of a thing.

He laughed and shifted into Drive. "Okay, how's this plan? Let's pick up some sandwiches in San Ramon and then just head out. When we're ready for lunch, we'll find a place to have a picnic. And for dinner, we'll just see what's around. If it's white tablecloth, we've lucked out. If all we can find is drive-through, then we'll just eat there."

Sarah looked at him like she'd never seen him before. "Who are you? And what have you done with Brandon?"

"Told you." He drove away from the curb in a smooth motion. "I'm a new man."

The day could not have been more perfect. Brandon drove to the sandwich shop like he had been there a hundred times. They stashed their sandwiches and bottles of tea in a small cooler Brandon took from his trunk.

"I borrowed this from Rita this morning. Wasn't sure we'd need it, but you never know." He put the cooler back in the trunk and slammed it closed.

They spent the rest of the day wandering. Brandon, who never liked to venture forth without a map, was the one who said, "Let's try this road" and "Why don't we see where this goes?" They had their lunch in a shady park in one of the little towns they drove through, and when it was time for dinner, they indeed found a white tablecloth restaurant. The same one, in fact, Brandon had taken her to the last night before he left for Chicago. Things had changed a bit. The patio tables had been taken inside for the season, and they had already begun clearing away the mesquite and sagebrush for the new retirement community, but somehow the changes didn't seem to be quite the outrage Sarah had felt them to be earlier. Change, as Gran had tried to tell her, didn't start and stop like a faucet; it was continuous, like a river.

Sarah floated on a cloud of well-being all the way home. It felt like their college days. She had not been looking forward to Brandon's visit this weekend, but it had really gone well—at least so far. Oh, the chest bumping between Brandon and Chris that morning at the Dip 'n' Dine hadn't gone unnoticed, but Sarah had grown up on a ranch and had brothers. She wasn't too perturbed by that. They'd get over it.

She could smell the wood smoke in the air when she got out of Brandon's car in front of her house. Someone nearby had a fire going. It was getting to be that time of year. The days were still warm, but at night the temperatures were already dipping into the forties. She shivered.

"Cold?" Brandon put his arm around her and drew her close as they walked toward her door. "We should have stopped by for a jacket when we took your grandma home."

"Brandon, if you had planned every minute of this day, you couldn't have done a better job. It was everything I love."

"I'm glad. I want you to be happy." Brandon stopped at the front door and lightly rubbed her arms. "You'd better get inside. It's cold."

"Aren't you going to come in? Maybe for some coffee?"

He looked into her face a long moment before answering. "Nope. It *was* a perfect day, and I want to leave you with that. I'll pick you up for church tomorrow."

"And then lunch at the ranch? Mom was so pleased you wanted to come out to see them."

"I'm looking forward to seeing them too." He slipped his arms around her waist. "I guess we'll have to take two cars. I'm going to have to leave for the airport right after lunch."

"It was a short trip. But I'm glad you came."

He tightened his arms around her waist, but when she looked up, he didn't kiss her. He looked deep into her eyes and smiled at what he saw there.

"Me too. Now, go inside before you freeze."

Inside, Sarah stood in the window and waved as Brandon got in his car and drove way. She would never have believed it, but he did seem to have changed, at least enough to have one spontaneous day. A day like this one, where they just followed the road, would never have occurred to the Brandon she knew.

She hummed a little tune to herself as she went to put the kettle on. When she stopped to try to figure out what she was humming, she recognized it as one of Chris's jazz pieces.

24

It had not been Chris's best Sunday since he came to Last Chance. First of all, Olivia had climbed out of bed on the wrong side and refused to get ready for Sunday school. She had begun to get along a little better with the other kids, but she'd never be Miss Congeniality, and today she was clearly not up to making the effort. Chris finally had told her that a week without Sunday school was a week without a riding lesson, and she had complied. But as she headed back to her room to get dressed, she gave him a look that said she thought he was playing dirty and she wouldn't forget it.

Then the whole Cooley clan turned up for church. Sarah's parents, Joe Jr., and Nancy Jo, didn't make it to church on a real regular basis because they lived so far from town, but today they came. And with Elizabeth, Sarah, and Brandon, of course, they took up the whole pew. Brandon sat squarely in the middle of the group and held a hymnbook with Sarah. Chris sat on the other side of the aisle near the back.

After the service, while others moved forward to meet the young man sitting with Sarah, her parents, and her grandmother, Chris left the sanctuary by the side aisle and went to collect Olivia, who was in no better mood when he picked her up than when he'd left her.

She didn't do more than roll her eyes when he tried to ask about Sunday school, and he gave up after a couple tries. Even after they got home, she still gave him the silent treatment.

"What'll we have for lunch?"

Olivia shrugged and looked out the window.

"How about some macaroni and cheese?"

She looked at him then and answered in a voice dripping with scorn. "It's not Thursday."

"Sometimes life calls for a little mac and cheese even if it's not Thursday, don't you think?" Chris took a box from the cupboard.

"With hot dogs cut up in it?" She seemed almost ready to let him back in her life.

"Why not?"

"And with two, I mean, three cookies for dessert?"

He just looked at her. "You're pushing it, you know that, don't you?"

A real smile broke through, and she threw her arms around his waist. He placed his hand on her head and stroked her hair. Maybe there was a time in his life when problems could be remedied by mac and cheese with hot dogs and cookies, but for the life of him, no matter how far back he searched, he couldn't remember that time.

Chris felt a little better later that afternoon, mainly because Olivia seemed to. He was lying on his sofa watching a football game when his phone rang.

"Kaitlyn. It's been awhile." He sat up and hit the Mute button on his remote.

There was a pause. Usually he let Olivia answer when her mom called.

"Olivia called. I'm just calling back."

"You mean last Monday? You must have had a busy week."

"Gosh, was it Monday? Are you sure? Wow. Well, better late than never, I guess. Can I talk to her?"

"I'll get her in a minute. I want to talk to you first."

"Oh no, what'd she do this time?"

"Actually, she's doing pretty well. I think she's starting to settle in. She loves horses and drawing. She's even had a friend or two over to play."

There was a long pause. "I miss her."

"She misses you too. That's why she called. Are you ready to come home?"

Another long pause. "Kaitlyn?"

"I'm here, just thinking." He heard her sigh. "I don't know, Chris. I do love Livvy so much, and I miss her. But when I remember how it was, how I could never go anywhere or do anything, I just don't know if I'm ready to take that up again. Not yet."

"I get that." He chose his words carefully. "I know how much you love Livvy. And I'm just now learning how much work it takes to raise a little girl."

"And you've just been doing it a couple months. Try seven years."

Chris had only a second for prayer, but *God, please help me here* had seen him through a lot of tough times in the past. "You were so young seven years ago. I remember how scared you were. But you were determined to have Livvy and be the best mom you could be. I was proud of you."

"And I've really messed up, haven't I?" Kaitlyn's voice was matter-of-fact and sad.

"You had Livvy, and what a gift she's been to all of us. I know you didn't get a lot of encouragement to choose that route. I remember Mom especially telling you what a foolish choice you were making. She was pretty adamant too, but you wouldn't be persuaded."

"You were with me. You were the only one."

"Yes, and then I moved to New Mexico and left you to do it yourself, didn't I? Great support."

"Don't say that. I've always been able to count on you. Even when I was little, I knew you were there."

"Then let me be here for you now." Chris repeated his prayer. *God, please help me here.* "I know you wanted to be a good mom, and we both know that hasn't always happened. So let me take that load off your shoulders now. Let me be the one who sees to it that Livvy has everything she needs."

"But you already . . ." Kaitlyn's voice trailed off as the meaning of Chris's words sunk in. "Wait. You mean for good?"

"I'm not talking about adopting her, if that's what you're worried about. You're her mom and always will be. I'm talking about taking legal responsibility for Livvy. You've always said you never had the chance to be young, to really grow up. This will give you that chance. And Livvy will have the stability she needs too. Add that to the love she'll have from both of us, and it sounds like a win-win to me. What do you think?"

In the silence that followed, Chris heard Kaitlyn sniff and knew she had started crying. He waited a moment. "Kaitlyn? Tell me what you're thinking."

"I do love Livvy. You know that, don't you?"

"Of course I do."

"Then why can't I be a good mom?"

"Kaitlyn, listen to me. What good moms do is put their children first. You did that when you had Livvy after everyone told you how much easier it would be not to. Letting her stay here with me is putting her needs before your own feelings too. Both of those decisions show a different kind of good mom than we're used to thinking about, but they're good mom decisions nonetheless."

"And I can see her whenever I want?"

"We'd both love to have you here as often and as long as possible."

"I'd still be her mom?"

"And I'd still be her Uncle Chris."

Chris had to listen carefully because Kaitlyn was crying in earnest, but he did hear her "okay."

"Don't cry. I think you're going to see that all this is the best thing we can do for Livvy, and for you too. You two are still the most important people in my life, you know."

"So what are you going to do next?" Kaitlyn sniffed and sucked in a long, shaky breath to steady her voice.

"I'll become Livvy's legal guardian, which means I'll be responsible for her welfare until she's eighteen or until we revisit this sometime down the road. I'll start tomorrow by making some calls. And I'll keep you posted every step of the way, okay?"

"Okay." Her voice was stronger now.

"You've made a brave decision, Kaitlyn, and a good one for Livvy. I'm proud of you. Now, blow your nose and pull yourself together. Livvy has been waiting for this call, and I know she wants to talk to you." He waited while she blew. "And Kaitlyn? Let me be the one to talk to Livvy about this, okay?"

"Okay."

Chris walked back to Olivia's room and tossed her the phone. "It's your mom."

As he went back to the living room, he heard Olivia's voice chirping into the phone. As sure as he was that he had taken the right step, he was equally sure he was completely ill equipped for the task. As he settled back on the sofa, he sent up his prayer one more time. *God, please help me here, because I sure can't do this on my own.*

—⁓—

Sarah had just slid her desk chair under her desk, slung her tote over her shoulder, and headed for the door after school the next afternoon when Chris stuck his head in.

"Are you busy?"

"I was just getting ready to head home. But come in. What's going on?"

"I hoped I'd catch you before you left. Sorry to drop in like this, but coming by after dropping Livvy off at your grandmother's is about the only time I can talk without Livvy around. Why don't I just walk you to your car?" He reached for Sarah's tote. "Let me carry that for you."

Sarah surrendered her tote, as much surprised at herself for doing so as she was surprised by Chris's gesture. She would have said she was perfectly able to carry her own belongings, and she was, but it seemed somehow natural for Chris to lift it off her shoulder and sling it over his own. He held her door open for her, and as she passed his shoulder, she looked up, still wondering why he'd come by.

He gestured with his chin toward the outside door down the hall to indicate he'd wait till they got outside before he'd talk, and she smiled to herself. Chris might have thought he was being discreet, but carrying her books silently down the hall like a shy middle schooler was anything but. There were still a few teachers in their classrooms who looked up as they trudged past.

"Okay, what's up?" Sarah waited till they reached the parking lot before breaking the silence.

"Sorry for all the mystery." Chris grinned down at her. "I haven't talked to Olivia yet, so I didn't want to be overheard. But since you're her teacher I thought you should know that I'm filing for permanent guardianship of Olivia. I talked to her mom yesterday, and we both agreed it was the best thing we could do for her."

"Really?" Sarah's face split in a huge smile. "That's tremendous news. Olivia is a different little girl from the one I met last summer, and I've got to believe that's because she's been with you. I only know a little about the life she was living before, but thinking she could go back to that at any time just tore me up. I know teachers aren't supposed to have favorites, but that little girl has had my heart from the get-go."

"It hasn't just been me." They had reached Sarah's car, and Chris put her tote in the backseat. "You've played a huge part in her life, so has Elizabeth, and even Juanita and Carlos have been there for her. And to tell the truth, if I were alone in this, I'd still do it, but with a whole lot more trepidation. I'm going to need all the help I can get. You don't need to tell Juanita I said that, though. She doesn't need any more encouragement."

Sarah gave him a quick hug. "Well, you've got it. We're all here for you. And we're praying for you too. So there's no need for all that trepidation."

"Thanks. I appreciate it." Chris did not look at all eager to go, but glancing at his watch, he shrugged. "I guess I'd better get back to the Dip 'n' Dine. They'll wonder where I am."

"Wait. I just wanted to say one thing." Sarah put her hand on Chris's arm as he started to leave. He stopped and raised a questioning eyebrow. "Remember last Saturday when Brandon and I were at the diner and he told you he didn't need the map to Papa's you drew after all because I didn't want to go back?"

"Yeah."

"Well, it wasn't that I didn't love Papa's. I hope you know I did. I just didn't want to go there with Brandon. I knew that it wasn't his kind of place, and I just couldn't bear to go there with him and listen to him get all snarky and critical. You knew that, didn't you?"

"I guess I hoped it was something like that. I did think you had a good time when we went." Chris leaned against her car. "So where did you end up going?"

As Sarah gave him a quick rundown of the day she and Brandon spent wandering aimlessly through the countryside and ending up at the restaurant outside Silver City, Chris smiled and nodded.

"I saw that day trip. It looked like fun. Livvy and I'll have to do it one day too."

"What?" Chris wasn't making any sense.

"I wasn't all that familiar with *Western Home and Garden* magazine, so I picked up a copy after the food editor came by the Dip 'n' Dine, and it was the issue with the day trips in southern New Mexico. The one that you and Brandon took looked to me like the best one. I'm glad it measured up to the copy." He looked at his watch again. "I really do have to go. Juanita and Carlos will be sending out a search party or, worse yet, figuring out they really don't need me. Just wanted to tell you what's going on with Livvy."

"And I couldn't be happier. Thanks so much for coming to tell me." Sarah tried to smile as she watched him cross the parking lot. Her mom subscribed to *Western Home and Garden*. She'd have to get the copy Chris referred to. It wasn't so much that Brandon had followed a day trip from a magazine. In fact, it might have been fun for the two of them to look at the article he found and decide together which trip they wanted to take. It was that he had led her to think that it was all spontaneous, had in fact lied to her about it, that made her feel so foolish. She had even congratulated him on his newfound ability to ease up on the reins, and he had accepted her praise as his due. How naïve he must think her—a real country bumpkin, incapable of picking up a magazine and realizing she'd been lied to.

—⁓—

A cold wind blew up when the sun went down, tugging at yellow leaves still clinging to the cottonwood branches and sending tumbleweeds chasing each other down the empty street in front of Sarah's house. Occasionally an especially violent gust would shriek past her door or whine its way into her spare room through a tiny space left by a window that didn't fit perfectly into its casing. Sarah knew that the sound of incessant wind put some people on edge, but she didn't get it. The nights she spent as a child snuggled in bed listening to the wind's unsuccessful assault on the walls of her life had left her with a sense of peace and well-being whenever she heard it howl.

A fire, the first of the season, crackled in her fireplace, and she curled up on the sofa under one of her grandmother's crocheted afghans and sipped from a mug of tea. She was still furious and hurt that Brandon had tried to make her believe their drive Saturday had been a careless ramble when in fact he had not only read it somewhere but memorized it. She was also beyond embarrassed that she had fallen for it so completely. But as the evening wore on and she added another log or two to her little fire while the wind outside howled around the corners of her house, she found it harder and harder to stay as mad as she wanted to be when she confronted him. After all, she had known for years that Brandon was not a spontaneous person. Almost, in fact, from the time they met. And if he had gone to such lengths to present himself otherwise, it could only be because he thought that's what she wanted. So who was trying to change whom? Of course, nothing altered the fact that he had concocted, and fed her, an elaborate lie, and she had no intention of letting that pass. Maybe she could learn to live with someone who loved a structured life, but no way could she live with someone she could not believe.

When her phone rang at 11:00, Sarah was still tucked under her afghan in a corner of her sofa, watching the last logs of her fire collapse into glowing embers.

She picked up her phone and settled herself a bit more comfortably. This could be a long and unpleasant conversation. "Hey, Brandon."

"Hey, babe." Brandon sounded like he was trying to be cheerful. "I've been thinking about you all day. I miss you already."

"I've been thinking about you too."

"That sounds promising." His voice picked up a trace of enthusiasm, and Sarah could almost see him smile.

"Well, Brandon . . ."

"Wait." He interrupted her. "Before you say anything, I've got to get something off my chest."

"Okay, what?" Sarah didn't think she could take many more surprises from Brandon today.

"That day trip we took on Saturday? It didn't quite happen like I let you think it did."

"Oh?"

"I wanted it to be the best day you've ever had, and since I don't know the area that well, I did some research. I got the idea for the trip from a magazine."

It took Sarah a second to regroup her thoughts. She certainly hadn't expected to begin this way. "But why did you let me think you were making it up as we went along?"

"I didn't mean to. I was just going to surprise you, but then you started telling me you didn't even know who I was, and you seemed so happy. I just couldn't give that up. I know I owe you a big apology. And I am sorry. I just couldn't base what I know is going to become one of my all-time favorite memories on a lie."

Sarah waited a moment. The day had been lining up to be one of her all-time favorite memories too, but that was gone, and nothing Brandon could say now was going to bring it back. She cleared her throat. "Thank you for telling me, Brandon. I know it was hard, and it means a lot that you did."

"I have to be honest with you, babe. If we don't have that, we don't have anything."

"No, no I guess we don't."

"So do you forgive me?"

"Of course." She had been preparing what she would say all evening, but so, it appeared, had Brandon.

"Terrific." She could hear the relief in his voice. "I can't tell you how great that makes me feel. I can't wait until Thanksgiving."

"I feel better too." Yes, Brandon had let her believe a lie, even if that hadn't been his original intention, but he couldn't let it stand. He had to tell her the truth. Didn't that prove something?

Brandon rang off, claiming a 6:00 a.m. flight back to Chicago in the morning. She set the fireplace screen firmly in place, turned out the lights, and headed to bed.

Just as she was drifting off, an image from yesterday floated across her consciousness and jolted her to wakefulness. She and Brandon sat on the sofa at the ranch after lunch, and in front of them a fan of magazines was spread across the coffee table. She had paid no attention, but *Western Home and Garden* usually held pride of place. Had Brandon seen it there yesterday? Had he confessed to his deception because he thought he'd likely be found out anyway? She'd never know, of course, but doubt crept in again, and not even the lullaby of the wind could carry her off to an easy sleep.

25

You know, I think this is the first Thanksgiving I'm not going to have all my children around the table."

Sarah and her mother sat at the big kitchen table shelling pecans the Saturday morning before Thanksgiving. Nancy Jo's sister in Las Cruces sent a big sack of pecans from their trees every fall, and for Sarah, shelling them with her mom had always heralded the approaching holidays.

"Really? Kimberly and Michael have never gone to his folks?" Sarah stopped to sweep some shell fragments into the big paper bag under the table.

"Not for Thanksgiving. Well, I guess it was bound to happen sometime." Nancy Jo never bothered much with crying over spilled milk. She got up to refill their coffee cups. "You are going to be here for Christmas, though, right?"

"Of course. I'm not moving to Chicago. Just going for Thanksgiving."

"Well, you never know. I'm bracing myself against the day you just up and move away. Chicago is so far away. I'm afraid I won't even know my own grandchildren."

"Mom." Sarah put down her nutcracker and pick and looked into her mother's eyes. "I'm not going to up and move away. I just got back to Last Chance and I like it here. And I don't know what grandchildren you're talking about, but you seem to know all of them pretty well. So I wouldn't waste any more time worrying about it."

"I still say you never know, Miss Priss." Nancy Jo scooped shelled pecans into a measuring cup and then poured them into zip-top bags. "You've been mincing around for weeks saying you didn't know what you were going to do about Brandon. And I say that's a lot of nonsense. If you don't *know* you love a man enough to spend your life with him, then you do know that you don't."

"What? Want to run that by me again?"

"You know exactly what I mean. You have to be one hundred and fifty percent positive that you're in love, or just let it go. Life's hard enough as it is. I never, to this day, have had a moment's doubt that your dad was the one, and I still want to shake him half the time."

"Maybe if either one of you had ever dated anyone else, you might not have been so sure. You started going steady when you were, what, fifteen?"

"When you know, you know. That's all I'm saying."

"Okay. Message received." Winning an argument with her mom was not any easier than winning one with Gran, and sometimes all Sarah could do was agree. They shelled pecans in silence for a while.

"How is Brandon, anyway? It was nice having him here for lunch when he was in town last month. I always thought he was a little hard to know, but he was just as pleasant as he could be."

"I guess he's doing fine. He's had to do some traveling for his company this last week and I haven't been able to talk to him, but he should get home sometime this weekend."

"Well, tell him I said hi and that he's more than welcome at Christmas, if he wants to come."

"I'll tell him you said hi. We'll worry about Christmas later."

"Oh, I think it would be real interesting to have him here for Christmas." Nancy Jo smiled a half smile. "Your grandmother's talking about having that nice Chris Reed from the diner and his niece up for Christmas Day. She tried to get him to come for Thanksgiving, but he's got other plans, I guess."

"And what does that have to do with Brandon, anyway?" Sarah tried to stare her mother down, but Nancy Jo was too engaged in cracking and picking and measuring to stare back.

"You know," Sarah went on, "when I was thinking about coming back to Last Chance to teach, I couldn't come up with a single drawback. But I've got quite a list now, and it's growing."

Nancy Jo looked up and smiled. "I'm sorry, darlin'. Did you say something? I'm afraid I wasn't paying attention."

Sarah gave up and returned to the pecans. Truth be told, her family, as exasperating is it could be, was number one on her list of reasons to come back to Last Chance. They got in her business, teased her beyond endurance sometimes, and were awfully free with advice, solicited or not. But they stood in linked-arm unity between her and anything that might harm her, just as she joined the protective wall of family that surrounded each of them.

Her mom might appear to be taking Sarah's absence from the Thanksgiving table this year lightly, but for Sarah it was a big deal. Next Thursday family and friends would gather around the two long tables set up in the dining room, just as they had every Thanksgiving of Sarah's life, and Sarah would be elsewhere. Knowing Brandon, she'd probably be at a cozy table for two in some popular Chicago restaurant eating something that had absolutely no connection to Thanksgiving whatsoever. She popped a few pecans into her mouth. He'd just better appreciate what she was doing for him, that's all.

"So when do you leave? Will I see you again before you go?" They had finally finished the shelling, and Nancy Jo was stacking the zip-top bags and rolling up the newspaper that had covered the table.

"Not unless you come to town, I'm afraid. I just have too much to do to get ready. I'm leaving straight from school on Wednesday."

"Well, we're going to miss you. And we'll be real interested to know how everything turns out. I know Thanksgiving was the make-or-break date you set for yourself."

"Who's this 'we' you're talking about who's so interested to know how things turn out?"

"Us. Your family. And we'll all be here having our pie Thanksgiving evening, so if you have an announcement to make or anything, why, just give us a call. We'll be waiting."

Sarah got to her feet and gave her mother a hug. "Well, don't wait. Because there's not going to be an announcement, I can promise you that. And in case you can't think of anything to talk about besides my love life, I'll make a list of topics and send it up with Gran. Now, I've got to go. I've got a ton of things to do."

Nancy Jo took her daughter into her arms and gave her a long hug. "I *will* miss you, sweet girl. It won't be the same without you. And for all the teasing I do, I want you to know that I am praying for you. Don't let anyone or any arbitrary date you set pressure you into making a decision you're not ready to make, you hear me? You have all the time in the world."

"Thanks, Mom." Sarah dug for her keys. "I'll call before I leave. And wish Dad a happy Thanksgiving for me, will you?"

"I will. Oh, and don't forget these." Nancy Jo grabbed some zip-top bags. "Would you take a couple of these to Gran? She's going to want to get started on her baking. And take one to Chris Reed too. I bet he'd appreciate it."

263

"Sure." Sarah gave her mom one last hug and headed for her car.

She was surprised to find herself batting back tears as she drove down the dirt road to the highway. *For Pete's sake, grow up, woman. It's just one Thanksgiving, not the rest of your life. Maybe Brandon is right; you do need to get out and see more of the world.* She bumped over the cattle guard and turned onto the pavement. *But I still say seeing more of the world on Thanksgiving was a really dumb idea.*

Olivia was in the lot next to the Dip 'n' Dine hitting at a scrubby bush with a stick when Sarah drove into the parking lot, and she ran to meet her. Sarah draped an arm across her shoulders.

"Hey there, Livvy. What're you up to?"

"Trying to find my lizard. I made it a home in a shoe box, but it got out and ran away."

"Well, lizards are tricky that way. Is your uncle inside? I have something for him."

"Sure." Olivia led the way into the diner. "Uncle Chris! Miss Cooley's here."

Chris looked up from the pie he was cutting and grinned. "Come on in. We're celebrating. Pie for everyone."

Sarah stopped just inside. "What's going on?"

"We're going to be in *Western Home and Garden* magazine, that's what's going on." Juanita, who appeared to have been having lunch with Russ, was helping the Saturday waitress distribute the slices. "Chris just got an email from that food editor, and they're going to do a whole article on the Dip 'n' Dine. Can you believe it?"

"Really?" Sarah looked at Chris for confirmation. She loved the Dip 'n' Dine. She had loved it all her life, but a whole article? In *Western Home and Garden*?

He nodded, still grinning. "Yep. They have a feature every month called 'Best of the Best' where they pick one thing in a western state—could be a park, or a plant nursery, or even a roadside stand—and call it the best of the best. Then they write an article about it."

"And next May, just in time for the next fiesta, they're writing about the best diner in the western states: the Dip 'n' Dine in Last Chance, New Mexico." Juanita looked like she could have turned a handspring.

"Chris, that's marvelous. Good for you."

He nodded. "They're sending a photographer out, and they've asked for the recipes for my mole verde and Carlos's chile rellenos. They want to make them home-cook friendly and feature them with the article."

"No one messes with my recipes." Carlos appeared in the window to the kitchen. If he was celebrating, he was doing it there, and from the looks of it, without pie.

Chris rolled his eyes. "Don't let him fool you. He's as pleased as the rest of us."

"Rita! We've got to call Rita. She'll bust out crying. I know she will." Juanita went for the phone, and everyone else in the diner turned to their pie.

"Well, this is certainly anticlimactic, but I brought you something." Sarah handed him the pecans. "These are from Mom—and my aunt Deb's pecan trees."

"That's nice." Chris turned the package over in his hand, looking a little puzzled. "How do I rate this?"

"Because you cook. Mom loves to share the wealth. I've got a couple bags for Gran too. I just wanted to drop these by before I left Wednesday. Great timing, though. Happy Thanksgiving and congratulations again. Sorry I don't have time for pie, but I still have a ton of things to do." She smiled up at him and opened the front door.

"That's right. Chicago for Thanksgiving." He and Olivia followed her out to her car. "That'll be different."

Sarah shrugged. "I'll say, but it's a little late to rethink now. What about you? Mom said they'd asked you to the ranch, but you've got other plans."

"Yes, we do. Although we certainly did appreciate the invitation, didn't we, Livvy?"

Chris did not seem inclined to elaborate, but Olivia piped up.

"We're going to cook a turkey. And make a pie from a real pumpkin."

Sarah raised a questioning eyebrow at Chris. "You're eating at home? You know there's always room at the ranch, and they meant it when they invited you."

The look Chris shot Olivia was both fond and exasperated. He put his hand on her head and waggled it. "Before your grandmother so kindly extended the invitation, I had promised Livvy we'd cook a Thanksgiving feast together. She's never had a traditional Thanksgiving dinner."

"Never?"

"No, my parents always took her and Kaitlyn out to their country club for holiday meals. So the little decorations she'd make in preschool or kindergarten never got used." He looked down at his niece. "But this year, we're going all out. Aren't we, kiddo?"

"You can come." Olivia grabbed Sarah's hand. "I'll make you a pilgrim hat too."

Sarah smiled at her. "That sounds like so much fun, and I'd love to, but I'm going out of town for Thanksgiving."

"I've already made the place mats, but I could make another one."

"I'm afraid I can't this year, Livvy. But you remember everything so you can tell me all about it when I get back, okay?" She gave them both a hug before she got in her car and started the engine.

Stopping by her grandmother's house to deliver the rest of the pecans and tell the good news about the Dip 'n' Dine, she found Gran planning all the dishes she was going to take to the ranch, and since Sarah was there, she wanted to go over the whole list with her, even though Sarah kept reminding her that she'd be in Chicago.

By the time she walked in her door and kicked off her shoes, Sarah had heard all she wanted to hear about Thanksgiving in Last Chance. She needed to hear Brandon tell her again about the wonderful weekend they were going to share. She glanced at her watch. He probably was still in the air on his way back from his business trip, but she could leave a message telling him she was going to be home all evening and he could call before 11:00 if he wanted.

Grabbing her phone and tossing a sofa pillow on the coffee table to cushion her feet, she stretched her legs out in front of her and crossed her ankles. She smiled to herself as she called Brandon's number. *My house, Mom. Feet on the coffee table if I want them there.*

When Brandon's phone started ringing, she composed a quick message in her mind. *Hi, it's me, and I can't wait to talk to you. So call as soon as you can.*

"Brandon's phone." A woman's voice.

Sarah opened her mouth and closed it again.

"Hello? Anyone there?" The woman's voice sounded impatient.

"Um, yes." Sarah found her own voice. "Is Brandon there?"

"He's not available right now. Who's this?"

"This is Sarah. Who are you? And where's Brandon?" What kind of game was this woman playing? And why was she answering Brandon's phone, anyway?

"Oh, he's up to his neck in mud right now, I'd say. But I'll certainly tell him you called. You wouldn't be his wife, would you?"

"His wife? No." Sara struggled to keep up with this conversation. Brandon wasn't married. Was this even the right Brandon?

"Okay. Well, I'm sure you'll be hearing from him."

"Wait!" But the voice was gone.

Sarah sat looking at the phone in her hand. Any second now it would come to life and Brandon's face would appear on the screen. He'd explain everything, maybe even have that woman get on the phone and tell Sarah that she was a co-worker and the world's lamest practical joker. But her phone lay in her hand like a dead thing. Finally she tossed it on the table, leaned back and covered her face with her hands.

There were a dozen possibilities that would innocently explain the phone conversation she'd just had, and she had no doubt that the story Brandon told would be a doozy. He had turned explaining his way out of trouble into an art form, and she, fool that she was, had helped him do it.

By the time her phone did ring, about an hour and a half later, she was almost disinterestedly curious about what he would say.

"Hi, babe!" He certainly sounded cheerful. "I just got off the plane and I'm headed for a taxi, but I needed to hear your voice. The trip was a bear."

"You have got to be kidding." He was going to pretend nothing had happened. Really?

"What?" Confusion. Bewilderment. Was that even pain in his voice?

"Give it up, Brandon. It's not going to work this time. Who was that woman, and what was she doing with your phone?"

"Honey, I don't know what you're talking about, but you sound a little nuts. Can we just back up and start over?"

Ah. The old no-sane-person-would-think-what-you're-thinking approach. Sarah knew that one well.

"Okay, Brandon, since you want to start over, we'll do it your way. One hour and forty minutes ago, I called you just to say I was looking forward to seeing you. A woman answered and said you couldn't come to the phone. She demanded to know who *I* was and asked me if I was your wife. So now that I've answered your questions, answer mine. Who was she and why did she have your phone?"

"Well, all I can say is that I've been on a plane for the last two hours and my phone has been in my pocket. You must have got a real joker of a wrong number."

"Brandon, you moron, do you think I sat here and poked in your number digit by digit? I did not get a wrong number. And exactly four days before I was coming to see you, you were with another woman. That is so sick."

Bandon was actually silent for a few seconds before he tried again. "Well, I don't know what could have gone wrong, but obviously something did."

"You got that right. But—and I thank God—it's not too late to fix it. I'm canceling my trip as soon as I hang up. Do not, and I mean *do not*, call me, or text me, and don't you dare turn up in Last Chance looking for me. I'll tell my relatives to shoot you on sight if you do."

"Oh, come on, Sarah. Don't you think you're overreacting just a little? Let me at least explain."

"You already did. Good-bye, Brandon."

"Sarah—"

Sarah held the Power button till the screen went blank before crumpling in a corner of her sofa and bawling. She had never been a particularly dainty weeper, and since no one could hear her anyway, she allowed herself to really let go. Three years! Three years of her life spent desperately trying to remain Sarah while Brandon with relentless persistence tried to shape her thoughts, her dreams, her looks, even her perception of reality. How could she have done that to herself? What could she have been thinking?

Finally, feeling totally spent and in dire need of a tissue, Sarah got up and padded down the hall for some toilet paper. Paying for her trip had completely depleted her tiny savings account and run up her credit card. She almost wished now that she had taken Brandon up on his offer to pay for everything. Then he'd be stuck with the bill, because she was pretty sure there'd be no refund from either the airline or the hotel, this being a holiday weekend. She unrolled a length and blew. Well, all things considered, if it saved her from making a mistake that she would regret every day for the rest of her life, it was a small price to pay.

Taking the roll with her, Sarah went back to her sofa. So she'd be home for Thanksgiving after all. And it looked like her love life wouldn't be the chief topic of discussion after all. No, it certainly would not, at least not when she was within earshot. All conversation would stop when she entered a room. She'd intercept tragic looks of compassion. This relative or that would find a moment to give her a squeeze and whisper that they never could stand Brandon anyway. Sarah shuddered. What a day she'd had. She'd gone from fighting back tears because she wasn't going to be spending Thanksgiving with her family to deciding that was the last place she wanted to be on Thanksgiving Day—well, the second to last. In between, she had completely eradicated Brandon from her life. And she had to admit that didn't feel as bad as she thought it might.

It took a can of chicken and rice soup, a long bath, officially canceling her travel plans—even though she did find out she was liable for the full cost—and blocking Brandon's number from her phone, but Sarah actually felt a little better by bedtime. She looked at her watch, decided it really wasn't all that late, and made one more phone call.

"Hi, it's me. Listen, I have two huge favors to ask. First, please don't ask any questions, and second, do you think you could ask Livvy to make me a pilgrim hat and a place mat, after all?"

She smiled as she hung up. Who knew "You got it" could be just what she needed to hear?

26

L ivvy, this cornucopia isn't going to work. It takes up the whole table, and we need at least some room for the food." Chris had no idea where she had seen one, but somehow Olivia had become convinced that a cornucopia was the only acceptable centerpiece for a Thanksgiving table. The problem was, their table was only about three feet by four, and even the smallest cornucopia they could find pretty much covered it.

"But we have to. There'll be room." Olivia picked up the tangerine that had rolled off the table and went back to trying to stuff it into the abundance of the cornucopia.

"Livvy. Listen." Chris squatted on his heels so he could hold her attention. "There is just not room on the table for this. I'm going to move it to the coffee table. I want you to turn it into the most beautiful, Thanksgivingy coffee table in the world. We'll do something else for the dinner table."

Olivia looked like she was digging in for the fight, so Chris got to his feet and turned her toward the table. "See, it's even covering up your place mats, and you worked too hard on them to hide them like that."

"But you're supposed to—" Olivia hardly ever cried, but Chris could see that this situation was escalating at a dangerous rate.

"Okay, what about this? We'll put the big cornucopia on the

272

coffee table, and then you can go get a piece of brown construction paper and the stapler and we can make a little one for the dinner table. Maybe just big enough for one apple, a tangerine, and some grapes. How would that be?"

Olivia considered his idea a moment and decided it would be an acceptable compromise. While she ran off to gather art supplies, Chris checked on his turkey. It was way too big for three people, of course, but Olivia had been as adamant about having a real turkey as she was about the cornucopia. And leftover turkey in the freezer was never a bad thing. He ladled drippings over the bird and checked the temperature. Perfect. Right where it should be for a 2:00 dinner.

Straightening, he looked around the room Olivia had decorated to a fare-thee-well. He had no idea that she had so much longing for celebration stored up in that skinny little body of hers. When it came pouring out, he gave her free rein and stood back. No telling what she'd do when she started in on Christmas.

"Okay, here." Olivia was back and handing him the paper and stapler. "I tried, but I couldn't make it work."

In a deft motion, Chris rolled the paper into a cone and stapled it. "Here you go."

Olivia grabbed the cone and went to create her centerpiece while Chris ran a sink full of suds and rolled up his sleeves. Sarah was due in an hour, and the place looked like a bomb had gone off.

He wondered why she wasn't in Chicago as she had planned to be. Unless she told him, he'd never know, of course, since he had promised not to ask any questions, but he was okay with it, whatever the reason. There was something about this Brandon guy that he just didn't like, and he didn't think it was entirely because of his history with Sarah. Brandon was too slick, too smooth,

273

and it could have been just for Chris's sake, but his attitude said, "I *own* this woman, so back off." He didn't deserve someone as remarkable as Sarah.

Of course, if pressed, Chris would have to admit that he probably didn't deserve someone as remarkable as Sarah either. But he'd spend his life trying, if given the opportunity, and Brandon acted like Sarah was the lucky one.

"Are you going to help me with this, or what?" Olivia was trying to move the cornucopia to the coffee table and spreading its contents over the floor in the process.

"Just hang on." Chris grabbed a dish towel to dry his hands. "Sorry, I got distracted. And you need to learn to ask for help politely, which would be, 'Would you please help me, Uncle Chris?'"

Olivia rolled her eyes and sighed. Chris put his hand on the cornucopia, anchoring it to the dining table, and waited.

She sighed again. "Would you please help me, Uncle Chris?"

"Glad to." He transferred everything to the coffee table. "Now are you good to set this up?"

Already in deep concentration, Olivia just nodded, and Chris went back to his cleanup. A half hour later he took the turkey out of the oven, slipped the sweet potatoes and the Brussels sprouts in, and stood back to survey their work.

"Livvy, everything looks amazing. You did an incredible job. It sure looks like Thanksgiving in here."

She just nodded and adjusted the place cards one more time. This must have been the way Rita started out.

He gave her a quick squeeze. "Miss Cooley's going to get here pretty soon. Let's go get dressed."

Olivia followed him down the hall. "I sure wish I had a pilgrim dress to put on."

"Well, we looked. Your pilgrim hat will make you look just like a pilgrim."

When his phone rang, the first thing Chris thought was that Brandon had convinced Sarah to come to Chicago after all, but it was his sister's face that filled the screen.

"Hey, Kaitlyn. Happy Thanksgiving." Sarah was due any minute, and Chris was in a very good mood. "Wish you were here with us. Livvy has this place looking exactly like Plymouth Plantation would have looked if construction paper and pipe cleaners had been invented then."

"Wish I were there too." Kaitlyn sounded subdued, but maybe he was comparing the way she always sounded with the way he felt at the moment.

"Do you want to talk to Livvy?"

"Sure."

"Livvy! Your mom."

She came running down the hall, grabbed his phone, and disappeared back into her room. Chris sharpened his carving knife. He would prefer to carve the turkey before they sat down, but Olivia had seen a picture of the turkey being carved at the table and had made it clear that that should be the procedure.

A few minutes later Olivia was back. "She wants to talk to you."

Chris glanced at the clock. Sarah was due this minute. He tried to make his voice easy and calm. "So, what are you doing today? Going out for turkey?"

There was a silence long enough to make Chris wonder if he had lost the connection, and when Kaitlyn did speak, he could hardly hear her. "Chris, I want to come home."

"Where? You mean Scottsdale?"

"No, I want to be with you and Livvy."

"Oh. Okay, I told you you'd always be welcome, so come. I'm afraid the welcome mat's not out for Jase, though."

"He's gone."

"Gone? Where?"

"I don't know. He just left."

"Kaitlyn, are you all right?" This wasn't just a heads-up that she intended to wander back west. "What's wrong?"

"Chris, I don't know what I'm going to do. I can't find work. I had to sell my bike, and now that money's gone." She started to cry, and through the front window, Chris saw Sarah pull into his driveway.

"Hang on." He covered the phone with his hand. "Livvy! Miss Cooley's here."

Olivia raced past him out the front door, and when she ushered Sarah inside, he pointed to his phone, mouthed the word *Kaitlyn*, and walked back to his room and shut the door.

"Okay. Do you have a place to sleep tonight and enough to eat?"

"Yes, but they're going to throw me out if I don't pay them something pretty soon."

"Everything's closed till tomorrow anyway, so this is what we're going to do. Give me the name of the place you're staying and how much you owe, and I'll see they get paid. I'll wire you enough money to eat and get to the airport, and I'll have a ticket waiting for you there. Think that would work?"

"When would I come?"

"Just as soon as I can work things out. Maybe tomorrow, maybe the next day. Are you good with that?"

"I'm good." Chris heard her sniff and take a deep breath. "Oh, Chris. I'm such a loser."

"No, you're not a loser, Kaitlyn, but I do think it's time you stepped up, don't you?"

"Yeah, it's time."

"Okay then, I'm going to go. Livvy and I have company. I'll call you first thing tomorrow, and we'll get this thing rolling."

Chris hung up and rubbed his eyes. *I love you, Kaitlyn, but your timing stinks.* He stood up, shoved his phone deep into his pocket, and squared his shoulders. Tomorrow he'd do everything he could to take care of Kaitlyn, but today was Thanksgiving, and Sarah had come to dinner.

When Chris scooped a sleeping Olivia from his big chair and carried her off to bed, Sarah took advantage of the moment to unfasten the top button of her pants and pull her sweater down to cover it. This was the second meal she had shared with Chris and the second time she had eaten to the point of pain. She was going to have to watch it if she spent much time with Chris Reed. And she was beginning to think she'd like that a lot.

Chris came back in and switched on some soft jazz before sitting next to her on the sofa. "She's out. I guess planning the world's best Thanksgiving takes it out of a girl."

"Chris, that was an amazing meal. If you tell my mom I said so, I'll have to deny it, but that was the best Thanksgiving dinner I've ever had in my life. What in the world did you do to the turkey to make it taste like that?"

When he started to tell her, she held up a hand. "No. That was a rhetorical question. I'm not going to cook a turkey, but I'll eat one like that any day."

Chris grinned and slid an arm along the back of the sofa. "Glad you liked it, and your secret is safe with me. Mom will never know."

They fell into an easy silence, and when Chris slipped his arm off the sofa and around her shoulders, it seemed the most natural thing in the world to lean her head against his shoulder.

"You know, if this were my house, we'd be looking at a fireplace instead of a blank television screen."

"I know. This is a first-class mobile home, but it does lack a fireplace. Maybe I should get one of those DVDs of a fire, so we could stare at that instead."

She leaned back to look up at him. "Seriously? A fireplace DVD?"

"Sure. Haven't you seen them? You just pop it in and you have a fire, complete with crackling."

"That's ridiculous." Sarah smiled to herself and went back to staring at the blank screen. Even sitting and talking about absolutely nothing with Chris made her happy.

She listened to the music for another long while before speaking again. "So what's with Kaitlyn? Everything okay?"

He sighed and shifted a bit. "Not really, but I don't want to bore you with my family stuff."

She tucked her feet up under her. "I'll tell you my tragic story if you tell me yours."

"Deal." He looked down at her. "Who first?"

"You."

"How far back do you want me to go?"

"I'm not going anywhere."

"I like that." Chris pulled her a little closer and started his story.

Sarah listened without saying much until he finished up by saying, "And so I guess she'll be living here, at least for a while."

"You'll be a little crowded, won't you?"

"I don't know what I'll do about that. I guess the best thing to do would be to give her and Olivia my room and take Olivia's, but Livvy is so proud of her room. I hate to do that. Maybe I can give Kaitlyn my room and take the couch. I don't know. I'll think of something."

"You know, when my cousin Ray ran the now-defunct High Lonesome Saloon, he had this little one-room travel trailer that he lived in. It's up at the ranch now. Maybe we could haul it down and park it outside here."

"You think that would be okay? It would sure solve my problem. Kaitlyn could have my room and I'd sleep out there."

"No, Chris." Sarah looked up at him. "This is your house; you're not giving up your room. The trailer is perfectly fine, and Kaitlyn can sleep out there."

He grinned. "You're awful bossy for such a little thing, aren't you?"

She settled herself more comfortably. "You have no idea."

"Okay, so you've heard my story, what about yours?"

"Ooooh." It was half sigh, half groan. "Well, first of all, Brandon and I are over."

"No going back?"

"No way. Not a hope, not a dream, not a prayer. We're done."

"Okay. How are you doing with that?"

"You know, not bad. I mean, when I ended things with him, I told him I never wanted to hear, see, or speak to him again, ever, and I meant it. But we'd been together since we were sophomores in college, and I really expected the hole that he left to be painful. I mean, wouldn't you think that?"

He nodded against her hair.

"But it's not. At least not much. And even that's getting better, not worse. I'm just now realizing how completely controlling he was, and I feel like someone has come along and clipped those strings. At first I just collapsed, but now I'm seeing that I can walk, and run, and dance on my own. I don't need anyone pulling my strings."

"It's only been a few days, Sarah. You might want to give yourself a little more time."

"It's been a long time coming, though. I tried to break things off when we graduated, but he would not let it go. I wouldn't take any of his calls, so he turned up in Last Chance one day and finally talked me into giving him one more chance." She slapped her hand over her eyes. "When I think of all the things he 'finally talked me into' in the years we were together, I feel too stupid to live."

Chris took her hand from her eyes and enveloped it in his own. "Don't say that. You're not, not by a long shot." Sarah heard the change in his voice. "Think he'll show up here again?"

"No. I think it finally sank in this time. I haven't heard a word from him since Saturday, and that is so unlike Brandon. I blocked his number right away, so he may have tried to call once, I don't know. But before, that would have slowed him down only long enough to reach for another phone. I'm pretty sure he's moved on. In fact, I think he was moving on before I even knew about it." She leaned away and looked up at Chris. "See? That's what makes me so mad. I was the one who said I wasn't sure, and I was the one pushing everyone else away to give us a chance."

"Don't I know it."

"And then here's Brandon. Calling me every night to tell me we belonged together and at the same time chasing every woman in the entire state of Illinois."

"Wow. All of this and a new job too. When did he sleep?"

Sarah saw he was trying to hide a smile, and she snuggled back against him. "You'd like me to stop talking about Brandon, wouldn't you?"

He drew her closer into the shelter of his arm. "As long as you stay right where you are, you can talk about whatever you want to."

They fell into a comfortable silence again, lost in whatever thoughts floated past.

"Chris?"

"Mmm?"

"Can we go to Papa's again? I love that place."

"Sure."

"Let's take Livvy next time. I bet she'd love to see all the brands."

"Okay. I didn't see mac and cheese on the menu, but maybe there's something there she'd eat."

Sarah leaned her head against his shoulder and closed her eyes. The soft wailing of a saxophone wound its way through a room still redolent with the aroma of Thanksgiving dinner. She could not remember feeling such peace and well-being.

When she opened her eyes and looked up, Chris was watching her. She knew he was going to kiss her. She could read it in his eyes. And this time, she closed her eyes and lifted her face to meet his.

27

It was still dark when Chris wandered into the living room Christmas morning and plugged in the tree lights. Since Kaitlyn had been with them, he had come to treasure his quiet moments alone in the morning like never before. When he turned on the coffeemaker, he could see through the kitchen window the little travel trailer where she slept. He'd been concerned that she might feel isolated, even banished by the arrangement, but she had welcomed it. She said she felt safe there.

He put in a CD of Christmas music and sat in his big chair to wait for the coffee. Kaitlyn was a different woman from the laughing, irresponsible sister who rode her motorcycle down his driveway and left him to raise her daughter. She was too thin, too listless, and something had changed in her eyes too. They were always sad.

"Is it Christmas yet?" Olivia stood by his chair rubbing one eye.

"It is indeed, Liverhead." Chris lifted her onto his lap. "And merry Christmas to you."

"Can I open my presents?"

"When your mom gets up. But you can look at your stocking if you want."

"Can I turn on the fire?"

"Sure." Sarah had presented him with a fireplace DVD a week

or so after Thanksgiving, and Olivia had hung her stocking over the screen.

He poured himself a cup of coffee while Olivia set the video flames to crackling and then sat down to watch while she dumped out her stocking on the floor.

This had been some year. Last Christmas Eve he had worn a white chef's coat and prepared a four-course prix fixe menu at a trendy restaurant in Albuquerque. This year he was living in a yellow-and-white singlewide in Last Chance, running his own soon-to-be-famous diner, and raising his niece. And then there was Sarah. He smiled every time he thought about her.

Of course, with his grueling schedule at the Dip 'n' Dine, Olivia's needs, and Kaitlyn to worry about, not to mention Sarah's own agenda, he hadn't been able to spend a fraction of the time he wanted to with her, but they had managed. And in just a few hours, he'd be seeing her at the ranch when the three of them went up to spend Christmas Day with the Cooleys.

"When's Mom going to get up?" Olivia leaned on the arm of his chair wearing the plastic earrings she found in her stocking and munching on a candy cane.

Chris glanced out the window. The sky had lightened and the sun was just about to burst over the crest of the mountains to the east. "Why don't you go get her? Put your slippers on first."

While Olivia scrambled to find her slippers and then tore out the front door, Chris got up to put the breakfast casserole in the oven. He smiled when he saw Olivia come racing around the corner and charge through the door of the travel trailer. Perhaps it was because of the change in Kaitlyn, or maybe Olivia still resented being left behind, but she had not warmed up to her mother like Chris expected her to. It pleased him to see Olivia chattering as she tugged Kaitlyn from the trailer and toward the house. Kaitlyn was even smiling.

"Here she is! Let's open presents now." Olivia and Kaitlyn came through the front door.

"Cool your jets, kiddo. We need to think about why we even have Christmas first." He sat back down and took his Bible off the end table. "I know you've been working on learning this in Sunday school, so I'll read and you say it with me, okay?"

Olivia came and stood next to him. He slipped an arm around her waist and the two of them began. "In those days, Caesar Augustus issued a decree . . ."

—⁓—

Sarah saw the Jeep coming up the road to the ranch house, trailing a long plume of dust, and went out on the porch to wait for Chris and his family. The air was cold and fragrant with wood smoke, but she found the stillness a peaceful respite from the chaos that had reigned inside since her nephews had roared through the house several hours earlier proclaiming the arrival of Christmas morning.

Chris smiled at her through the windshield as he stopped in the drive, and Kaitlyn, sitting next to him, returned her wave. Sarah had been ready to dislike Kaitlyn on sight. After all, who just goes off and leaves her kid? But far from being the heartless narcissist that Sarah expected to meet, Kaitlyn just seemed lost, and totally crushed. Sarah stepped off the porch to greet the Reeds and slipped her arm around Kaitlyn's waist to lead her into the house.

"Come in this house, and merry Christmas." Nancy Jo met them at the door wearing a holly-sprigged apron over white wool pants and a red sweater. She held up her cheek for a kiss from Chris and grabbed Olivia in a quick squeeze.

"Mom, this is Kaitlyn, Chris's sister and Livvy's mom."

"I'm so glad to finally get to meet you, Kaitlyn." Nancy Jo enveloped her in a warm hug that held no hint she had ever heard a negative word about her guest. "Welcome to the zoo. We'll have dinner at about 3:00, but meanwhile, if you're hungry, there's all sorts of goodies laid out on the table in the den. So help yourself."

"Mom's one of those people who thinks if you're not actually eating, you're probably starving." Sarah smiled at Kaitlyn.

"A woman after my own heart." Chris gave Nancy Jo a one-armed hug.

"I got some boots for Christmas." Olivia, who had been out of the conversation about as long as she could stand it, held up her treasure for inspection. "Uncle Chris said I had to wear shoes since we weren't riding today, but I brought them just in case. Can I ride?"

"Livvy." Chris glared at her.

Sarah laughed. "Not today, I'm afraid. Everyone's got the day off, even the horses. Maybe later we'll go see them though."

"We'll take her." Two boys, maybe a little older than Olivia, skidded to a stop in the entry hall.

"Great." Sarah put a hand on each shoulder. "Livvy, these are my nephews, Michael James and Jacob. You may have seen them at school."

"We know you," Michael James said. "You're the one who beat up Emma Anderson."

Olivia's face fell into a scowl.

"Sorry you got kicked out of school for that," Jacob chimed in. "She's kind of a crybaby. So do you want to go see the horses?"

"Shut the door and don't"—Nancy Jo sighed and finished her sentence too late—"slam it."

"Listen." Sarah held up a finger and tipped her head. "That's called silence. It only happens when the boys are outside. Come on, I'll introduce you to everyone. Now, the first thing you need to know is that this is a house right out of the nineteenth century. We'll find all the men sitting around like third base in the den, and we'll leave Chris, the best cook in the county—sorry, Mom—with them. Then we'll go join all the women in the kitchen, busy cooking dinner. They'll put me to work unwrapping the butter or something. I know. It's an odd system. But they seem to like it that way."

"Sarah Elizabeth, you just wear me out." Nancy Jo shook her head and headed back to the kitchen.

"Hey, everybody." Sarah led Chris and Kaitlyn into the den, where a huge Christmas tree dominated one corner. "Here are some very special friends of mine. I think most of you know Chris Reed, the new owner of the Dip 'n' Dine, and this is his sister, Kaitlyn."

One by one the men half rose from where they were sitting playing dominos or just talking to shake Chris's hand and nod at Kaitlyn. When Sarah reached the last two, she smiled and reached up to drape an arm around each of their shoulders.

"These are my two favorite cousins, Ray and Steven Braden. Ray is an artist in Santa Fe. His wife is Lainie and she's you-know-where. You'll meet her in a minute. And this is Steven." She gave him a little shake. "Steven shocked the daylights out of all of us this morning by telling us the State Police has said they'll have him. He's in the next academy class. Who knew?"

"We all had a feeling he'd be getting up close and personal with the law one day." Ray grinned. "We just didn't think it would be from the good side."

Steven ignored the jab. His eyes were on Kaitlyn, and he took one of her hands in both of his, smiling so his dimple showed. "Kaitlyn, was it? Are you in town for long? I'd love to show you around."

"No! Steven, don't even think it." Sarah got between them and gave Steven a little shove. "Kaitlyn, stay away from him. I'm warning you. He thinks he's God's gift, but he's a lump of coal if ever there was one. If you see him coming, just run."

"Wow, if that's what you say about your favorite cousin, I'm glad I'm not further on down the list." Steven smiled his aw-shucks grin and ducked his head.

Sarah saw him check to see if Kaitlyn had noticed and rolled her eyes. "Come on, Kaitlyn, I'll introduce you to the kitchen help now. Gran's in there and she's been waiting for you. Chris, I'll see you later." She smiled up at him and squeezed his arm before leading Kaitlyn off to the kitchen.

—∞—

Chris watched them leave and turned to find every eye in the den on him. Clearly, they had not missed the warmth of Sarah's touch. And the youngest daughter of the area's biggest rancher had a roomful of bodyguards. He smiled. No one moved.

Finally, one of the hands spoke. "There's some fudge there on the table, if you want some."

"Um, no thanks. I'm good." Chris looked around, but the only chair he could see was at the desk. He turned it around and sat in it.

"Big fella like you play any football?"

"I played in high school." Chris tried to remember the name of the man who asked the question.

"Any good?"

"Well, the team was. We won the state championship my junior and senior year."

"You don't say. What state?"

"Arizona."

287

An almost palpable wave swept over the room, and Chris saw everyone relax. Well, Sarah's dad still looked pretty stern, but clearly Chris had passed some kind of test with the rest of them.

The conversation drifted from high school football to college ball, and Chris was starting to feel a little more comfortable when Ray cleared his throat. "Uh, Chris, I think you're getting a page."

Chris looked up to see Sarah standing by the front door holding his jacket and trying to get his attention. He stood up. "Excuse me, gentlemen. It's been a pleasure. I'm sure I'll see you later."

Joining Sarah, he helped her into her coat and put his own jacket on. "What was that all about? Why didn't you just come in and get me? Or holler or something?"

Sarah shrugged and led the way onto the porch. "I don't know. I thought maybe I could catch your eye and you could just slip out unnoticed."

Chris laughed and reached for her hand as they stepped onto the drive. "Well, I'm sorry, but that was the most noticed exit I've made in a long time."

"Was it awful in there?"

"It wasn't bad. Your dad doesn't seem real happy with me, though."

"Oh, don't worry about him. He'll love you when he gets to know you."

"Be sure to tell him that, will you? I don't think he's all that convinced." They headed down the road that led to the corrals. "Where's Kaitlyn, by the way?"

"In the kitchen. She and Lainie hit it right off. I think they're peeling potatoes or something. They were going to make me help too, but I escaped. I always cut myself."

"You don't need to cut yourself, all you need to do—"

Sarah held up a hand. "Do not go there. In fact, let's get one thing settled. If I need a cooking lesson, you are the one and only person I'll come to. If I don't ask for one, you can bet I don't want one. Agreed?"

"Okay." They walked awhile in easy silence. "But I'm beginning to think you see me as just another pretty face who knows his way around the kitchen."

Sarah burst out laughing and threw her arms around his waist. "I love you."

Immediately she dropped her arms and jumped back, hands over her mouth. "I didn't mean to say that. I mean . . ."

Chris took her face in his hands and looked into her eyes. "It's okay. I know what you meant." He smiled. "You know, if I didn't know it was impossible, I'd say you were blushing."

"It's possible. I feel like such a doofus. I'm surprised that thundering sound isn't you running for the hills."

"Nope. I'm not running. That thundering sound is them." Olivia had spotted them and was leading Jacob and Michael James in a charge their way. "And I wouldn't thunder if I did run. What kind of thing is that to say?"

Sarah laughed again and took his hand. "A pretty face, a great cook, and someone who makes me laugh. I like that combination."

"Hey. What are you guys doing?" Olivia skidded to a stop in front of them with Jacob and Michael James close behind.

"Just walking." Chris held his other hand out to Olivia. She took it.

"Where are you walking to?"

"Just walking, that's all."

"Want to come see the horses?"

"Maybe later."

Olivia looked up at him. She was clearly torn between running off with her two new friends or staying with Chris and Sarah and "just walking." The friends won, and in a few seconds they had thundered off again.

"She's a different little girl. So much happier." Sarah watched her go.

"She still has a long way to go, but we're making progress."

"How does Kaitlyn fit in the family picture?"

"I don't know what's going on with Kaitlyn. I do all the parenting, but that's an agreement we made before she ever came back. And truthfully, I don't think Livvy even notices. She's just glad to have her mom where she can see her."

"What's Kaitlyn going to do?"

"She was in such bad shape when she got here that I've just let her be for a while. But after New Year's, I'm going to have her come work at the Dip 'n' Dine with me. She needs to start putting her life back together."

Sarah nodded and walked next to Chris for a long while without saying anything.

"You're awfully quiet." Chris stopped and looked down at her until she looked up into his face, shielding her eyes against the glare of the sun with her hand.

"Your life is so full. You have Livvy and Kaitlyn and the Dip 'n' Dine. I don't see how you have room for anything else."

"Sarah, listen to me." Chris brushed a curl from her face, letting his hand linger on her cheek. "My life has, or had, a huge emptiness, no matter how full my days were. I'd say big enough to drive a truck through, but you're nowhere near that big. This I do know, though—since you've been in my life, that emptiness is no longer there."

Sarah started to open her mouth, but Chris laid two fingers against her lips. "Wait. I'm not done." He took a deep breath and blew it out in a gust. "I spend a big chunk of my time kicking myself for dumb things I've said or done, and this may wind up being one of those times. But I'd a hundred times more rather kick myself for something I did than something I didn't have the guts to do. A little while ago you said 'I love you.' I know what you meant. You meant you loved the way I made you laugh, or the way I can play the fool sometimes. But listen to me. I *love* you. And if love is that punch-in-the-gut feeling that never goes away, I've loved you since I first saw you in the Dip 'n' Dine last summer. All it does is keep getting stronger until I can't think of anything but how I want to spend my life loving you. Now if *you* want to run for the hills, go for it. But know that I'll be here waiting for you."

Sarah didn't say anything for a long moment, and Chris was beginning to wonder if he hadn't really blown it when she said, "You know, I had always pegged you as the strong, silent type, but you sure talk a lot."

He stared. "That's it? I pour my heart out and you just tell me I talk too much?"

"Oh, I didn't say too much, just a lot. And by the way, I'm done having someone else do my thinking for me. If I want to run for the hills, I'll do it without anyone's permission. And if I say, 'I love you,' I'll be the one to say what it means. Got that?"

"Got it. So . . . what did you mean?"

She looked up at Chris, and the smile that filled her face and shone in her eyes radiated through him like sunshine.

"I mean I love you."

There was nothing for him to do but kiss her then, and he lifted her off her feet to do just that. It was a good kiss, warm and deep and passionate.

"Gross. Would you guys stop that? Miss Nancy Jo says dinner's almost ready and you have to come in now."

But not very long.

A Special Peek at

❧ ⬥ ❧

Book 3 in

A Place *to* Call Home

series

❧ ⬥ ❧

Coming Spring 2015

1

Pure and simple, Kaitlyn Reed hated her job. She hated getting up in the early hours of a cold, dark January morning to get there. She hated the curious to outright hostile looks of the diners she served. She hated that she didn't really have a choice about whether to work at the Dip 'n' Dine. But most of all, she hated taking orders from Juanita Sheppard.

Truth be told, she wasn't very good at taking orders from anyone. Her reputation back in Scottsdale as a creative, avant-garde stylist had gained her positions in some of Scottsdale's toniest hair salons, but those jobs never lasted long. And neither did the jobs she'd held after she left Scottsdale. Kaitlyn simply could not stand being told what to do. And employers always seemed to think they had to give directions. Nine times out of ten, if they had just given her five seconds, she'd have completed the task before they even mentioned it. But they'd go and bark their orders, this white-hot flare would shoot through her, and before she even realized she had said anything, she was out the door, purse and final paycheck in hand.

"Here. You need to refill this and make the rounds." Juanita shoved a nearly empty coffeepot into Kaitlyn's hands. "And tables four and six need busing. Let's keep our eyes open, Kaitlyn, and try to stay on top of things."

Kaitlyn's eyes narrowed. True, her brother had asked Juanita to show her the ropes, but Kaitlyn was about ready to grab that rope and strangle her with it. Holding the pot in both hands, she started after Juanita, who hadn't even paused as she breezed by.

No telling what pyrotechnics the early breakfast diners at the Dip 'n' Dine might have been treated to if her brother, Chris, who owned the diner, hadn't intercepted her.

"Why don't I take care of the coffee?" He took the coffeepot from her and gave her a wink. "You go ahead and clean those tables. And Kaitlyn? Try not to throw the dishes in the bin so hard you break them, okay?"

His grin lightened his words but not her temper, and after shooting one last murderous glare at Juanita, who was chatting with a customer and clearly clueless about the apocalypse she had so nearly brought down upon herself, Kaitlyn ducked into the kitchen to find Carlos, her one friend and ally in this awful place.

"How can you stand her?" Kaitlyn could almost feel steam coming from her ears. She shot another look into the dining room as Juanita's voice reached them.

"Who? Juanita?" Carlos Montoya pulled a pan of biscuits out of the oven and straightened to look at her. "She's okay. Gets a little bossy sometimes, but you don't need to let it bother you. I don't."

"Well, you don't have to. You're in here. I'm the one she's treating like her own personal servant."

On cue, Juanita appeared at the window to the dining room. "Kaitlyn? Those tables still need busing and we have people waiting for a table. Let's save the chatting for our break, okay?"

Kaitlyn's mouth popped open on its own accord, but before she could say anything, Carlos spoke for her. "She'll be right there, Juanita. I needed her in here for a minute. The bins are right there, though, if you want to go ahead and get started."

Juanita was silenced, but only for a second. "She wasn't hired to help you, Carlos. She was hired to help me. And I need her out here."

She pursed her lips and raised her eyebrows at Kaitlyn before whirling away, leaving Kaitlyn fighting yet another flash of rage. Carlos shook his head and turned back to his biscuits.

"Take a second and cool off. Here. Eat a biscuit. Then go on out there and bus some tables. Just do your job and let Juanita roll off your back. I mean that." His voice took a serious tone Kaitlyn had not heard before, and she paused in mid-bite. "This place doesn't belong to Juanita. It belongs to your brother. He's a good man. And if you think you owe him anything, keep the cat fights out of his restaurant."

His dark eyes held hers for a long moment before she dropped her glance and took a thoughtful pull off her biscuit. She hated it that Carlos wasn't just taking her side against the insufferable Juanita, but she had to admit he was right. She did owe Chris. Big-time. If there was one person in her life who had always been there for her, it was Chris. When they were growing up, it was he who tried so hard to take the place of their always-busy parents. When she got pregnant at sixteen, it was he who stood by her decision to have the baby when everybody else told her what a bad idea that was. Seven years later, when she decided she was tired of motherhood and had dropped off her daughter like a puppy at a pound, he had taken Olivia in and given her a home. And several months after that, when Kaitlyn found herself alone and penniless and beginning to understand what a world-class idiot she had been, Chris, without a word of recrimination, brought her home and took her in too. Yep. One could say she owed her brother.

"Kaitlyn?" Juanita had appeared at the window again with a brittle smile. "Are you coming?"

Kaitlyn took a deep breath and held it before exhaling in a long slow whoosh. She smiled too and squared her shoulders. "Coming."

She stopped just before pushing her way through the door into the dining room and turned to Carlos. "For Chris."

He raised his spatula in salute. "For the boss."

If Juanita noticed her new, cooperative attitude, she certainly gave no sign. In fact, her instructions, always frequent, seemed more curt and brusque that ever. More than once during the day, Juanita had backed Chris into a corner, and from her glances in Kaitlyn's direction and the fact that she had actually lowered her voice to a near whisper, Kaitlyn could only surmise that the discussions were about her.

Chris listened as he always did. He lowered his head to better look into Juanita's face, nodded thoughtfully as she spoke, then smiled, straightened, said a few words, and put his hand on her shoulder before walking away. Whatever he said could not have been what Juanita was looking for, because she always glared in Kaitlyn's direction before huffing off.

For Chris. Kaitlyn took another deep breath and held it as long as she could before slowly exhaling. *For Chris. For Chris. For Chris . . . and for my sweet, abandoned Livvy.*

Cathleen Armstrong lives in the San Francisco Bay Area with her husband, Ed, and their corgi. Though she has been in California for many years now, her roots remain deep in New Mexico where she grew up and where much of her family still lives. After she and Ed raised three children, she returned to college and earned a BA in English. Her debut novel *Welcome to Last Chance* won the 2009 American Christian Fiction Writers Genesis Award for Women's Fiction. Learn more at www.cathleenarmstrong.com.

Meet
CATHLEEN
ARMSTRONG

online at
www.cathleenarmstrong.com

 AuthorCathleenArmstrong

@cathleen_arm

"A wonderful debut novel."
—New York Journal of Books

Don't miss the first book in the
A Place to Call Home series!